Forever Young

Venetian Blood: Book One

Barbara Stanzl & Brett Fitzpatrick

Forever Young

A Novel

Bibliografische Information der Deutschen Nationalbibliothek:
Die Deutsche Nationalbibliothek verzeichnet diese Publikation in der
Deutschen Nationalbibliografie; detaillierte bibliografische Daten sind
im Internet über http://dnb.dnb.de abrufbar.

© 2019 Barbara Stanzl & Brett Fitzpatrick

Herstellung und Verlag: BoD – Books on Demand, Norderstedt

ISBN: 978-3-7519-3523-4

For our parents, Christine and Werner, and Gladys and Jim

"I stood in Venice, on the Bridge of Sighs,

A palace and a prison on each hand:"

Lord Byron

Jasmine was alone in the compartment, enjoying the first sight of Venice in the distance. Her train was crawling slowly across the long bridge that connected the island of Venice to the mainland of Italy. She saw bell towers and domes, picked out in the beams of bright spotlights and reflected in the dark water of the lagoon. Only the towers and spires could be seen, the other buildings remaining dark silhouettes, almost indistinguishable from the surrounding blackness of the night.

Jasmine stood up and pulled down the top half of the train window. With no glass between her and the view she could suddenly see a lot more. Only the lagoon refused to give up any more of its secrets. The water was so dark that anything could be hiding down there and she wouldn't know.

The interior of the carriage was still warm from the heat of the day, but the wind on her face was cold. The train was inching toward the city and Jasmine felt a shiver run down her spine as she saw more and more of it. There were street lights, each one illuminating little more than a small patch of wall, or alleyway floor, and there were the lights of the oncoming station platforms, but beyond that there were only the silhouettes of buildings against a starry sky.

Less than twenty minutes later, Jasmine was lost among the dark mass of buildings. She had never been in a city without roads before, which was disconcerting enough, but this city seemed also to be almost entirely without people. She stopped to look at the map displayed on her phone and tried to work out where she was.

Only one street in four seemed to have a name, and none of the names she read on the side of buildings were the same as the ones on the map. The wheels of her suitcase grumbled noisily over the cobblestones behind her as she picked a direction, almost at random. The blue dot marking her position suddenly jumped three streets as her app updated her position based on esoteric factors known only to itself.

"You're lost as well, aren't you?" she said to the small, inanimate device. A figure appeared at the end of the alleyway, and Jasmine drew a breath to ask for directions, but then shut her mouth again. The figure was an old man, stooped and drunken, and he was growling invective at himself. Jasmine didn't understand his words, her Italian was pretty good but the man's words weren't Italian, they were something else, a local Venetian dialect Jasmine guessed. She may not have understood the dialect but it was extremely clear to her that the words the man was saying were bad words. She put her head down and continued walking, coming uncomfortably close to the man in the narrow alleyway as he stumbled past her. She breathed a little sigh of relief as she emerged onto yet another small square, with yet another canal bisecting it. There was a single stone bridge across, leaving Jasmine no option but to climb the steps, her suitcase banging against each step as she went up. She reached the center of the bridge, the apex, and was suddenly confronted by a wall of noise. It was the throaty roar of hundreds of voices, and it was coming from a small alleyway on the other side of the small square. From where she was standing, at the highest point of the bridge, she could see that the alleyway was short and there was a huge open space beyond.

The voices she now saw were coming from a huge group of young people. They were drinking, Jasmine saw, and they were packed in so tight it was going to be difficult to make her way through the throng. Jasmine just stood there on the bridge, her phone in one hand, the handle of her suitcase in the other, the classic pose of the lost tourist.

She was a young woman with black, super curly hair, and below her curls, her dark brown eyes were shining with irritation. She descended into the alleyway and started pushing her way through the crowd.

"Hi," Jasmine said, picking somebody at random from the crowd and proffering her phone. "I'm trying to find this address."

The address on the screen was typical of Venice. It was just two lines, the area of the city and the building number.

"I don't know it," the young man she had chosen said, with a shrug.

"I know it," a young woman said. "It's nearby. Come with me, I'll show you where it is."

***

The alley that the young woman led her down was yet another one that her phone's app didn't recognize, so she just dropped it in her bag and forgot about it. She hurried her steps, having to walk quickly to keep up with her guide. Jasmine followed her down alleyways, under arches, and round turn after turn, but then her guide had gone. One moment she had been there, leading the way, and the next Jasmine was on her own in a tiny, dark alleyway. Half way down the alleyway was a dark gateway. There was a garden within that was obviously very overgrown, even in the darkness, and the house too was dark and empty looking. It could be the building she was looking for, her accommodation, she decided.

She pulled out her phone and opened the maps application. It showed her location as a red dot, and the address she had been given as a blue dot. They were pretty much, but not exactly, on top of each other. It was starting to look like the creepy old building was the place she was supposed to stay the night.

She cursed softly to herself and pushed her face up against the ornate swirls of the metal gate so she could get a better look inside. She saw a big house, with three stories. And she saw that there were windows in the roof above too, hinting at some kind of attic space. But the place was completely dark. The windows had a touch of North Africa in their complex arches, and the chimneys had the bulbous tops of the middle ages. The building looked ancient, half-derelict, but so did all the other buildings.

She cursed gently to herself and gave the handle of the gate an experimental nudge. She jerked back in shock as the gate came slowly open on screeching hinges. She was even more sure this was the right place now, otherwise, surely the gate would have been locked. She stepped through the gate, onto the short path that led across the garden to the front door, her suitcase still trundling noisily after her. She felt a wave of cold and neglect coming from the building. It was just a huge, crumbling pile of masonry, unloved and uncared for. She felt the damp radiating from the ancient stones, like the breath of a monster.

She went up a small stone staircase to reach the front door, and her eye was immediately caught by a bull-headed door knocker. It reminded her of something she had been reading on the long train ride. She had been reading about Aegeus, king of Athens, the goat-man who gave his name to the Aegean Sea. Aegeus had engineered the death of the son of King Minos, who declared war on Athens and only agreed to end the war if Aegeus would send seven young men and seven young women every nine years to Crete to be fed to the Minotaur.

She shuddered and reached for the knocker but her hand froze half way when she heard a click. The door swung wide on screaming hinges that were obviously oiled just as infrequently as the ones on the gate. Jasmine could now see a cavernous hallway with a high ceiling and a huge chandelier. There was also an enormous window opposite the front door, dominating the far wall.

By the light of the big window she could dimly see the opulence of the wallpaper, and the ornate carving of the furniture, but also big dark stains of mold, and some chips in the plaster. Two doors led off from the massive hall on either side of her, and a giant staircase led up to the floors above. Jasmine took a step across the threshold.

"Hello," she yelled, "anybody home?" No answer came, so Jasmine put her suitcase by the front door and walked further inside, yelling as she came. There was still no answer, and soon she was all the way across the hallway, at the giant window. The view was magnificent. This side of the house looked directly out onto a canal. The waters actually lapped at the face of the building, which explained why everything felt so cold and damp. She hadn't seen any sign of life yet, so she guessed she would have to investigate the building a bit more, to see where everyone was hiding. She reluctantly turned from the view through the huge window, and then she screamed, loud and long.

There was a single figure standing right in front of her, in the dark, silent room. She managed to pinch her lips together and force herself to stop screaming, it had just been shock, and she had to get a hold of herself. The figure in front of her wasn't monstrous or intimidating, quite the opposite. It was a young woman, no taller than Jasmine herself, and slim, slight even. But there was something about the way the moonlight through the window caught her face. There was a slimy, cold cast to the skin of the young woman in front of her. Or was it just raindrops reflected from the glass of the huge window that made her face look weird? When had it started raining?

Jasmine couldn't focus, couldn't bring the features of the woman into sharp relief, no matter how much she squinted into the half light. She could hear her own heart thumping hard in her ears. Time to take charge of this situation, she thought. She opened her mouth to speak, but the young woman spoke first. There was a presence and an anger in the voice.

Jasmine felt that, even though she couldn't understand the girl's raging-fast Italian.

She caught a word or two, but not the sense of it. She just stood slack jawed, her mouth hanging open, but her mind was racing. The voice was dark and husky, almost dry. Jasmine thought the young woman looked like a rocker, dressed in some sort of weird collection of dark, vintage clothes.

"Shit," Jasmine hissed, the ugly word as involuntary as the scream had been. The effect was instant. The moment the woman heard that single word of English, she stopped in mid sentence. Her eyes narrowing suspiciously.

"You are English. I once knew an Englishman," she said, but didn't go on to elaborate.

"Shit," Jasmine hissed again. Such lack of control over her own body, over her own lips, felt frightening. Who was this Englishman she was talking about? Was he some nutty expat who had crossed her path? And what had he done to her? And why was Jasmine going to have to pay the price for his misdeeds? She briefly considered barging past the girl and making a run for the front door, but some aura, like a nasty smell was emanating from the girl, blocking off all escape.

"What brought you here?" the girl asked. Jasmine had no idea how to answer the question. She was increasingly starting to suspect that this wasn't her accommodation.

"I'm not sure what brought me," Jasmine said, and emphasized the last two words. They felt strange and old fashioned in her mouth. But then she thought again, thought about how she had lost her guide from one moment to the next. "Blind chance?" she said.

"Blind fate," the young woman corrected her. Jasmine was unsettled by the vehemence with which the young woman had just spoken. She wanted to get out of this creepy old mansion, but the girl looked upset. It looked like she would have to try to calm her down, to make sure she didn't feel the need to call the cops or something.

"My name's Jasmine. What's your name?" Jasmine said, forcing a smile onto her face.

"I do not introduce myself to thieves, or vagabonds, or worse." The girl's eyes seemed to burn with indignation. Jasmine had heard the expression, of course, about eyes burning, but she had never seen what almost looked like actual flames in someone's eyes before. "What is your purpose here?"

"Are you going to call the cops?" Jasmine asked. "I just arrived, and I don't want to get into trouble with the police."

"You should have considered that before invading my sanctum."

"C'mon," Jasmine implored, drawing the word out to add emphasis.

"For the last time," the girl barked, "what do you want here?"

"I just wanted a place to stay. And my crazy old professor gave me an address that is impossible to find, and I thought the address was this place. I'm sorry I should have known it wouldn't be this decrepit old building."

The girl was visibly shaken by the words. "You think my home so strange," she asked, "does it look rotten to you?"

"Not strange exactly," Jasmine said, "and certainly not rotten... exactly." Jasmine felt awful about her clumsy words, overcome now by pure embarrassment, an emotion strong enough to banish all fear. She was no longer frightened of the strange young woman, didn't care whether she called the police or not. She just wanted to make sure she hadn't hurt the girl's feelings too badly.

"Go," the young woman said, "leave this place and go back to your gadabout life."

"Gadabout?" Jasmine couldn't resist a snort of amusement at the choice of words, even though she knew it was rude. The girl's English was so strange.

"Yes," the girl said, "gadabout, hooligan, rowdy. Somebody who does thoughtless and damaging things for their own mindless pleasure. I think the word fits you very well."

Jasmine couldn't take it any more. She dropped her head, pushed past the girl and made for the front door at an embarrassed trot. She was almost running by the time she reached the door, her face blushing red, but at the door she stopped, forcing herself to try one last time. For some reason she couldn't leave this bizarre stranger with the idea that she was some strange thrill seeker, who spent her time breaking into rich people's houses for kicks. She turned. "I'm not a gadabout," she said, "I don't do this."

"You did it tonight," the young woman said.

"Yes," Jasmine admitted, "but I thought this place was..."

"Decrepit?"

"No," Jasmine almost groaned with frustration. "I thought it was the place I was supposed to stay. Accommodation, you know..."

"This is my home," the young woman said, with a flourish of the hand. The gesture looked theatrical, with the huge window behind her making into her a dark silhouette.

"I don't think anybody should live like this," Jasmine said, "in the dark."

"Sometimes," the young woman said, "it's unavoidable. Sometimes you just end up alone, in the dark, and there is nothing to be done about it. Like I said, unavoidable."

"It's never unavoidable," Jasmine said. The smile she had forced onto her face was still there, though it was fading. But she meant what she had said. This was something Jasmine was convinced of. No matter how bad things got, you could always hang on in there, and wait for things to get better. Sitting in the dark feeling sorry for yourself was absolutely not the answer. "Let me at least turn on the lights."

"That would alleviate the darkness," the young woman said, "but what about the loneliness."

"That's easy," Jasmine said, because in her experience it was. Making friends was the most natural thing in the world. She'd never understood at all how anyone could end up being lonely and alone.

She smiled, walked a little way back across the hallway, and raised her hand for the young woman to shake. "Let's be friends."

"I don't make friends with every wandering lunatic that breaks into my home for their amusement," the young woman said, and Jasmine was disappointed to see that her mood hadn't softened one iota. Then something occurred to her.

"But I didn't break in," Jasmine said.

"What do you mean?" the young woman asked, genuinely surprised.

"The door, the gate, they weren't locked," Jasmine said, "I just pushed them open."

There was a long pause, as the girl stared at her. Some trick of the light was catching her eyes, picking them out like the luminous discs of a nocturnal carnivore, a wolf perhaps, or a panther. "You just pushed them open?" the girl said at last, pensively. "You say you were brought here by blind fate?" There was more silence, the two young women regarding each other. The stranger was still some way away across the hall, silhouetted against the big window.

"If you don't make friends with gadabouts," Jasmine broke the silence, her words loud and confident, "Who do you make friends with?"

The girl hesitated to answer. "I've made very few friends," she said at last, "in my entire cursed existence in this world. I even may have forgotten how to make friends. I find I have no earthly notion... Do you have a visiting card?"

Jasmine laughed out loud. She was really beginning to enjoy this odd young woman's company. Where had she learned to speak English. Her grammar book and dictionary must be from the previous century or something. Probably from the shelves of some moldy old library she undoubtedly had hidden away in the house somewhere. "No," she said kindly, "no visiting card. Just tell me your name, then come on over here and shake my hand." Jasmine still had her arm up, and she wiggled her hand, invitingly, beckoning for the young woman to shake.

The young woman stared at the hand, shy as a deer. She wanted to come and shake hands, Jasmine could sense that, but she didn't yet feel secure enough.

"Come on. Don't leave me hanging," Jasmine said. She had been holding her hand out for so long her arm was getting tired, but it was working, the girl was coming closer, slowly, timidly, one step at a time. When the girl had closed half the distance between them, she stopped. She lifted her head proudly, put her hand to her breast and introduced herself.

"My name is Violetta Marquesa Romanziana."

"Erm, OK," Jasmine smiled, "Would it be all right if I just called you Violetta."

"Yes," she said. And then, after a pause, "That would probably be best. I would prefer it if you did not use my family name."

"Which of those was your family name?" Jasmine meant it as a joke, but she could see by Violetta's raised eyebrow that she had misjudged it. "Ignore me," she said. "I've got a big mouth." She wiggled her hand, it was still hanging there waiting for a handshake. Violetta raised her hand, and Jasmine could swear she could feel Violetta's hand approaching hers as she closed the final few steps that remained between them. It was like a wave of cold, like pins and needles, but made of darkness. My hand must be falling asleep, she thought, as they touched. "My god," Jasmine yelped. "Your hands are freezing."

Violetta smiled sheepishly, as if ashamed at the temperature of her hands. She was standing in a shaft of light now, and Jasmine got her first good look at her. Her dark hair was unkempt, bunched up on her head in no particular style and held in place with big silver pins. She wasn't wearing any makeup and her skin was pale. She was thin, almost gaunt, with a pair of piercing green eyes staring out of slightly hollow sockets. Her clothes were an eccentric mix of vintage items from various epochs, half hidden by a dark, heavy cloak.

Jasmine knew a thing or two about clothes, being a fan of various fashion blogs about vintage clothing, and she could tell from the weight of the fabrics and detailing that the clothes had been expensive when new, but she also spotted inexpert patching and sewing. It was clear that Violetta was a very odd bird, which just made Jasmine warm to her more.

"You can not stay here," Violetta said, releasing Jasmine's hand. "Show me the address you were given."

***

Violetta was showing Jasmine the way to the address on the sheet of paper when they crossed the large square again. It was still very full of people. "You know, Violetta," Jasmine said, "I could use a drink."

"For the nerves," Violetta said, raising an eyebrow.

"Yes, exactly," Jasmine nodded, "unless you're in a hurry to get back home."

"I have all night," Violetta said. "Most of these places will be closing soon, but there is a bar that is open later. Café Noir. It is nothing more than a disreputable drinking den."

It was only a minute away, and Jasmine thought it was a cozy place, no matter what Violetta had said about it. It had exposed beams and brick, and laminated menus with an extensive selection of snacks and drinks.

"It's not so bad," Jasmine said, glancing around, taking it all in. "What is that radioactive-looking orange drink that everyone is drinking?"

"It's called Spritz Aperol," Violetta told her. "It's sweet, and they make it strong here, so it burns. I'll get us each one, if you like?"

"Very much," Jasmine said, "I would very much like a... what did you call it?"

***

It was much later before Jasmine was at last in the little apartment that had been rented for her. It was just one small room, crammed with a sofa bed, a wardrobe, a kitchen, a washing machine, and there was also one tiny bathroom. It was only just big enough for one person, but Jasmine was amazed to discover, it had an absolutely enormous terrace. It was a terrace that was as big as the apartment itself.

"Wow," she said, rushing out into the open air.

"This is the address, I'm afraid," Violetta told her, as she followed her onto the terrace. "Tiny and dreadful, isn't it?"

"Are you joking?" Jasmine yelped. "It's the best. The front looks out onto a tiny canal and the back has this terrace. It's wonderful. Wait there."

Jasmine worked quickly, switching on the music app on her phone, and finding a corkscrew and a couple of glasses for the red wine Violetta had bought at the bar. Soon there were two half-full glasses resting on the wall of the terrace, along with the bottle and the corkscrew, with the freshly liberated cork still impaled upon it. The first song of her jazz playlist was coming from her phone. It was Miles Davis, a lonely trumpet only just perceptible, coming softly from the phone's small speakers.

Jasmine saw movement out of the corner of her eye, a neighbor closing the shutters on their apartment's windows. Then she noticed that all the neighboring buildings' shutters were closed. Jasmine didn't understand it, but Violetta explained it was the Venetian custom to close the shutters at night.

"It must plunge the home into absolute darkness," Jasmine said, aghast. "It seems almost medieval to me."

"It is Medieval, of course," Violetta said, and took a sip of wine. "Excellent she said, dances on the tongue. Quite a discovery at such an ordinary bar." There was a short silence, just the two young women, the wine and the jazz. Then Violetta glanced at Jasmine. "You're quite the night owl," she said. "A lot of people would just want to go to bed, after arriving in a strange city and having an adventure."

"You bet I'm a night owl," Jasmine said.

"I think I'm going to like having you as a friend," Violetta said, as though finally making a decision. The two young women clinked their glasses together, two figures illuminated on the terrace of a tiny loft apartment among looming shadows. It was the only oasis of warmth and light amid the shuttered windows and deep darkness of the surrounding city.

CHAPTER 2

Despite her late night, Jasmine was up early. The sun had started to penetrate to the bottom of Venice's narrow allies, but it was a pleasantly shaded and refracted version of sunlight. Jasmine shaded the screen of her phone, as she made her way to her appointment at the university. Venice certainly was beautiful, Jasmine noticed, as her eyes flicked from the map on her phone to the streets around her and back. As she walked through the streets it was impossible to ignore another side to what she was seeing. She became aware that there was homelessness and begging in the street, all mixed in with the hordes of wealthy tourists and locals. She was extremely early, finding the university much more quickly and much more easily than she had expected. She decided to kill a few minutes in a cafe, so as not to be embarrassingly early. It seemed like there were three cafes in every street, which made it difficult to choose one, but soon she had picked one that appealed to her and chosen a table in the sun, where she ordered with the friendly Chinese lady who worked there.

At her table in the sun, checking her email and reading the online versions of British newspapers, she lost track of time, and had to pay and leave in a rush. The university, when she reached it, was a huge structure of raw concrete, that had somehow been hidden by its architect among the backstreets and alleyways of Venice. Jasmine hastily navigated through its corridors, and was a few minutes late by the time she found the office of the professor she had been sent to Venice to assist, a woman named Professor Gabizon. Gabizon's office door was ajar and she was at her desk.

Jasmine saw a face that was all hard angles, as if it had been chiseled, reading something on a laptop screen. Jasmine knocked on the door and popped her head into the room. Even seated behind a desk, Jasmine could see that the professor was tall and slim. Jasmine introduced herself. "Was your journey all right?" the professor asked.

"Not really," Jasmine replied, "but that was my fault. I missed my connection, so I didn't end up arriving in Venice until nearly midnight."

"The witching hour," Gabizon murmured. "I'm sorry to hear that."

"It's okay," Jasmine said.

"How do you like the apartment we arranged for you?" Gabizon asked.

"It took some finding," Jasmine said, with an involuntary smile as she once again remembered her adventure from the night before, "but I made a friend and they helped me locate it in the end. Anyway... I've been sent to assist you. What is it you would like me to do?"

"I'm not sure I can tell you just yet," Gabizon replied.

"Oh," Jasmine said, a little nonplussed. "It's just I've been sent half way across Europe, just to assist you. I'm not sure how much help I can be if you don't tell me what I need to do."

"My research is quite sensitive," Gabizon said. "I need help, but I need somebody I can trust. I need someone with the right qualifications, and I was told you might have what I'm looking for..." Gabizon's voice trailed off as she looked Jasmine up and down pensively. Then she glanced at the screen of the laptop and then back at Jasmine. "I guess it is stupid to have you come all this way and then get all precious about my research. It would be a waste not to have you do anything," Gabizon said. "I suppose I could start you out with something tangential to my studies and see how you do."

"Great," Jasmine said.

"It's just boring research," Gabizon warned her, "no fieldwork. We will have to work our way up to that, very slowly. For now, I need you to do some reading in the library for me."

"Okay," Jasmine said, "so what do you want me to read about."

"Ghosts," Gabizon said.

"Ghosts?"

"Yes," Gabizon nodded. "Like I said, I can't tell you too much, not yet, but I can tell you that an important element of my research is the relationship between ghost stories and a society's taboos. You'll enjoy it, there's lots of juicy stuff to put your teeth into."

"Sink your teeth into," Jasmine corrected, then cursed herself. Why was she correcting the almost perfect English of her new boss?

"Really? Sink... like a ship? Huh..." Gabizon's expression was suddenly appraising again. She stared at Jasmine for a few seconds, then touched a button on her laptop's keyboard. There was a printer in the corner of the room that softly ghosted out a sheet of paper. "Okay," Gabizon said. "Grab that list of books. I'll be here for a few hours. Pop in when you're finished in the library and tell me how you are settling in."

"Will do," Jasmine said.

She awkwardly squeezed past Gabizon to get to the printer and despite not wanting to, she glanced at the computer screen over Gabizon's shoulder. There were two documents open on the desktop. One was the list of books Gabizon had just printed and the other was some kind of report. At the top was her own name, and below were blocks of text with headings like skills, qualifications, character, and most strangely, moral fibre. Gabizon closed the document, and Jasmine immediately started to wonder if she had read it right. It had looked almost like a resume, but she didn't think it was one she had ever written.

The library was just a few doors down from Gabizon's office, but it was a very different space. Both Gabizon's cubbyhole and the cavernous library had the same raw concrete walls, but the library was much bigger, much colder, and much more impersonal. It was a modernist temple of learning with long wooden reading tables and metal shelves. She glanced at the list Gabizon had printed for her and went over to some shelves containing oral history, privately printed books and essays on folklore. The dark and musty books were incongruous on the clean, dust-free, beige metal shelving. She let her finger wander along the spines, looking for the first book on her list. At last she found it, a large-format book with an ornate design on the spine. Her fingers wrapped round the old leather. She took the book over to one of the cold tables and leafed through it. There were fifty stories collected within, and numerous essays about them. There were also three other books on the list Gabizon had given her, so there was no way she could be expected to read it all today. She supposed she was to use her intuition, and decide what among all this material might be useful to Gabizon. Then she corrected herself, it was inconceivable that Gabizon wasn't intimately familiar with these books. She had probably been told to read them as a test. Gabizon was not what she had expected at all. She had been hoping to make a friend of her new boss, but instead the woman had been cold and suspicious. Maybe she would thaw, Jasmine decided, if she found some interesting new angle on the material she had been given to read, something Gabizon hadn't considered before. The problem was that the book was like nothing she had ever read.

As far as methodology went, there was only a short note explaining that the ghost stories in the book had been collected by an anthropologist from among the fishing communities of the Venice lagoon. It was about as far from academic writing as it was possible for a text to be. There was nothing for it though, and she lowered her head to the book and started concentrating. One of the stories caught her eye, and she started reading.

The story told of an old fishing boat, operated by three fishermen. Joining them for the first time that night was one young lad. The fishermen took the boat very far out into the lagoon, and they carried on fishing long into the night. It was the first time the young lad had been out fishing so late. The three older men noticed that he was uneasy and frightened, and the rough old men found this hilarious. Still, they needed him to get over his fear and work, so they put a bright lantern at the front and back of the boat. "Look, it's almost as bright as day," one of them said to the boy.

The young boy wasn't very reassured, but he went and joined the men at the side of the boat. However, when he reached out to help them throw the nets into the water they could see that his hands were shaking. To try and calm him, one of the old men pointed at the horizon, to where the lights of the city of Venice could be seen in the distance.

"Look," they said, "you can still see the lights of the city. One of them is your bedroom window. We can't be so very far from home, can we?" Again the boy wasn't very reassured, but he did stop shaking enough to help the others throw out the nets. The night wore on, and the boy began to relax a little. The chill of dusk lifted once the sun had gone down, and the long night itself really wasn't as cold. The stories of the old men were funny, and the lad started to cheer up. Now and again, the fishermen would take a small nip at a bottle of some fiery, lemon-flavor drink they had brought with them. "Just a bit," one old man said, as he passed the bottle. "A little bit will keep you awake, but you can't drink too much till we've reached our little island, and we're safe for the night."

"We're not going straight back to Venice?" the boy asked.

"No lad. We're too far out. We'll spend the night in our hut and head back at first light, or maybe the day after that, depending on the catch." In the shallows of the lagoon there was a maze of wooden fences, sunk in the mud to trap fish and ensure there was good fishing, even when the tide was low.

Each maze of fences had an island at the center, and on each island there was a little hut, built of cane and plastered with mud. The huts were nothing more than one square room, a door, and two windows. Each isolated hut was the only structure visible for miles around, except for Venice itself, way off in the distance. It was in one of these little structures that the fishermen intended to spend the night. But first, they had to haul in the nets.

The catches were huge back in those days, and it needed all of them working as a team to get the nets onto the boat. They all four reached into the freezing water together, got a good hold of the nets together, and all hauled at once, spilling fish onto the deck of the boat with every heave. They sang traditional songs to keep the pace, and it was warm work even with freezing water splashing about their ears.

The young lad already knew the songs very well, they were a part of him. He'd been singing them since before he could walk, and he bent and heaved mechanically in time with the song. He reached into the cold water, then straightened his back to have fish come gushing all round him. Then he again reached into the water, for another mighty heave. This time, instead of fish, something big and heavy came crashing onto the deck. The old men cursed, and the young boy screamed.

It was a dead body, dressed in the fine clothes of a nobleman. Its eyes were open, staring directly at the boy. A hand, thin as bones but still with some flesh, seemed to reach for him as he struggled to move backwards away from the terrible thing.

"Calm down lad," one of the men said.

"It's just a dead body," another said. "Is it the first one you've ever seen?"

"Yes," the boy admitted.

The old men moved the dead body away from the catch, and the nets were now light enough that they could be pulled on board without the young lad's help.

As the others carried on their work, singing and heaving, already seeming to have forgotten the corpse on the deck of the boat, the young boy was left alone with it, staring into its gruesome eyes. When the older men had finished their work, they all had a nip of the fiery yellow liquor, including the young lad, and then the old man with the bottle smiled and offered it to the dead body lying in the bottom of their boat.

"What are you doing?" the young boy screamed.

"He's not very talkative," the old man grinned, and the others laughed long and hard. "I just thought it might wake him up a bit."

When the rough old men had stopped laughing, they rowed to the island for some rest. The young boy immediately began to beg the old men not to spend the night at the island. He wanted to go straight back to Venice.

"It's too far," they told him. "We'll rest and have a bite to eat, and we'll get off on our way home before you know it." They'd been fishing not far from their little island and it hardly took twenty minutes to row to it. They hauled the boat into the shallows and dropped anchor, then they jumped out into the freezing water, ready to wade ashore.

"I don't think we should leave him in the boat," the young boy said.

"I agree," said the man with the liquor, the one that had offered their guest a drink. "He might spoil the catch." The young boy helped him lift the dead body gently out of the boat and they started to drag it through the water, over to the makeshift building.

"Ouch," the young boy said. There was some wood sticking in the dead thing, protruding right in the center of its chest. It had caught the young boy's hand and gashed him. The lad angrily pulled it out of the body and threw it to one side, so he wouldn't cut himself again before they had finished moving the corpse.

The other fishermen were already inside, and judging by the flickering light coming from the windows had already gotten a fire going. The boy could even smell fish cooking on the fire.

"Let's just prop him up against the wall out here," the old fisherman said. "It's not like he minds the cold, now is it?" When they had the dead body propped up against the wall they went in to join the rest of the fishermen inside. There was just enough room in the makeshift building for a fireplace and a single table. The boy joined the rest at the table and took a long, gulping drink of the lemon alcohol he was offered, to the great amusement of all the rest. They had a few herbs growing in pots on the island, and there was some oil, but beyond that there weren't many ingredients, so the fish were very simply cooked. The cook knew nobody would care though, because they were all hungry after a hard night's fishing. At last he plucked his metal skillet from the fire, smelled the contents suspiciously, then pronounced the meal ready, which was greeted with cheers from the rest of the crew.

"You'd better pop out and tell our guest that dinner's ready," one of the old fishermen said to the boy.

The room went silent.

"What did you say?" the young boy asked, a tremor in his voice.

"You heard me, lad," the old fisherman said. "Just nip outside for a second and tell our guest that dinner is ready. He's invited in, if he'd like to eat."

The young boy got unsteadily to his feet. Something in the older men's eyes told him that he would not be forgiven if he didn't follow orders. The lad walked out into the night to extend the cook's kind invitation. The boy wasn't gone for a minute before he came running back in, to the great amusement of the older fishermen.

"He says he accepts your kind invitation."

The men turned pale, their laughing suddenly silenced. Outside they heard footsteps coming slowly round the hut. The door was pushed open, and the dead man came in and sat down in the boy's place, the only empty chair at the table. The eyes of the others were fixed on their guest. They all felt terror in the hearts, but they couldn't move or speak. The blood flowed chill in their veins, and their dinner guest smiled.

When the sun rose, there were three dead men sitting round the table in the room, and a young boy, half mad with fear, who had a story to tell that nobody would ever believe. The dinner guest, the boy said, had gone.

Jasmine shuddered, and started to make some notes. This was exactly the sort of thing Gabizon was looking for, she decided. A story intended to warn fisherman about what behavior was and was not tolerated on the boats.

***

Gabizon declared herself pleased with Jasmine's first day's work, studying the notes Jasmine had made and grunting in satisfaction in a few places. "This is very significant," Gabizon said. "What made you read this particular story?"

"It was a hunch," Jasmine admitted.

Gabizon looked up from the report and stared at Jasmine. "A hunch? What is that?" she asked.

"A gut feeling, intuition," Jasmine explained.

Gabizon then waved her away with a mumbled goodbye. Jasmine had half been expecting to be invited for a coffee or a glass of wine, so she could get to know her professor better, and so her professor could get to know her, but Gabizon didn't seem interested. Jasmine at last left the university as night was falling, not quite knowing if she had impressed or disappointed her new boss. She decided not to worry about it, after all if the professor didn't want to go out for a drink, she would just have to find somebody who did.

***

Jasmine surprised herself with how easily she found Violetta's house, and once again the gate opened at a push. The door was less accommodating, and refused to open as easily as it had the night before. Jasmine didn't want to use the giant iron ring to knock on the door, she thought it would make too much noise, so she tried knocking with her bare knuckles. There was hardly any noise at all, like a trapped insect banging its head on a window. She could hardly hear her own knocking, even though she was standing right there. How was Violetta supposed to hear her?

"Okay," she muttered to herself. "Here goes." She reluctantly took the iron ring of the knocker in her hand, feeling the chill of it instantly enter her fingers, penetrating to the bone. The noise made by the knocker was deafening. She knocked once, twice, three times, each time louder than the next. She was almost worried that she would wake the whole street. 'Wake the dead', the words suddenly occurred to her as she let go of it, and saw a slick of slime on her fingers, dark and undefinable in the dim light. She sniffed at her fingertips, quickly, not wanting the door to open and someone to catch her smelling herself. The smell was metallic, like rust, or blood.

She'd made a lot of noise, but it was a large house, would anyone have heard? Jasmine didn't have an appointment, and it was entirely possible that Violetta hadn't heard her knocking at all. How long would she give it before she went away again? Jasmine was staring into the eyes of the bull door knocker as these thoughts crossed her mind, almost hypnotized by its blank-eyed gaze, trying to work up the courage to knock again. It was difficult to tell what material the bull's head was made of, and she couldn't even work out how it was held onto the door. The bull was like something organic that had burst its way out of the wood of the door, its blank eyes just stared back at her.

She shrugged and reached to knock again, but before she got her fingers to it the door started to open inwards. An indistinct figure was revealed by the dim light within, a figure that seemed to merge with the darkness, Violetta. Jasmine strained her eyes against the murky light to pick out some details of her friend's clothes, which were all vintage, again. Violetta certainly had a look, like so many of the

Italian students, though most usually went for something a little more modern.

"I like the outfit," Jasmine said.

"These clothes are my most recent purchases," Violetta said, and opened the door wider to let more light in and allow Jasmine to see her outfit more clearly. She was wearing slacks, a dark crimson tailored jacket, ballerina shoes, and had her hair held up in a satin headband.

"My, my," Jasmine said, "that's an awesome look."

"Thank you," Violetta said, and Jasmine felt herself being looked over and appraised in turn. Jasmine joined Violetta in looking down at her own leggings, floppy cardigan, and boots.

"Your clothes are also very impressive," Violetta said. "I suppose they are very modern."

"I suppose they are," Jasmine agreed, suddenly feeling a little underdressed. "Well, come on, it's cold, invite me in."

"But you may come and go as you please," Violetta said. "An invitation is not required for one such as you to cross the threshold. You have even been in this building before... uninvited."

"Huh?" Jasmine grunted, confused by what Violetta was saying. It sounded a little complicated and bonkers.

"Very well. If you wish." Violetta said, standing back with an impressive sweep of the arm. "Enter, of your own free will." Jasmine took a step inside, and the acrid damp of the place hit her in the back of her throat.

"I didn't know if it would be okay to come round. It's quite late," Jasmine said. "In fact the sun has set already."

"Don't worry about that," Violetta said with a smile.

"I was working on an important assignment and I lost track of time," Jasmine continued with her apology.

"Hmm," Violetta said half distracted, half encouraging Jasmine to continue. She motioned for Jasmine to follow her, and walked off down the hall, to a kind of cloakroom.

"I'm reading ghost stories for my new boss," Jasmine said, peeking over Violetta's shoulder at her collection of coats. "They are supposed to provide an insight into the taboos and codes of society."

"Ghost stories?" Violetta said.

"Yes," Jasmine said. "Actually I'm enjoying them immensely."

"As you should. A lot can be learned from such stories," Violetta said, "I've just got to find my hat and my cloak. When we get to the bar, you can tell me more about your ghost stories, I would enjoy hearing about them."

"You have a cloak?" Jasmine said with a wide, impressed grin.

"Yes. Is there anything wrong with that?" Violetta asked.

"No, no. I've seen a few people here in Venice wearing cloaks. I wish I had the confidence to carry it off," Jasmine said.

"You don't seem to be lacking in confidence to me," Violetta said. She emerged from the cloakroom a moment later with her cloak, an eye-catching garment of bright red wool with hand holes in the front. "Let's be off," she said.

CHAPTER 3

The bar was only half full and there were plenty of empty chairs for Violetta to lay her cloak over and for Jasmine to bundle up her cardigan on. "So," Violetta said, "You promised me a ghost story."

"What?" Jasmine said. "Oh. No. I've had plenty of them for one day. I was in that library for hours."

"I understand. I sometimes spend a lot of time in the library, too," Violetta said. "I'm always reading."

"For your studies?" Jasmine prompted.

"No, just trying to pass the time," Violetta admitted. "I never completed my studies. I'm on a sort of extended sabbatical at the moment." A young woman came over, wearing the black t-shirt that was a kind of uniform for the bar staff, and they ordered drinks. They each received a spritz, and the young lady brought a small bowl of popcorn too. Jasmine reached for a handful of the popcorn, tossed one of the irregularly-shaped salty spheres into her mouth and munched loudly.

"Well," Violetta said. "Now I suppose we should discuss the issues of the day."

Jasmine snorted a laugh. "But I'm not even sure what the issues of the day are."

"Oh dear," Violetta said. "I have rather lost track of current events myself. I was hoping to learn a little of them from you. It all starts to get so repetitive; war then peace, then war, then peace again. Boom then bust, then boom, and then bust again."

"Cycles," Jasmine nodded.

"Yes cycles," Violetta repeated. "I read somewhere that cycles are caused by animal spirits, by behavior outside what is considered rational. The theory is that society isn't trying to attain rational goals but is instead driven by animal spirits."

"Speaking of animals," Jasmine said, not quite following what Violetta was talking about, but enjoying listening to her accent, "that bull on your door is quite something."

"Oh that ugly thing," she wrinkled her nose. "It was chosen by my father."

"It looks so old," Jasmine said. "How long has it been there?"

"It is indeed ancient. In fact this isn't the first door it has graced."

"I thought so," Jasmine said, triumphantly. "I've got a nose for such things. You should see me at the flea market. Vienna has a huge one. I've found quite a few treasures there."

"I envy you," Violetta mumbled. "It is some time since I went to market."

"Oh," Jasmine said, suddenly concerned. "You didn't say why you are on this sabbatical of yours? I hope you're not ill or anything."

"No," Violetta said, "I'm not ill. Not really. Not exactly. In fact I think it will be quite some time before I'm finally dead and buried. No, it's more about taking time for myself... to discover who I am."

"Finding yourself," Jasmine nodded.

"Exactly," Violetta said, "but I do worry that I might have overdone it. I may have spent too much time brooding on my own. We don't exist outside of society. Do you see what I'm trying to say? If you are not part of society, you may as well not exist at all."

"Sure," Jasmine nodded.

"Who we are can only be seen when we are surrounded by other people," Violetta continued, seeming to enjoy putting her feelings into words. "It's something like the way a breath can only be seen when condensation forms on a cold mirror. Without the mirror, you can't see the breath, without society, you can't understand who or what you are."

Jasmine raised her empty glass and used it to signal to the young lady at the bar that they wanted two more drinks. "You can knock that back sweety," Jasmine said, pointing at Violetta's still half full glass. "She'll be over in a second with a fresh one. I hope she brings crisps this time. I'm not a fan of popcorn in a bar. It's kind of the sort of thing that you're supposed to have in the cinema, you know what I mean?"

"I haven't been to the cinema in a while, and I certainly didn't have popcorn," Violetta said.

"Right," Jasmine said, "Cinema it is, and tonight, even if we have to catch the late show. If you don't watch a movie at least once a month your brain shrivels up and dies. It's the medium of our age."

"What?" Violetta said, "just like that?"

"Just like that," Jasmine said.

"Okay," Violetta nodded. "It's a nice night and there is a cinema near here. It's just over the bridge at Academia." The two new spritzes arrived then. Jasmine glanced down at her smart phone, opened the browser, went to the local cinema listings site, and looked through the movies with a late show.

"It's anime or superheroes, I'm afraid," she said. "Everything else will have started before we get there."

Violetta finished her first drink and reached for her second. "I don't know what either of those two things are," she said.

"Superheroes then," Jasmine decided, and dropped her smartphone back in her bag. "The movie's about a psychopath in a leotard who hides down dark allies... and he's the hero."

"Sounds... interesting," Violetta said, uncertainty tinging her voice, but Jasmine thought she seemed interested.

***

The cinema was built inside a hollowed out workshop, the concrete structure of the cinema concealed behind a much older brick facade. "How wonderful," Violetta said, not bothering to explain exactly what it was about the cinema that she liked.

They climbed a staircase of raw-concrete up to the box office, and bought tickets. There was no queue at that time of night, and only a few other nocturnal cinemagoers waiting to go in. The concessions stand was right next to the box office and Jasmine bought coke, popcorn, gummy bears and a packet of M&Ms. "There are enough calories in this little lot to last us a week and a half," she said to Violetta, apologetically. "I saw you're not a fan of popcorn, you didn't touch any at the bar, so I'll eat it, if you want. Don't feel you have to have any if you're watching your weight."

Violetta took the big tub of popcorn off the counter where the guy behind the concession stand had left it. She took a generous handful and stuffed it into her mouth. Jasmine started laughing. Violetta made muffled sounds and waved at the coke.

"Need something to wash it down do you?" Jasmine taunted, "Kind of salty isn't it?"

Violetta nodded imploringly, strangled noises coming from her mouth, making beckoning motions with her hand to get Jasmine to stop faffing around and give her a drink. Jasmine punctured the plastic lid of the cup of coke with a straw and passed it to Violetta, who sucked greedily on it, clearing her mouth of popcorn. They were both giggling now, Violetta's giggles mixed with spluttering and coughing.

"I hope he takes his shirt off," Jasmine said, pointing at a poster with the leading man jumping from an exploding car. "He has an awesome six pack."

"Six pack?" Violetta said, wiping her lips.

"You know, abs." Jasmine said, pointing at the actor's stomach area.

"Abs?" Violetta's English vocabulary was good, but it seemed lacking here and there.

"Well developed abdominal muscles," Jasmine said, "The kind to set the heart a fluttering."

"Oh I see," Violetta said. Her coughing and spluttering suddenly got worse, making Jasmine giggle, which in turn made Violetta giggle. A green square started flashing on a monitor above the box office.

"Time to go in," Jasmine said, and she gathered up the rest of her goodies from the concession stand counter.

***

The film had been pretty good and Violetta had made Jasmine promise she would come round the next night so they could go to the movies again. The way she had asked was so imploring that Jasmine was still smiling when she thought about it afterwards, out on her terrace. She could still see Violetta's big puppy-dog eyes.

"Ouch," Jasmine yelped. She slapped her neck and was surprised when her hand came away with a smear of blood. She had been bitten by a mosquito, its tiny, now crushed and ruined body was mixed in with the bloody mess. It was amazing to her that there were already a few mosquitoes around, so early in the year. As an English woman who had grown up in a climate way too cold for mosquitoes she knew they bothered her a lot more than the locals, who were used to their depredations. She had decided she would just get used to them too. Along with the mosquitoes, there were also the predators that fed on them. She couldn't see them, but she heard bats going in and out of the eaves of the houses all around, diving and turning as they snatched mosquitoes from the air.

Jasmine smiled as she sipped her wine. She was particularly pleased, every now and then, when she heard a bat swoop across her terrace and flutter around her head. It meant that another mosquito had been picked off. She saluted with her glass each time and said thanks to the unseen hunters at work around her. The bats were just an impression of movement and an occasional half-heard click of sonar, so high pitched it was hardly even a sound at all. Jasmine stayed out on the terrace until the bottle of wine was finished and then turned to go into her apartment.

It was then that she became aware that something wasn't quite right. There was a kind of whirring presence in the room. A shadow in constant motion, faster than the eye could see. It took her a few moments to realize what it was. A bat had flown into her apartment and now couldn't find its way back out again. It was flying round and round in circles. Even though the door to the terrace was open, it didn't seem able to see it. It couldn't find the escape route, even though it was so obvious to Jasmine. She went in and opened all the windows, two in the living room and two in the kitchenette, separated from the living room by a pair of wardrobes but still part of the same space. The bat's frenzied circling took it into the kitchen area and back out, round and round, over and over again. Opening the windows didn't help, the bat seemed blind to all the new escape routes she'd created for it. It just kept whirring around. She could feel the wind coming off its frantically beating wings as it flew past her head.

"You're going to tire yourself out," she said, "or have a heart attack, you poor little devil." Jasmine ducked to avoid getting the bat in her hair, picked up a big soft cushion from the sofa and tried to shoo the bat out with it. The bat seemed to be able to change direction in a split second and avoid the cushion, almost like it was flying through it. Even her biggest sofa cushion was not enough to redirect the bat or dissuade it from going round and round. And then there was silence. The bat wasn't flying anymore.

One minute there was an indistinct shadow and a fluttering noise, the next nothing.

"Have you gone?" Jasmine asked. She searched her apartment carefully for any sign of a bat, but there wasn't anything. "I guess you must have found your way out at last."

***

The next evening, Violetta was already waiting in the cinema bar with tickets for the both of them and a half-drunk spritz when Jasmine arrived. This time the movie was terrible, and the two girls were talking of other things as they wandered back to Violetta's place. Violetta opened the big door to let them in and the chandelier in the entrance hall was already lit. There were some small flickering lights on the walls too, though the light was much less than you would get from modern electric lamps. "Are those candles?" Jasmine asked.

"Of course not," Violetta replied. "We have gas."

"Gas lighting?" Jasmine said, incredulous.

"Yes, that's right," Violetta confirmed, a note of something akin to pride in her voice.

"Surely you've heard of electricity," Jasmine said, slightly flabbergasted.

"Yes," Violetta said, "but the house was never connected."

"I guess Venice is pretty bad for getting connected," Jasmine mused. "I asked about getting an Internet connection, and they told me it would take six weeks."

Violetta nodded sympathetically but didn't respond. "So," Jasmine said. "How much time do you spend here, in the dark, away from electricity?"

"All of it. All of my time," Violetta said. "I no longer travel. Since I came to Venice, some years ago, I have never felt the desire to travel again. So this is my main, and only, residence. But enough about that. I have refreshments waiting in the other room."

"Refreshments," Jasmine said, "I like the sound of that." Violetta led the way into a side room where there was a teapot, sugar, cups, milk and a cake stand with macaroons, all on a low table between two high-backed chairs. The chairs looked well upholstered without being particularly comfortable. It all looked like the sitting room of a very old lady.

Jasmine was glad to see the cake stand. She was slowly starting to worry a little about Violetta's eating. Apart from a few ostentatious displays, like the time she filled her mouth with popcorn the night before, she hadn't seen Violetta eat very much of anything. She hadn't known Violetta long, and she didn't want to jump to conclusions, of course, because if her friend did have an eating problem, she probably felt ashamed and fearful of others finding out and judging her. She certainly didn't want to come over as judgmental or insensitive, so she decided to bide her time.

There was a cat curled up on one of the easy chairs. She had seen a similar, fat, black cat on a neighboring roof the night before, she remembered. The mangy old moggy had probably been attracted by the bats, she guessed. This one looked too fat and lazy to even get up on a roof.

"Let's drink some fragolino," Violetta said.

"What's that?" Jasmine asked.

"It's a sparkling red wine from the local region. It is made using special grapes called uva fragola, strawberry grapes. Some compare it to a fine Muscat," Violetta explained.

"I see. Well, give us a glass then," Jasmine said, brightly. Violetta poured some fragolino and the girls sat down, in the uncomfortable chairs. Jasmine smelled something on Violetta's breath as she leaned close to hand her a glass. It was a smell like decay, but not bad decay. It wasn't like the stink of rotten milk for example, it was a sweet smell. The way strawberries can smell even better when they are overripe. The smell of the strawberries gets even sweater as the fruit decays, the color also gets more vivid, even as the taste deteriorates. You can enjoy the smell of the rotting strawberries, even though you wouldn't think of trying to eat them. 'Must be the fragolino' she thought. "Do your parents live here with you?" Jasmine asked.

"My mother is resting in peace now, and Father is reclusive," Violetta said. "Once upon a time they were minor nobility, in a country that no longer even exists."

"I'm sorry to hear that, Do you miss your mother?" Jasmine asked.

Violetta snorted, "I never even knew her. All anyone has ever told me about her is that she was beautiful, as if she were a statue or painting. It's as if she never did or said anything, as if her role was purely decorative. My father has been a much bigger influence on my life, and he still influences me now."

"It was the opposite for me," Jasmine said. "My father was out of the picture before I was even born. My parents' marriage hardly lasted more than a summer. It feels like I can count the number of times I've seen him on the fingers of one hand. A few birthdays, a few weekends, he's much more interested in work. Even his new family takes second place to that."

"He works?" Violetta said, clearly surprised.

"Sort of," Jasmine said. "It isn't exactly work, per se. He sets up tax havens in the tattered remains of the British empire." Jasmine noticed the candle light catch Violetta's sharp cheek bones, throwing her face into shadow, which only emphasized the dark pits of her eyes.

She looked beautiful, Jasmine admitted to herself, but unhealthy. "Is it okay if I take a look at the view?" she asked.

She went over to the drapes, moved them to take a look, and gasped. The view was stunning, even better than through the big window in the hall. It had to be one of the best views in Venice. The lights reflecting on the waters of the canal were almost unreal in their beauty. Jasmine let the drapes fall back into place. "Nice view," she said, smacking her lips. "This wine is really, very sweet." She guessed she could get used to the taste, but it was heavier and sweeter than she liked, or she was used to. "So did you used to go to one of the universities? Before your sabbatical?"

"I attended some lectures," Violetta said, "but I never started an official course of study."

"So why go to the lectures?" Jasmine asked.

"I like to keep up with developments in science and philosophy," Violetta said.

"Philosophy?" Jasmine said, intrigued,

"Mmm, yes. There are a great many matters that are, as yet, not well known to science," Violetta said, "but philosophy can help allow a glimpse of them."

"What do you mean?" Jasmine thought of science as having cleared up a lot of nature's mysteries, and she was interested to hear what Violetta was getting at. She certainly didn't think that philosophy would be able to provide answers where science failed.

"Well," Violetta paused for a moment, collecting her thoughts. "For example, when you look at me, what do you see?"

"I see a young woman," Jasmine said.

Violetta smiled. "But that, philosophy tells us, is what you are programmed to see, what your senses are designed to detect. Sometimes a shadow on a wall will look like a young woman, but it is just a shadow."

"I'm gonna need another glass of wine," Jasmine said.

The two girls carried on talking long into the night, but eventually Jasmine decided it was time to head off home.

**

Violetta remained in the room drinking wine until long after Jasmine had gone. Violetta really enjoyed talking to Jasmine and still had a little smile on her face. The room was dark now. The candles had been blown out by a little gust of wind, but Violetta hadn't noticed. She was sitting alone now, in the shadowy drawing room. The drawing room had once been the center of the house, a place to display family status, gentility, good taste. It was handsomely furnished, without being showy. It had sofas, ottomans, upright chairs and easy chairs, stools, a ladies' writing desk, occasional tables, and a screen, but the centerpiece was the round drawing room table. In one dark corner was the piano, covered with felt and cluttered with odds and ends of china and bowls of flowers. Another corner was set up as a 'cozy corner', a niche with small sofas, cushions and knickknacks.

The door to the room was ajar, and drafts from the badly insulated window were nudging it this way and that, less than a centimeter one way then an almost imperceptible little nudge back the other way. There was a gas light outside in the corridor, and the dim illumination it cast into the room moved with every shift of the door. Shadows around portraits lengthened and shortened, deepened and lightened. The trees outside, tossed by the wind, added to the shadows and the dark. A sofa fell into shadow for a moment and then a branch swayed back out of the way again and moonlight fell on the sofa. The sofa was no longer empty, a young man was now sprawling there.

The man was in his late teens. He was tall with an immaculately shaved face, despite the lateness of the hour. He was dressed in tight chinos, slip-on shoes, a shirt, scarf and jacket. His hair was tousled, but in a way that suggested he had invested ten minutes with product to get just that tousled look.

His face went beyond handsome, into the range of beautiful, in a way that few masculine faces did, but he was also sneering. "Hello dear," he said.

Everything about him, even his voice, simply repulsed her. "I am not your dear," she said.

"Oh, but that's where you're wrong," the man said, "We're blood."

"Your ways disgust me and if I could revoke your invitation to just wander into this home whenever the fancy takes you, I would," Violetta hissed.

"If you really want to keep me out, why don't you just move?" the man said. She knew he was taunting her, but his voice sounded filled with real concern. What an accomplished liar. "But then again, I suppose it's not quite so simple, is it?" He was chuckling to himself now. "Some of our personal effects might raise eyebrows with the movers, mightn't they?" She didn't answer him. "I do love coming round to visit," the man said. "You're really the only person in Venice I can properly talk to."

"I don't appreciate the lateness of the hour," Violetta said.

"The lateness of the hour?" the young man said. "You are droll."

"I'm serious," Violetta said.

"But when else am I supposed to come see you?" the young man laughed.

"You aren't supposed to come see me, at all," Violetta hissed. "You have disgraced yourself too many times to ever be forgiven."

"But whose was the original sin, my dear, disciplined, perfect, innocent Violetta," the young man said. "And so who is entitled to pass judgment?"

"You are nothing to me," she said, her voice threatening.

"But we are blood," he said, as he got up and looked deeply into her eyes. His face was uncomfortably close. "So tell me, who's the new girl?"

"I haven't the slightest idea what you mean," she said, holding his gaze.

"I'm watching you my dear, I'm always watching you" he whispered and slightly caressed her face.

CHAPTER 4

Jasmine visited Violetta almost every day over the next few weeks. It was when she was on her way to Violetta's house, a route through the narrow streets of Venice which was becoming second nature, that from the corner of her eye she spotted something unusual, somebody she thought she knew, but she didn't know from where. She'd made a few friends among the students by now, so she said, "Hello," without even thinking.

"Hi," the young man said as Jasmine realized that she didn't recognize him, that he was a stranger. She felt an urge to lower her gaze and hurry on her way, but something stopped her. There was something slightly hypnotizing about his eyes.

"Would you like to join me for a coffee, or a snack, or something?" the young man said.

"Erm," she said, hesitating.

"I'm buying," the young man said.

"That doesn't make any difference to me," Jasmine said.

"Sit with me, my name is Sebastian," the young man said. "Who are you? What do you do?"

"I am an anthropology student," she told him, still hesitant to join him. There was something off-putting about him. "I'm interested in folklore and history. I particularly like ghost stories."

"I like ghost stories very much, too," Sebastian said. "I know many. Many forgotten stories. The ones that were never written down are the most terrifying of all."

"That would actually be helpful to me," Jasmine said, at last slipping into a chair opposite him. "Where do you live?" she asked.

"That's not important," Sebastian waved a hand dismissively. "You would like to hear about ghost stories, yes?"

"Yes that's right," Jasmine said, fantasies of finally getting in her professor's good books going through her mind. She dove into her handbag for her smartphone. As soon as she found it, she summoned up the voice recorder app and set it going. She placed the shiny little device on the aluminum of the café table between them.

"Are you intending to record my stories?" Sebastian asked.

"Yes. That's how we work. It's common practice in anthropology," Jasmine explained.

"But this is not how stories work," Sebastian told her. "They must be allowed to grow and breathe, in the mouth of the teller and in the ear of the hearer. If you capture the story in this little box, it will die. It will no longer be able to spread itself enough to encompass the truth."

"But, without the recorder, how will I remember the story?" Jasmine asked.

"You must listen to the story again and again. You must listen to every version. Only when you can remember the story in your heart, do you know the story and can see the truth," Sebastian told her.

"How many versions are there of a story. How many times will I have to listen?" Jasmine asked.

Sebastian didn't answer. She reached for the smartphone and ostentatiously switched off the recorder app. She slipped the phone into her bag and leaned back. "Are you sitting comfortably? Then I'll begin," she said, under her breath.

"What?"

"It's the traditional thing we say, where I'm from, at the start of a story," Jasmine said. "I like to say it, even if all I'm doing is listening."

"I like that," Sebastian smiled. "Are you sitting comfortably?"

"Yes," Jasmine nodded, "That's right."

Then Sebastian began to tell his story. First he told her that the country he came from was not Italy. He told her that it was a country that was plagued by vampires. To be more exact, the country used to be plagued by vampires. He told Jasmine about a time when vampires were as common as blades of grass, or berries in a bowl. The population was always very fearful, and the vampires wandered at night, mingling among the people.

There were no restaurants or bars back in those days, so people got together in a barn or a farmhouse, sometimes traveling miles when there was news of a gathering. There would be a selection of small dishes, various meats, sausage and cheese. Each place was only open for a limited time, usually two or three weeks, in the season when the first wine had been produced. People generally knew when a place was open through word of mouth, but a sign was also used. The sign was a couple of conifer or fir twigs bound in a circle and hung above the door.

Once, when one of these evening gatherings was in full swing, an old man wandered into the village, and he looked sad. He noticed the sign of the circle of fir twigs, and he went to investigate. He found the people of the village eating and drinking in a barn. He sat with the village people, told them stories and even danced. He was very thin and clumsy because he had not eaten in a long time, but this was not unusual in those days. The people at the feast offered him food and drink, and he sat down among the people having a good time. He was not like the simple farmers of the village or their sons, he was a sophisticated man, from the city.

The stranger stayed at the party until the early hours. He mostly ignored the people there, but there was one girl who gained his special attention. She started to get uncomfortable. She asked him to stop looking at her. She asked if she had done something to upset him. The man said nothing, but he didn't look away.

Then the girl looked down, and saw that the man's feet were cloven hooves. He wasn't one of the living at all. He was one of the undead, a vampire. She immediately screamed for everyone to run away, but she saw that she and the man were the only ones still there. She backed away, and went outside. She was careful not to start running till she was outside, so as not to make him suspicious. Then, as soon as she was outside, she ran into a nearby forest, a forest as old as the world and black as her fear.

The vampire followed her. He walked through the forest the girl had taken refuge in. He searched for hours, never giving up, until at last he found her under a tree. He scolded her for leaving the party so early and the girl started quaking with fear. She tried to say that the party was over already, but her teeth were chattering so much the words wouldn't come out.

The vampire told her that if she was shivering so much, she should come back to his house, where he would make her some nice soup to warm her. He told her that his home was right there in the forest. He took her to a hole in the ground, in the depths of the forest. The hole was too small for her to squeeze through, but she put her head in and saw that this was indeed the home of the vampire. His open coffin was in pride of place in the center. He motioned politely for her to enter first. But, equally politely, she declined and told him that she would follow after him.

So the vampire went in first. He turned into a thousand cockroaches, all tumbling and scuttling on the ground. The dirty creatures ran through the hole and then all jumped up on the other side, coming together to form the vampire again. He looked around and tutted, and began to sweep up and clear away his things. The girl, however, stopped up the hole with a wine cask, and ran quickly away. She didn't know where she was going, she just wanted to stay ahead of the vampire till daybreak.

As she was running she saw a little light a long way off, a house. She ran towards the light. When she got to the house, she found it empty. She didn't know if it was best to go into the house or keep running. She entered the house, climbed up on to the stove, and went to sleep, worn out from the run, and from fear. She slept even though she could hear the vampire crashing through the forest as he looked for her. He had smashed the cask, and rushed out of his hole, mad with rage.

He came towards the house, but he had forgotten the time in his rage. It was almost sunrise, and he had to turn back, howling in frustration. When the girl awoke the only sound to be heard was the chirping of the crickets. The girl now saw all the beauties of the forest, and heard all the sounds of all the living things there. It was so lovely it made her smile and feel at peace. She set out for her parents' house, hoping they wouldn't be too worried that she had been out all night.

She reached her home village, and went directly to her family's home. She told them about the vampire and how she had cleverly escaped him. She also told of the beautiful things she had seen in the woods. But her parents were not glad to see her. They were not happy to hear her story. Suddenly the girl started to sink into the ground, deeper and deeper, for she too had become a vampire. She had stayed too long with the vampire, and he had bewitched her.

"Did you like my story?" Sebastian asked.

"I liked your story very much," Jasmine said, "It's exactly the sort of thing I need for my studies. I'd like to hear more stories in fact."

***

Jasmine was even later than she anticipated, but she took hold of the ring through the door-knocker bull's nose and knocked on the front door loudly and confidently. She had been to this door a few times now and she was starting to believe that she belonged.

The door opened and Violetta was standing there in the gloom of her hallway, looking subdued, even by her standards. She looked over her shoulder, deeper into the house, then back at Jasmine without saying a word.

"Well," Jasmine prompted, "Can I come in?"

Violetta stood aside, to let Jasmine come in, then led her towards the living room. She still hadn't said a word. As Jasmine followed Violetta into the room, she saw that there was a visitor waiting. The visitor was the boy she had just been talking to. It was Sebastian. He was standing by the fireplace, one elbow resting on the shelf. He was playing absently with some small ornament he had picked up. He raised an eyebrow as Violetta brought Jasmine into the room. "Hello," he said. He put down the knickknack that he had been playing with and held out his hand.

She looked at him, and this time it wasn't just for a short moment. His eyes were fascinating. She had the sudden feeling of drowning when she looked into them. They were deep like an endless, bottomless ocean. But there was also an arrogance about him which annoyed her deeply. She had never met anybody like him before. She wondered if her meeting with him had been accidental after all. Violetta noticed the moment between them. She didn't know what to think.

"Don't shake his hand," she said, "You don't know where it's been."

"That's a little uncalled-for," Sebastian said. "After all, I am family, aren't I? Isn't that right old girl?"

"You are certainly not family, and never will be." Violetta turned her gaze to Jasmine, "He's just leaving."

"I don't know that I am," Sebastian said.

"Get out," Violetta screamed at him, staring at him, her hands balled into fists. It was obvious to Jasmine that Violetta did not like this boy at all, or was at least trying very hard to pretend that she didn't. So why was he here? Why had he engineered the meeting with her? Why was he keeping it secret from Violetta?

"You can't just dismiss me, as you would a servant," Sebastian said, "and I demand to be introduced to your friend." he moved a little closer to Jasmine. Jasmine didn't know what to do. Was this some sort of boyfriend, a relative or just a friend? Should she intervene to help Violetta deal with him? She decided to take a step towards her friend, to show her support by standing beside her.

It didn't seem to have any effect on this boy called Sebastian. He was still standing there, as confidently as ever, despite Violetta's harsh words and obvious anger. Jasmine stared at him, trying her best not to be intimidated by his arrogance and sense of entitlement. She fixed him with an evil look, intended to make him uncomfortable. Sebastian noticed and smiled. He started advancing on Violetta and Jasmine. Violetta seemed to flinch away from him, but Jasmine stood her ground. He kept on advancing, and Jasmine found herself almost toe-to-toe with him. He was a little taller than Jasmine, but he was thin, perhaps even thinner than she was.

"Cute but feisty," he said. "You've found a very interesting little friend for yourself here. I'm so glad I popped round. If I hadn't, I wouldn't know you'd been out enlarging your circle of acquaintances."

Jasmine did not like being talked about as if she wasn't even there. "Is he your guest?" Jasmine asked.

"Yes," Violetta said, "In a way. And, unfortunately, some guests can't be disinvited."

Sebastian's face, up until that point a picture of relaxed ease, had tightened a little. He obviously didn't like being talked about as if he weren't there either. He cleared his throat, and the girls' eyes were drawn to him, almost against their will. He smiled, content to be the center of attention again.

"You know, Sebastian," Jasmine said, "anyone who isn't a friend of Violetta's, isn't a friend of mine."

"Then I suppose we shan't be friends, which is a shame," he said, "because I don't know that many nice people in this city." He looked deeply into her eyes.

"I think my friend asked you to leave her house," Jasmine repeated.

"Yes she did. But I don't really think she meant it. You see, she always lets me back in again. She gets so bored here all on her own, year after year. It must feel like it's been centuries."

"She'd have to be extremely bored to put up with somebody as rude as you," Jasmine said.

"I've been nothing but civil. It's she that is giving me the cold shoulder, to coin a phrase," Sebastian said.

"To coin a phrase," Jasmine repeated, imitating Sebastian's cultured but slightly accented English, "What kind of dumbass says 'To coin a phrase' these days." His face fell ever so slightly. It was almost imperceptible, but she could tell she had hurt him a little.

"It appears my English might be a little outdated," he said, "and perhaps my manners are too. It is, of course, the right of the hostess to decide if she would like a caller to stay to tea. And you, darling Violetta, are most definitely the hostess. Would you like me to stay to tea, dear Violetta? If it's not too late. We have afternoon tea quite late at this house, don't we? I can't remember the last time we sat down at the table before twilight. The table is already laid, of course, with all the best things and a fat pink rose at the side of each cup. There are hearts of lettuce, thin bread and butter, and pretty little cakes. So, should I stay to tea?"

"What should I say?" Violetta asked Jasmine. She seemed to be almost hypnotized by Sebastian's words. Jasmine felt she was falling under some kind of spell herself. It was his eyes, she decided. His brown eyes, darker than any she had ever seen before. It was like looking up into the night sky, except there were no stars. Combined with his sing-song accent and pretty words, it was easy to fall under his influence, but Jasmine was a very strong willed young woman.

"Tell him to fuck off," she told Violetta. Violetta laughed, and Sebastian drew a sharp intake of breath. The spell was suddenly broken.

"Fuck off," Violetta said, between giggles.

"You'll regret this." His face was set in a grimace of anger, like a little child who has lost a game of checkers.

"Don't say you'll be back," Jasmine joined Violetta in her laughter, their voices ringing in Sebastian's ears as he left the house and disappeared into the night.

"I had a run in with that guy earlier, in the street," Jasmine said, once he had left and she had regained her composure a little.

"He accosted you?" Violetta asked, putting a hand on her arm.

"No. He told me a ghost story. It was useful, actually. Who is he?" Jasmine asked

"He is one of the waifs and strays taken in by my father. There is a lot of anger in Sebastian. He did not really want to fall into my father's orbit. He would have preferred never to have even met my father, I'm sure. But my father took him under his wing. He was so different then, but he changed. He became bad, degenerate."

"It sounds like you used to like him," Jasmine said. "Before he changed."

"Sebastian is very easy to like, but you must resist that impulse. I blame myself. I never used to want to go hunting with my father, you see, and so he went and found someone who was willing to go hunting with him. Sebastian is a very skilled hunter. A born hunter, my father said. He said it was because he has the killer instinct."

"Hmm, so he's bad, got it," Jasmine said, pensively. "If Sebastian is the bad guy, who is the good guy?"

"There is no good guy," Violetta said. "There is just him and me. I wish he would go away and find his own way in life, but he doesn't. He just keeps turning up like a bad penny and making my life miserable."

"Can't you call the police," Jasmine suggested, "or get a restraining order?"

"Unfortunately not," Violetta said. "It's complicated. He's not family, but he's like family. He's the only family I have left, and there is a very strong bond between us. Perhaps not family in the conventional sense, but a blood relation, sort of."

"Was he here to see your father?" Jasmine asked.

"No," Violetta said. "My father is not as active as he used to be. He no longer goes out much."

CHAPTER 5

Jasmine was at a cafe, thinking about Sebastian. In reality he was little more than an arrogant stranger who apparently popped round Violetta's house sometimes, but somehow it felt like he was more than that. She already knew his mannerisms so well and she already knew his voice. It was very low and velvety. She responded almost physically when she heard it, even at a distance. Just remembering him speaking made her mood lighten, like eating expensive chocolate.

Jasmine took a sip of her cappuccino and, as she drank, she looked up. She noticed one of the saints atop the church facade across the square. The saint was sculpted with its eyes looking humbly down. The roofs of Venice are well populated by statues of saints and angels, and even the smallest of alleys is usually watched over by a saint or two. Jasmine thought about how they looked like pure white marble protectors.

She finished her coffee, paid and went off to the university, and then later the cafe closed, and then later still, night began to fall. The statues of saints that had looked so pure in the daylight started to look different as dusk encroached on the square, and on the alleyways around it. Now the saints looked as time-worn and flawed as the rest of the crumbling architecture of Venice.

The statue Jasmine had noticed was the patron saint of lawyers, barristers, clowns, and torture victims. The statue seemed to wink as a dark, pill-like shape crawled from the saint's eye socket. It was a woodlouse, looking for something rotten to devour. It crawled over the face of the saint, and then it was followed by another, and another.

Soon the saint was alive with the tiny creatures, hundreds of them, but they were just a few of the millions of woodlice that infested the buildings of Venice, eating away at it, feeding on the corruption of the city.

A water taxi came along the canal that bisected the square, and drew up to some stone steps. The passenger stepped from the taxi and the boatman instantly gunned the engine of the water taxi, and waved a friendly goodbye.

"Ciao, Alessandro," he called over his shoulder to the passenger, as he departed.

Alessandro gave a brief wave in return, more of a salute, and then headed down a nearby alley. It wasn't a long alley but the buildings on either side of him were tall, making it surprisingly dark down at the bottom of the alleyway, and he almost didn't see the figure that stepped out of a doorway up ahead. It was just a silhouette, slim, far from imposing, but all the same he still felt a shiver run down his spine. "You're quite a specimen," the figure said.

"I beg your pardon?" Alessandro said. He was forced to stop a few paces in front of the figure. It was either that or barge impolitely past. The alley was too narrow for any other option.

"I'm talking about you. I know all about you," the figure said, and even this close, Alessandro couldn't tell if the figure was a man or a woman, young or old. "You've just finalized a big deal. You must be on quite a high. I bet there are a lot of endorphins in your blood, and a dash of adrenaline too." The figure was right in front of Alessandro now, in his face. Alessandro took a step back now, moving toward the nearest streetlight at the end of the alleyway. He wanted to see who he was dealing with. But before he got there, the figure was on him. He wanted to defend himself, to push this frail but menacing stranger away, but somehow he didn't have the strength. He suddenly felt wrong, as if something terrible was happening to him, but he didn't know what it was.

It was like insects, tiny insects, crawling into his nose, into his ears. Then everything went black. Alessandro lay there for twenty minutes before somebody noticed him and helped him to his feet. The thing that shakily stood up looked exactly like Alessandro, but it was not him.

"Are you all right," the kind stranger asked.

"No, no," Alessandro said, "I feel terrible, not right at all, and now I have to go to the office."

"At this time of night?" The kind stranger said. "But you just had a fall. Why could you possibly need to go back to the office?"

"It's something important," the thing that had been Alessandro assured the helpful stranger.

***

The thing that had been Alessandro walked into the office building, and breezed past the little reception desk with a nod. He went past the elevator and took the stairs up to his floor. The place was half deserted, almost everyone having gone home already. He made directly for his office and opened the door, revealing an anteroom with a secretary. "Hello Mr De Luca," she said. He recoiled. He had not been expecting her still to be there. Weren't secretary's supposed to go home before their bosses?

"Hello Ms. Maletti," Alessandro said.

"You have a few messages. I've left them on your desk," she said, the personification of professionalism. "I'm sure they'll all wait till morning. Did you forget something?" Then after a pause, "Would you like to hear my latest composition."

"I'm sorry?" the thing that had been Alessandro said. What in the name of heaven was she talking about?

"You know how you like to hear my latest compositions, as soon as they're finished," Ms. Maletti said. "I've never told you before, but you're always the first to hear them, even before my mother."

"All right," the thing that used to be Alessandro said. The words were long and drawn out, unsure, unconvinced. Ms. Maletti smiled instantly and reached between two filing cabinets. She fumbled for a second, not quite able to pull out what she was seeking, and then, slowly, a violin case was extracted.

She placed it on her desk and unhurriedly opened it. Then she lifted out a small sheet of turquoise velvet. Underneath this cover was the violin, the bow, and a few other odds and ends in little compartments.

She lifted out the violin, adjusted it, then snuggled it tight beneath her chin. The bow started sawing away and suddenly the little vestibule with the secretary's desk was filled with music. He had never heard anything like it. He'd heard people play the violin before, of course, usually on stage, but this was something different, something intimate. He could feel the noise on his skin, making the hairs on his arms stand up. He could hear tiny vibrations as pictures were rattled, almost imperceptibly, by the noise, as a pair of wine glasses on the desk sang in tune to the violin.

The composition was exquisite. What cruel turn of fate had deposited such a talent in the vestibule of a lawyer's office? When it was over, he applauded quietly, but his applause was heartfelt. She blushed and quickly jammed the violin into its case. She didn't take time to do it properly and the lid wouldn't close. She just moved it to one side and reached into a desk drawer. She pulled out a bottle of Fernet Branca, a brand of intensely bitter, aromatic spirit. It was an acquired taste that he'd never acquired. He put his hand over the top of one of the glasses. "No thanks," he said, "the music was enough."

He left her smiling and blushing in the vestibule and went into his office, though, of course, it wasn't his office. He had taken the form of the true owner of the office, the man who the violin music was actually intended for, Alessandro the lawyer, his latest victim.

There were always sides to a person's life that nobody knew about, things so private they would forever be secret to the outside world. Who would have guessed that the lawyer would be an audience of one to concerts of such beauty and genius. He sat down at the desk, agitated, distracted, unable immediately now to get on with the tawdry business that had brought him here.

CHAPTER 6

Jasmine was wedged up against the wall in the apartment of two friends she had made, Andrea and Marco. She loved visiting the boys, even though their place was such a miserable hole. It had stains on the wall, blood streaks of swatted mosquitoes and even a bloom of black mold below their only window.

The layout of the place was like nothing Jasmine had ever seen in any city ever before. It was one single room, even smaller than her own, and she had thought that was tiny. In their room they had a TV, a small table, a sink, a couple of electric hobs and two beds. The beds were part of some kind of horrendous storage unit with one bed on top and another sticking out the side. It filled the entire place like an art installation filling a gallery exhibition room. Jasmine gasped in horror every time she entered the flat and was confronted with the monstrosity again.

They were eating some meat and cheese they had bought at the supermarket and washing it down with wine from plastic bottles that a local merchant filled for the students for a couple of euros a bottle.

Being Italy, this back-street, plastic-bottle wine was surprisingly good.

"Where have you been?" Andrea asked, "You haven't been around Uni much, and you've been missing lectures."

"You look thin," Marco chimed in, "Have you been looking after yourself?"

"My two Italian mothers!" Jasmine said.

"Be careful," Marco continued. "This city has a way of getting to people. It's like the normal rules don't apply. You might think you are lost in a dream, but you still have to look after yourself. You still have to eat, and you still have to wash."

"Hey! I wash!" Jasmine said.

"I'm not judging." Marco said, "I live with Andrea and his socks."

"No seriously," Jasmine said. "I wash. I showered this morning."

"It's the humidity," Andrea said, though it wasn't clear if he was giving this as a reason for his malodorous socks, or as an excuse for Jasmine.

"It's my new friend," Jasmine said. "She lives in a big old creepy house, and it does have kind of a smell, and I guess maybe it has rubbed off on me. She's why I haven't been around as much as well. Violetta says you've got to either get up early or stay out late in order to truly see the city. It's after the cruise ships have left for the day, when the crowds are thinner, that you can hear the noises of the city. You can hear the sound of the quiet canals lapping at the walls of crumbling palaces. Your eyes become accustomed to the dark and you can see into the shadows."

"I'm not sure I want to see into the shadows of Venice," Marco mumbled. "You never know what horrible things you might find there."

"You have to drag Violetta out into the sun," Andrea added. "It's not healthy to spend all your time in the dark, even if you can hear the canals sloshing about and see the piles of garbage in the corners."

"Pour me some more of that hooch," Jasmine commanded.

"It's not hooch," Marco said. "It's actually a very nice white wine, wasted on your palate."

"C'mon," Jasmine said, "splishy splashy!"

"All right," Marco said, and poured Jasmine out a generous measure from his plastic bottle.

"I'm going to see her again tonight, if you boys want to come along. I'm sure she wouldn't mind. I introduced you to her, remember, that night at the bar."

"No thanks," Andrea said. "I remember, that night at the bar."

"That's all right," Marco agreed. "She's a bit weird. The language she uses is archaic."

"I guess she just learned English from an old text book," Jasmine said.

"It's not that," Marco went on. "Her Italian is very peculiar, too. Violetta speaks Italian like my old grandma, before she died."

"I noticed that too," Andrea agreed, and turned to Jasmine. "Do you know anything about the old Venetian dialect?"

"Not a hell of a lot," Jasmine admitted, which Andrea took as his cue.

"It has the influence of Celtic and the languages of the Germanic tribes, the Visigoths and Ostrogoths. It is the language of books from as far back as the fourteenth century. I chatted with her for a time, and she said a strange word to me. She said I should trincàr, that's more like German trinken, or English drink than the modern Italian version of the word, bere. And she called her chair a trón."

"Like... throne," Jasmine said.

"Exactly," Andrea said.

"Is that so strange?" Jasmine asked.

"You bet," Marco said. "Nobody speaks like that except old ladies. She also said barbastrìo for bat, an ugly word. In standard Italian it's pipistrello, a beautiful little word."

"Why were you talking to her about bats?" Jasmine asked.

"Because she has, how do you say, bats in the belfry?" Marco laughed.

Jasmine thought better of challenging him, even though she didn't like the way they were talking about her friend. It would just encourage them to rib her all the more.

"Okay, she's a bit odd, but I like her and I'm off to see her as soon as this hooch has run out."

"It's not hooch!" both boys yelled.

But Jasmine didn't make it round that night after all. It got too late and she was too drunk. She didn't pop in to see Violetta until the next night.

***

Violetta's door was opening as Jasmine walked up the short garden path. "You didn't drop by last night," Violetta said. Jasmine didn't hear any reproach in her voice. It sounded like she was just making conversation.

"You know how it is. I was with the boys and we were drinking," she said. "In the end, it just got a little to late to come round."

"Oh, I see," Violetta said, then, "You know, you needn't necessarily worry about the lateness of the hour if you want to pay a call on me. I'm a notorious insomniac you know, and I'm often up reading a book or catching up on my correspondence."

"Facebook, you mean? I'm the same," Jasmine told her. "It's robbed me of so much sleep. It's like crack."

"I'm serious. If you see a light in my bedroom window, I'm most likely up and you can feel free to ring the bell."

"I'll bear it in mind," Jasmine smiled.

"Do," Violetta smiled back. The two girls were in the receiving room of the old house now, and Violetta poured out two glasses of the red and sweet fragolino that she loved so much. They sat down, opposite each other. "I'm sure I'm at least as nocturnal as you are, if not more so."

"Okay then," Jasmine said with a smile, and held up her wine glass. "Let's toast." Jasmine enjoyed the conversations with Violetta. They were so different to the conversations she had with other students. Jasmine smiled to herself when she thought of the heated political conversations that could often be heard in the university canteen.

"What are you smiling about," Violetta asked.

"Oh," Jasmine said, "just thinking about my conversations with the boys, and how soon everything always turns to politics."

"I've known boys like that," Violetta nodded.

"But we never seem to talk about politics," Jasmine said.

"True," Violetta said, "but politics are a dangerous business. Getting involved in politics attracts attention. It's something I've begun to pay less and less notice to."

"You mean from the NSA?" Jasmine said.

"Who are the NSA?" Violetta asked. Jasmine's eyes went wide with shock, and Violetta's became uncertain. Jasmine knew her friend was a little disinterested in current affairs and pop culture, but surely everyone had heard of the NSA. But then she remembered that the CIA were called the Chia in Italy. She reasoned that Violetta knew them but by whatever their Italian name was.

"You know," Jasmine said, "the spooks that listen in on everyone. The spies who snoop on private conversations."

"Oh, I see," Violetta said, "is that the latest name for them? The names keep changing but the function is always the same."

"Too true," Jasmine smiled. "This is great. Now we're talking politics."

Violetta smiled back, not quite as enthusiastically as Jasmine. She seemed reluctant to be drawn into talking about such things. She took a sip of her sweet wine instead.

"Hey, Violetta," Jasmine said.

"Yes."

"You and Sebastian aren't really family," Jasmine said, "I've gathered that. But you aren't exactly strangers either. Has there ever been anything...? You know...? Between you and Seb?" Violetta paused for a long moment before answering. "I would like to answer you truthfully," she said at last, "but the thing is, I don't really know the answer to that myself anymore.

If there ever was anyone for me, and I'm not sure there ever was, then Sebastian is probably the closest approximation."

"When we first met," Jasmine said, "you mentioned something about an Englishman. Did you mean an ex?"

"Sort of," Violetta nodded, "but it was all very innocent by today's standards. It never really had time to develop into anything scandalous, and it would have been doomed if it had. They are very sad memories for me."

Jasmine found herself distracted by the words Violetta was using. Today's standards? Doomed? Sad? She was confused and didn't quite know what to ask about next, but at that moment they were interrupted by the door.

There was a short pause, both girls looked at each other, and then Jasmine heard another knock at the door. The metal ring through the bull door knocker's nose clunking against the old wood. Violetta stiffened ever so slightly at each impact but made no move to go and answer it. "You have a visitor," Jasmine said, her heart starting to pound.

"It would appear so," Violetta said. She rose slowly and headed out of the room, on her way to answer the front door. The knocking could be heard again, impatient sounding, before she had even made it half way across the room. Violetta continued out and Jasmine heard the big front door being opened. Then there was a muffled conversation, Violetta's voice and the voice of a young man. Violetta's voice sounded resigned while the male voice sounded forceful. There was the sound of the door being closed and then Violetta came back into the room, immediately followed by Sebastian. Jasmine was surprised to see Sebastian at Violetta's house again, especially considering how emphatically he had been ejected last time.

"Why don't you take a seat," Violetta said. Her voice icy with disdain.

"Why don't I," he replied and lowered himself gracefully onto a sofa, his angular knees kept politely together. Jasmine noticed how different he was to most of the boys she knew, who would sprawl all over a sofa, arms and legs going in all directions.

"Speak of the devil," Jasmine said.

"Hardly," Sebastian said. "You have a pretty smile."

"Don't get used to it matey," she replied wiping it from her face. "I can see Violetta hates you. I don't know why you keep on coming round here."

Sebastian turned his attention to Violetta. Her eyes avoided his gaze. "Could such a thing be true?" he asked her. Violetta eventually met his eyes but she did not respond. "Do you hate me Violetta?" Sebastian asked, unwilling to relent until he had received an answer.

"It's not hatred," Violetta's voice seemed to have warmed, but had still not approached anything like friendly. "Not exactly."

"Then what?" Sebastian sounded genuinely interested.

"I pity you," she told him.

"I'm a pitiable creature, am I?" Sebastian asked.

"Yes you are. You give in to your base desires, your needs and urges. You could be so much better, so much more, if you could just manage to curb your..." Violetta paused, "your debaucheries."

"And what debaucheries are you referring to?" Sebastian asked.

"I can't even bring myself to say," Violetta shook her head slightly.

"Then let me," Sebastian said, as he turned to Jasmine. "What my dear Violetta is trying to say-"

"No," Violetta said, her voice raised, commanding. "Hold your tongue. And I am not your dear anything."

"I don't understand," Jasmine said. "What is all this about?"

"Would you like me to explain," Sebastian smiled, "or would you like to do the honors?"

"Oh, why won't you leave me alone?" Violetta muttered. "You make everything so complicated."

"I suppose everyone would be much more comfortable if we just changed the subject," Sebastian conceded, relenting at last. There was a short, uncomfortable silence, then Sebastian spoke again. "Why don't you see if there aren't some nice cakes in the pantry?" Sebastian suggested to Violetta. "Or some of those delicious macaroons you keep around the place but never eat."

Violetta stared at him, her eyes dancing in rage. "Run along old girl," Sebastian taunted, "hospitality and all that. Let's not be churlish." Violetta made no move to follow his wishes, just sat and stared, her lips a tight, thin line. "Or are you worried about leaving the two of us alone together?" he asked.

"I'll help you with the macaroons," Jasmine volunteered, and got up from her seat.

Violetta smiled. "Yes," she said, "that's a very good idea."

"Isn't it customary for somebody to stay and entertain the guest?" Sebastian said.

Violetta hesitated a second, but Jasmine just grabbed her arm and dragged her from the room. "He'll be fine," she told Violetta. "Grab a book if you get bored," she said to Sebastian and nodded at the bookcase as she dragged the hostess from the room.

***

They took their time walking to the kitchen. "What's going on?" Jasmine asked Violetta as they walked, "Why don't you just throw him out?"

"It's hard to explain," Violetta said. "This house is just as much his as it is mine. I don't really have the authority to throw him out. And even if I did, I'd just be worried about what became of him."

"What do you mean?" Jasmine asked, secretly pleased that they were talking about Sebastian. He seemed to push Violetta's buttons, but he was interesting.

"I'm not exaggerating about him," Violetta said. "He is terribly debauched and has hurt many people very badly. Worse than I can say."

"Drugs?" Jasmine guessed. It would explain a lot, she thought.

"Probably that too," Violetta said. "Without my influence I fear he would lose his last shreds of humanity and become a monster."

"He seems to be just a polite young man," Jasmine said. "A bit pushy, but basically okay."

"As I explained before," Violetta said, "looks can be very deceptive."

"Does he live in Venice?" Jasmine asked.

"I presume so," Violetta confirmed, "though I haven't asked him about his living arrangements in quite some time. I confess I'm somewhat afraid of what I might find out."

"So what happened between you two?" Jasmine asked.

Violetta paused before answering. They had reached the kitchen and Violetta led the way inside. There were cupboards and working tables, but it wasn't a modern fitted kitchen. The cooker in particular looked old, a gas range with iron skillets and brass pots hung above it. There was a big, sturdy table in the center of the space, big enough for multiple cooks to work round at the same time. "Back in the old country," Violetta said at last, "my father wanted a companion to share his interests." She paused again. "Hunting and the like."

"I think you mentioned that," Jasmine said.

"Did I?" Violetta said absently. She paused again. They had crossed the kitchen and were now standing beside a sturdy wooden door. Violetta pulled a key out of a pocket and unlocked it.

"You keep the pantry locked?" Jasmine said.

"It's a silly old tradition," Violetta said and shrugged her shoulders apologetically. "You're not the first to comment on it."

At first, Jasmine didn't see any food. The pantry had china, glassware, and silverware, and also a sink for washing up, but not much else. There were large wooden shelves, but all that was stacked on them were a few small boxes and jars of expensive sweets. There were shavings of orange peel coated in chocolate, maraschino cherries, Turkish delight and many other delicacies but not even a single can of soup.

"You were telling me about Sebastian," Jasmine said.

"Oh yes," Violetta nodded very slightly. "I suppose I was quite a disappointment to my father. I wasn't the slightest bit interested in hunting, or any other of his pursuits." She picked out a box of macaroons. The box was heavy card, with gold edges and fancy writing. It was obviously quite the most expensive type of macaroon it was possible to buy. "Then father found Sebastian."

"That is complicated," Jasmine said.

"Yes," Violetta gave a wry smile, "isn't it." She opened the expensive looking box and extracted one of the macaroons. Jasmine's eyes were drawn to the two sweet meringue biscuits made with egg white, icing sugar, and ground almond, filled with a buttercream center. "Have one," Violetta offered. "The red ones are raspberry. My favorite."

Jasmine took the proffered sweet, getting some of the central raspberry-cream layer on her fingers as she took it. As Violetta let go, her nail caught in the smooth sugar dome of the top half of the macaroon, leaving a very slight crease in the surface. Jasmine popped it into her mouth and within a few seconds it was gone, melted on the tongue like a snowflake. "Delicious," she said.

Violetta's half smile became a full-blooded grin.

***

Sebastian had taken Jasmine's advice and was reading when they returned. "You girls were away for ages," he said. "I've been left to my own devices for a deuced long time."

"I hope you managed to amuse yourself," Jasmine taunted.

"As you can see," he said, holding up the book, "I did as you suggested."

"Well," Violetta said, "I've never known you to be much of a reader."

"There's no need for cheek," Sebastian said, pretending to be offended. "I ended up reading Proust," he flipped the book over to read the spine. "This one is called... erm... Remembrance of Things Past. I hope you feel sorry for me and thoroughly ashamed of the predicament you left me in. Sitting on my own, reading Proust." Sebastian shook his head at the very thought. "I suppose I have been told it ought to be read by everyone, but the sentences are so long I nearly fall asleep before the end of each one."

"Proust? No way. That thing is unreadable, I once tried to read it but the same happened to me. I actually did fall asleep," Jasmine laughed. "You can put the book down now. We have your macaroons."

"Then all is forgiven," Sebastian grinned, throwing what was obviously an expensive leather-bound edition nonchalantly aside. "Just put the plate down on the table here, somewhere within arm's reach."

Violetta, who was the one actually carrying the macaroons, artfully displayed on a three-tiered service among pretty paper doilies, smiled to herself as she put them on the table.

"Hey," Sebastian yelped. "Who ate the raspberry ones?"

***

By the time Jasmine left, it was very early morning. She walked to the front, the place where the buildings of Venice met the open lagoon. She saw huge lines of ducks flying low over the quicksilver water. She watched the waves for a while then turned around and headed home. She found herself briefly thinking about Sebastian. His eyes were really very dark and hard to get out of her mind. She saw a robin redbreast when she cut through the park, looking for food at the edge of a flower bed. It let her walk right up to it before it flew away. She heard a woodpecker somewhere among the trees, but she didn't see it.

A baker came out of his shop, a man in his sixties with horn-rim glasses and a stylish sweater. He put a white paper package in a little wicker basket hanging down from a second-story window, and the basket was lifted upwards. She couldn't see who it was who was getting their morning bread. Just as some people were pulling up their freshly baked bread, others were letting down long ropes with their household waste, a couple of plastic supermarket bags here, a big paper supermarket sack there, bulging with trash. The bags of scraps and packaging weren't allowed to descend all the way to the ground, where gulls and pigeons would soon eviscerate them, but dangled instead at shoulder height against the walls of the buildings.

A window opened on the first floor of a house and a woman put out three little pots of white spiky flowers. Jasmine had no idea what they were, she was no gardener, but the morning was chilly and she supposed the woman must have kept the flowers indoors for the night because she had been worried that they might be killed by frost. It didn't seem worth going back home so she went to university.

Jasmine was one of the first arrivals at the university, the exposed pipes of the modern building were crackling and popping, making noises as they expanded within their silver jackets. Hot water was now flowing within, coming from the giant boilers in the bowels of the structure. Students and professors were arriving in small groups and the waking world was gradually coming alive, reclaiming the territory from the nocturnal creatures.

CHAPTER 7

There was no chalk outline round the body because of the soft clay of the building site. Among all the mud and confusion it was a real stroke of luck that the body had been found before the new jetty was constructed on top of it. Accurso, the lead detective, had decided it was very likely a dump site rather than the murder site. The deceased, Accurso had noticed, was wearing shoes by A. Testoni. They were, he knew, stitched with custom-made linen twine and lined with glove-soft goatskin to make a shoe as light as a feather. They were shoes unashamedly aimed at gentlemen of means who insisted on the very best the world has to offer, regardless of price. He couldn't imagine anyone voluntarily coming to this muddy place in such nice shoes. No, the man had definitely been transported here and dumped.

The photographer was still at work, the site intermittently illuminated by his camera flash every few seconds. Accurso always made sure to get to the crime scene before the forensics experts if he could, or as soon afterward as possible if not. He had a very low opinion of Italian forensic science. The main issue was the collection of samples, and avoiding contamination of evidence. Strict protocols had to be applied during the inspection, collection, and sampling of all items at the crime scene, which basically meant he had to be there to stop police officers walking backwards and forwards over everything. He'd already had to physically manhandle two rubbernecking officers out of the way.

The wound was unusual. The edge of the wound was torn and jagged. Accurso wondered if a particularly hungry rat from the canal might have simply jumped at the man's neck and nibbled him to death. Accurso smiled at the thought, but the wound did have a nasty tattered edge to it.

***

Later that day, Accurso was looking for wounds with similar characteristics, but it wasn't going well. Accurso could eliminate gunshot killing and knifing of course, they would leave wounds that were too clean, but that left an awful lot of murders. He had to download the pictures for each one and look for similarities with his dead lawyer. But there were just too many to look through. He tried narrowing his search using keywords that described the neck injuries. Ripped, slashed, gashed, torn, and similar words. He was making progress, he supposed. He had transformed his task from something hopeless to something merely Herculean, but it would still take far more time than he would have liked.

About an hour later he got a hit that caught his eye. It had been included in his search because of a match from the body of the text. The wounds were different to his victim, but there were similarities. He clicked on the download link for the file the photographs were from. A progress bar appeared, but instead of slowly creeping to download completion it disappeared again and was replaced by an error message. "File not found."He banged his desk in frustration. This didn't happen often but it wasn't completely unknown, and troubleshooting the problem was a little beyond Accurso's computer skills. If he wanted that file, the quickest way round a computer problem was to go and find the paper version.

***

Accurso went to the other side of the building, to the records department and started systematically checking the spines on the files. He noticed a gap. The files jumped from JH015678 to JH015680. With everyone relying so much on the computerized versions of the files and with the case being so old, he doubted that the file was being used.

He got the sudden sick feeling, more than a feeling, a certainty, that the file had simply disappeared, from both the computerized and the paper records.

"Marco," he yelled the name of the records clerk hovering nearby, keeping an eye on him. He pointed to the shelf. "Any idea where this one might be?"

"I'll take a look," Marco said. He plunged his hands in among the files on the shelf and rooted around. "Looks like we have an escapee," he said. "How badly do you need it?"

"It might be connected to something I have going on now," the inspector said, vaguely, "but, then again, it might not." "If it turns out you really need it," Marco said. "you could check with the investigating officer, they might have a draft of the report on their computer, or in a backup. I'll find out who the investigating officer was, if you come to the desk with me. It'll only take a minute.

***

The detective's name was Berlin. He had recently retired, so Accurso decided to call round and see him at his home. He couldn't go that day, but he made sure to visit the very next day. There was only one bell on his door and he answered in just a few seconds. After a warm greeting Accurso was led up some stairs to a spacious first-floor flat. Accurso was surprised to see that there were several book shelves. Most cops weren't big readers. It was rare to find a policeman's house with more than five books in the whole place, including cook books and maybe a famous footballer's biography. Berlin opened a bottle of grappa with no label on it and two small shot glasses were poured out.

"So, Mr Berlin, did you find a copy of your report."

"I'm sorry, no," Berlin said, "but I did find some notes." There was a plastic file on the coffee table, alongside the grappa glasses. Accurso picked it up and flicked it open.

"The thing that interests me most is the weapon," Accurso told him. "The wounds are similar to ones I saw on my most recent deceased. Definitely not a knife or gun. Did you ever come up with a theory about the murder weapon in this case?"

"No," Berlin said. "We never did find it. And we didn't come up with a convincing theory about what it was."

Over many years of interrogation, Accurso had become expert at spotting incongruous choices of words. It was these strange choices, he believed, that could be unlocked to unleash floods of information, if you noticed them and if you had the knack. "So you had a theory," Accurso said, "but nobody else was convinced?"

The old man's eyes became guarded. He poured them both another drink. He sat silently for quite some time, then spoke. "Why don't you take that away with you and give it a good read. If you still think it has any connection to your case, you contact me again and ask all the questions you want. How about that?"

"Sounds fair," Accurso said.

CHAPTER 8

Violetta was sitting at the window. She was doing embroidery by the light of a candle on the table in front of her, but her concentration waned for a moment, and her eyes drifted to the view through the window. The big black cat opposite her, curled up on a sedan, shifted its head and opened an eye, as if to reassure itself that she was still there. Violetta bent her head back to her needlework. She was working in red silk, painstakingly stitching a verse from A Lovers' Quarrel by Robert Browning.

He has taken a bride
To his gruesome side,
That is as fair as himself is bold:
There they sit ermine-stoled,
And she powders her hair with gold.

Violetta lifted her head and her needle paused in its endless motion. "What am I doing?" she screamed at the cat, her words tearing the silence. The cat raised its head again, and again opened an eye. "I'm wasting my time, when life is out there to be lived!" She threw her embroidery to the floor, got up and stomped across the room. "This isn't living. This is worse than death. That damn clock constantly counting all the wasted seconds, all the wasted minutes, all the wasted hours, the days, the weeks, the months, the years. Years and years and years and years. And what do you do?"

She walked back across the room, advancing menacingly on the cat. "You just lie there, laughing at me. You're an animal, a debased fiend." The cat's eyes went wide as she picked it up and threw it across the room.

It twisted in mid air and landed instinctively on its feet. "Oh bravo," Violetta screamed. "Well done."

She ran over and aimed a kick at the cat, but the cat was already running for the exit. She looked around the room, grabbed up a candlestick from a side table raised it and hurled it down on the wood flooring. Even throwing the heavy metal object with all the might in her skinny arms, she wasn't able to leave the slightest mark on the hard wood floors. There was no damage, no evidence of her rage. "This damn place is a jail. I hate you. I hate you!" She was screaming now, wails of torment punctuating her words.

A shape appeared in the door. It was a tall man, his hair slicked back. He was wearing a gray flannel suit with a drab tie. "What is all this unrest and commotion?" he asked.

"You know exactly what it is," Violetta replied.

"Cease this behavior immediately," the man said. "Calm yourself."

"I will not stop!" Violetta spat. She lunged for the candlestick, gathered it up from where she had thrown it and raised her arm to throw it again. The man quickly crossed the room and slapped her across the face as she threw it, disturbing her aim so that instead of the window she hit the wall, leaving a very slight dent in the wallpaper. The man's blow wasn't particularly forceful but it still sent Violetta reeling backwards. She recovered her balance near the table where she had originally been sitting. She was standing with one foot on her embroidery, lying forgotten on the floor.

"You ungrateful child," the man said. "I have done everything for you. You know that you are the lucky one, from all your friends. Where are they now? And where are you?"

"I am in hell," Violetta hissed.

"Don't be so melodramatic," the man scolded. "You know what the world is like. You have seen it. You must be kept safe and the world must be kept out." His voice softened and he came nearer. "Look at you," he said touching her cheek, "you are all skin and bone daughter.

I wish you would eat."

"Get your hands off me, you monster," she hissed. She turned her back on him and went over to the window. She stared out at Venice. The man watched her for a few moments. He opened his mouth to speak but his daughter preempted him. "Get out," she said.

She didn't move from the window, or even turn her head to see if he had gone. She just stayed at the window staring out. Then she saw the garden gate open, and saw Jasmine walking up the garden path. A wide grin spread across her face as the sound of the iron door knocker against the wood could be faintly heard.

When Violetta got to the door, the smile disappeared from her face. The man was chatting to her friend at the door. "You are spending a lot of time with the lady of the house," he said. "Talking of many things." Jasmine looked confused.

"Get away from her you old fool," Violetta shouted. "Stop bothering my guest."

"Of course," the man said, and wandered off through a side door.

"Who was that?" Jasmine asked.

"A servant," Violetta said. "It seems he just came out of retirement. Hey, do you want to go out?"

"That's the spirit," Jasmine said. "We can't sit around in the drawing room drinking fragolino and nibbling macaroons every night."

They headed out to Cafe Noir, where they now had a usual table. They chatted and drank spritz but there were times when the conversation would falter, when a silence would intrude. In those moments Violetta often felt herself dragged down by her memories, sometimes painful memories. She felt embarrassed at having such dark things in her head sitting in a place of such happiness and enjoyment. The laughter and conversation was such a contrast to the silence and gloom of her interior life.

When the gloom overwhelmed her, Jasmine's jokes and stories seemed to slowly wash it away, like the sea washing away dirty sand to reveal beautiful shells on the beach.

But the gloom always came back. Often the memories were of the castle, a very dark period for her, perhaps the darkest. She often tried to remember the time before the castle too, but that was all such a long time ago. She remembered her parents, not her father, her parents. She remembered their smiles, but not their faces exactly. She remembered the sun, like candle light, like electric light, but much, much brighter. She remembered the way it made flowers look, remembered her mother collecting flowers for her, how such a simple gift given freely by mother nature and simply collected by her own mother had made her so happy.

Then came the castle. She had been given ludicrously expensive gifts since then, jewelry, paintings, palaces, even tracts of land big enough to show up on the political maps of Europe, but they were dead things compared to those flowers. Her father stalked the halls and corridors at night, which was unbearable, or he just wasn't there at all. He disappeared from sunset to sunrise, leaving the castle gaunt and irascible and returning fat and content.

Violetta, that hadn't been her name back then, but she couldn't remember what her name had been, was it Ellyn or had that been her friend's name? Violetta was always hungry. The castle was full of the most delightful food, and she liked the taste, but it didn't fill her, it didn't satisfy her. The hunger never really went away.

She would eat with her father at the huge table, just him and her, or were there a few servants attending? They brought course after course of food, with fine, strong wine, wine fit for nobility. And it was all finished off with a wonderful desert of pastry and raspberry preserve. They pushed their metal plates away and servants rushed to take them out of the room.

"I'm still hungry," she said to her father.

"I know," he said, "Me too."

"But you know how to still the hunger, don't you?" she said. She didn't really know what she was talking about, the words were half instinct. Her father's eyebrows bunched up in discomfort, his lips pursed, but he didn't deny it. He pulled his knife from his belt and picked at his teeth, getting out a few morsels of the fine food that were lodged there. He wiped the blade on his sleeve and returned it to his belt.

"It is a secret," he said, "and it can not be unlearned. Only speak of this again if the hunger becomes so great that you can not bear it."

"But my hunger is great," she said. "I feel like I have never eaten, like my belly has never been filled."

"Then tomorrow night I will teach you," he said. She thought for a moment that the hunger would still with his words but it didn't. It surged, threatened to overwhelm her like a wave. As soon as dusk came the next night she was there, at the castle gates in her Sunday best, making sure that he didn't leave without her. She saw him come out of the little door in the keep, descend the staircase and cross the courtyard to the gatehouse where she was waiting. He noticed her, then looked her up and down.

"Those clothes won't do," he said. "Where are your riding clothes?"

"Should I change?" Violetta glanced apprehensively back and forth between her father and the castle keep.

"Yes," he nodded. "Don't worry. I will wait for you." She ran across the courtyard to the keep, scrambled up the staircase to the little door and squeezed through. She was back out, in a completely new outfit of riding clothes and boots in just ten minutes. She could hear her father's laughter as she hurried back across the courtyard.

There were now two horses by the gatehouse, her father already mounted on the larger of the beasts. A servant helped her into the saddle and the giant gate was opened and portcullis raised. She followed her father down the precipitous path that led down the hill, away from the castle.

She knew the path well and was a confident rider, but she had a fright or two on the way down because her father was going at a fast pace.

He galloped through the village, where the shutters were all closed and the doors barred, and then out into the countryside, cantering across his land, mile after mile. They turned off the main road and trotted along pathways and through orchards. There were hardly any fences back in those days, she remembered. A rider could go pretty much wherever they wanted to.

Violetta couldn't do anything except do her best to keep up. She sensed that her father was in a very determined mood and she wasn't sure he would stop for her if she fell behind. She began to think it was some type of test, to see if she was worthy of what he had to show her. They reached a remote hamlet, just four or five houses, surrounded by orchards. Her father stopped and dismounted. He slung his reins round a tree branch and gallantly helped his daughter down from her horse.

"Apples," she said, "fresh from the tree. Is that the secret?"

"No," her father shook his head. "It would be much better if it were, much easier, but no. That is not the secret." He stared at her for a moment, then continued. "We must be very silent from this point on, so, if you have any questions, or if there is anything you want to say to me, it would be best to do it now."

"What would I ask?" Violetta whispered.

"In about an hour you will have a great many questions," her father told her. "Save them until after. Do not open your mouth, do not cry out, do not gasp, whistle, or hiss, until you are back in this spot," he gestured to indicate the spot where they were standing, beneath the tree. "Do you understand?"

"You have my word," she said, as he took her hand and led her towards the nearest house. It was only one story high and the windows were shuttered. There was a single large door with iron studs in it, which Violetta thought was likely to be barred. There didn't seem to be any way of gaining entrance short of a battering ram. Houses like these were designed to keep out brigands, and were built round a little internal courtyard. Her father pointed upwards, and Violetta looked up to see that the roof was steep to shrug off winter snow. There was a tiny skylight, enough to let a little light into an attic, but there was no way in through there, it was too high.

Her father smiled and lightly put the index finger of his right hand on her left eye, and the ring finger on her right. He moved his fingers downward, closing her eyes. She felt herself lightly held round the waist, her father's arms, and then felt herself lifted from the ground and hoisted high into the air. She immediately felt the urge to open her eyes and see how this magic was being done, but she resisted. She couldn't close her ears however. There was an insectile scrabbling sound, coming from the wall and following them up. The sound changed as it transitioned from the plaster of the wall to the tile of the roof. Then it stopped and she was put down. She felt the rough tile of the roof through her riding breaches and felt the air, fresher and windier now they were above the trees. A hand curled round hers. It maneuvered her hand to a handhold, one of the metal brackets on steep roofs in areas of high snowfall intended to prevent dangerous falls of snow from the roof. She grabbed it and hung on. Then she felt gentle fingers on her eyes, and so she slowly opened them.

As she had expected, she was beside the small skylight. Her father motioned for her to look inside. There was a simple peasant's room with a young man lying, fully clothed, on a straw bed. Her father then retreated down the roof, his arm and leg movements hidden by his riding cloak.

Violetta couldn't see how he was moving so surely on the steep roof, but she could hear the nasty scrabbling noises. He disappeared over the edge of the roof, one hand momentarily exposed in the guttering as he held onto the drain pipe. The hand was wrong somehow, bony, or shiny, or perhaps hairy. She couldn't see what it was and decided it must have been a trick of the light.

After a moment she couldn't hear anything except the wind in the apple trees. She turned her attention back to the skylight and was startled to see that the young man was looking right at her. She snatched her head back, waited for him to yell, but there was no sound. Had he seen her after all? She peeked again, and although the man was giving the roof and walls some suspicious looks, he was settling his head back onto the pillow to sleep. He hadn't seen her through the dirty little skylight.

She watched for a while, watched the young man fall asleep, then noticed something strange. Something was leaking under the door, like somebody had spilled milk outside but it wasn't milk. The widening stain spreading from the door was moving too slowly and was too dark. It was more like blood. It was something terrible, she understood that immediately, something unclean. Then she noticed that lumps were forming in the horrible viscous fluid, lumps with legs, like cockroaches. The pool of fluid was flowing towards the bed, and the roaches multiplying, they climbed on each others' backs, gradually fusing to form a solid mass. As the mass grew, with wave after wave of roaches crawling from the ooze, climbing, and joining the mass, it became taller. It grew two arms, its lower part split into two legs and it became her father.

It took every scrap of self-control Violetta had not to scream. She watched horrified and fascinated as her father took one tentative step after another towards the young man's bed. When her father was just a few steps away, the young man woke up. He raised his head, looked in the direction of her father and jumped in shock.

She saw her father hold up a finger, catch the young man's eye, she heard muffled words as her father started talking, but she couldn't discern any meaning in it. The young man seemed to relax a little, as though there were some rational explanation for finding a man in your locked room in the middle of the night.

Her father took a step forward, approaching the man as if he were a skittish wild animal and might bolt at any moment. The man's posture was strange, stiff somehow. His face was slack, his eyes glazed. Her father had reached the man and now put his arm round him. She could see her father's lips moving, she could tell he was whispering, but she couldn't hear anything from outside on the roof. Then her father placed his lips against the man's neck, and bit his teeth into the man's jugular. Violetta put her free hand, the one that wasn't holding her in place on the roof, over her mouth. It was the only way to prevent herself from crying out in horror and disgust.

There were two spurts of blood before her father managed to encompass the whole wound in his mouth. His neck was pulsing as he swallowed down the blood pumping from the man's neck. The man seemed to be coming out of his trance, seemed to dimly be aware of what was happening, but he had already lost a lot of blood. He was becoming weaker and weaker as the life ebbed out of him, and as the man weakened, her father grew stronger, becoming visibly meatier and healthier, plump even.

Violetta turned away, she'd seen enough. She had no interest in watching anything else that might happen in that room. So this was the meal that would satisfy her. So this was what was required to make the terrible hunger go away. A blood meal. For her to slake her thirst, some other living being would have to die. Violetta closed her eyes.

"Hey," Jasmine's voice roused her from the memory, dispelling it. "You're quiet tonight. Are you okay?"

Violetta looked at her and a tiny smile appeared on her lips. "I think I will be okay, yes," she replied. "Thank you."

CHAPTER 9

Accurso was in a small cafe near the station eagerly waiting for his polenta when he got the call. His phone rang just as the meal was arriving, making him groan with frustration. The waiter smiled sympathetically and left the steaming hot food in front of Accurso while he fished around for his phone. It was the dead lawyer's secretary, ringing him on his personal phone.

"Pronto," he said, his voice terse, after swiping to accept the call.

"It's Miss Maletti," came the voice on the other end. "Remember you asked me to find the name of the last file that the deceased had worked on before... before his death."

"That's right," Accurso said. "Do you have the name for me?"

"Yes," she said. "Do you have a pen. It's a little unusual."

"Sure," Accurso replied, digging a pen and pad out of his jacket pocket.

"The name is Ratchis Romanza."

"That is unusual," Accurso said. "And what did this Ratchis need a lawyer for?"

"I'm sorry I can't tell you any more, Inspector. Client confidentiality," she explained. "You understand, I hope."

"Of course," Accurso said. "Thanks again, and don't hesitate to ring me if you think of anything that could be of assistance."

He rang off, and slipped the phone back into an inside pocket. He looked at the name he had scribbled in his pad. He rang the station, asked them to see if there was a file on Ratchis, then turned his attention to his polenta.

There was a file, and it was waiting for him on his desk when he arrived in the office. Accurso groaned when he opened it. It bore all the hallmarks of being a fake identity. There were just the basic documents required to formalize an identity, birth certificate, identity card, domicile status registration, and nothing more. No notes, no medical records, no criminal records, no driving license, nothing. It was just too thin to be the file of a real person.

CHAPTER 10

Sebastian was standing in the center of the square watching the water seep through the drains, but it wasn't seeping into them, it was seeping out of them. It always started in the middle of the square, where the weight of the central fountain made a very slight depression in the pavement. The concavity wasn't obvious in dry sunny weather, but in wet weather that was where the water collected, and that was where the tide waters made their first appearance during the regular flooding Venice was subject to. The phenomenon occurred mainly between autumn and spring, when the local tides were pushed by a seasonal wind called the bora. Sebastian was forced to take another step back, it was that or allow the murky lagoon water being forced through the drains to engulf his expensive shoes. They were alligator skin, durable and soft, and not at all robust enough to be exposed to the dark waters of the lagoon.

The rising waters were an ill omen, he thought, although he wasn't sure why he was suddenly seeing doom in a simple, natural phenomena he'd observed countless times before. It had to be Jasmine. He hadn't felt this unsettled in a long time. This business between Violetta and Jasmine was bound to end unpleasantly, he was sure of that.

It was a shame, of course. He liked Jasmine. He had encountered her a few times now, at Violetta's place and a couple of engineered meetings around the city. He found her irreverence and lack of understanding... what was the word? Refreshing? Disturbing? She was intelligent and knowledgeable, and a little too interested in ghost stories, but she didn't know the truth, how could she? And what would happen when she did?

Sebastian took another step back, again forced to retreat by the oncoming water. For all the skills he had acquired over the years, there was nothing he could do to hold back the encroaching waters. His only options, if he wanted to cross the square any time soon, were to go home and change into his boots, or to let the lagoon waters ruin his shoes. Or he could simply wait. High tide wouldn't last all night. He could simply stand there, his umbrella held protectively over his head against the rain and wait. Waiting was a good option, so much more dignified than messing around with rubber boots, but it was so passive.

He found his thoughts turning to Jasmine again. There was something so instinctive and powerful about her. She had brought a sea change in Violetta. Violetta was now so much more alive, thanks to Jasmine's influence, so much more interested in the world around her, in a way she hadn't been for a long, long time. But she was also more independent, less likely to do as he suggested. She seemed to be toying with some act of rebellion, Sebastian thought, but he had no idea what that might be, or what consequences it would have for them all.

Sebastian didn't have the same feelings for Violetta as when they first met, she had betrayed him too completely for that, but he was still oddly fond of her. He should hate her by rights, but he didn't. He wished her well. He wanted her to be happy, if such a thing was possible for her, and he liked the way Jasmine was making that possible. But no good could come of her rebelling too much. And then there was Jasmine. His feelings for Jasmine were more complicated than his feelings for Violetta.He was forced to take another step back as the lagoon waters lapped up against the toes of his shoes. Just when you thought the waters had reached their highest point, they surprised you by going a little bit further, and even an extra half a centimeter could make a huge difference.

An extra half a centimeter could make the difference between a building staying dry and being completely flooded. Once the waters went higher than the threshold they could flow unimpeded into the entire house. Sebastian was faintly aware that his fondness for Jasmine was building in a similar way, but what level would it reach? Would it breach his threshold and overwhelm him?

Such sentimental thoughts, he chided himself, probably because he had been skipping meals. He knew he should be eating a lot more if he was to keep up his strength, but it was complicated. He just couldn't bring himself to do it.

Sebastian raised his eyes from the waters and looked around the square, which was beginning to look more and more like a lake. The electric lights were reflected beautifully in the black water. There wasn't a breath of wind, so the only disturbance to the surface was the beginning of ripples caused by the raindrops that were falling. It wasn't heavy rain, just enough to make an umbrella necessary. There was an alleyway on the other side of the square where people kept emerging, most dressed in the plastic socks you could buy from tourist kiosks and street traders. They waded through the water, emerged onto dry land alongside Sebastian and carried on their way without giving him a second glance. He wouldn't be the only pedestrian they had seen trapped by inappropriate footwear along their route. They were heading for Rialto, most of them, and had quite a way yet to go. The waters would deepen again as they got to Rialto, the oldest part of Venice. The waters were always deepest there: it encroached there first and took longest to leave.

Where was it that he was going, Sebastian asked himself, as he watched the tourists stride purposefully through the water. He didn't even know anymore. He had left the house with some destination in mind, but now he had no idea what it had been. He was just killing time. His life had become an exercise in killing time, distracting himself from the endless onward march through history.

He had become passive and lost. Listless and aimless, just like Violetta. If Jasmine could awake Violetta, why not him?

He took another step back. If you just glanced at the water you wouldn't realize it was on the move. You had to stare at it to realize it was slowly creeping forward. You had to pick a point on the ground, the edge of a flagstone, the toe of an expensive shoe, and keep your eye on it. It was only in relation to the fixed point that the motion of the water became noticeable. He had become a fixed point, he realized. He was the edge of a flagstone, the dirty toe of a shiny and expensive, hand-made shoe. He was waiting to be overtaken and engulfed by time. There would come a point when he was completely lost in time, all at sea, set adrift and far from any reference point or landmark.

"I have to start..." he paused, startled by the sound of his own voice out loud. He was talking to himself now. "I have to start... Doing things." He needed achievements. He needed to have his name up in lights, carved in stone, shouted from the rooftops. He had been lurking in the shadows for far too long, virtually his entire life, and if he continued he was fairly sure the shadows would swallow him up. He had to get out into the limelight, into broad daylight, out into the world.

"I need the ring," he said. He took a step into the water. He knew the water was freezing but he didn't feel it. He knew his expensive shoes would be ruined but he didn't care. He was going somewhere now.

CHAPTER 11

Jasmine was dog tired after being out late with Violetta. They had stayed out at every type of drinking den Venice had to offer, starting with a relatively harmless pizza place, then when that closed they had moved on to the usual Cafe Noir and then later to a horrible little club, little bigger than her own flat and decorated in white tiles like a cheap Greek restaurant. They had only given up and gone off home just before daybreak and Violetta had seemed reluctant even then.

A lot of the night was a blur, but she remembered that Violetta had mostly been telling her about local history. Violetta had been talking about a local tradition called the Flight of the Angel. A tradition that was still carrying on to the present day, but her stories were so vivid it was almost like she had been there at the very start. She talked about a trapeze artist, who amazed the Venetians assembled below by walking along a rope from the top of the huge bell tower to the topmost balcony of the Doge's Palace.

He wore angel wings, Violetta said. Jasmine smiled as she remembered the words.

She slept for a long while, then decided to go in to university, to see Gabizon, her unfriendly boss. Her boss, usually so reserved, surprised her by clasping her hand and looking into her eyes. "I'm a little worried about you Jasmine," she said. "There are black circles under your eyes and you are getting skinny. It's two in the afternoon and your breath still smells of alcohol from last night."

Jasmine was now more than a little annoyed with this woman. "I'm doing my work well, aren't I?" she asked.

"That's the thing," Gabizon said. "It is impacting your work. Your work for me is starting to suffer, and it is very important work."

"Ghost stories?" Jasmine said.

"Ghost stories, yes," Gabizon said. "If you want to go out all night, and have fun, and explore life, you have to find a way to do it without it negatively impacting this work. Look," Gabizon gestured at a window. "It is already getting dark. What work can you do now?"

"I can get another ghost story for you," Jasmine said, "a good one."

"I doubt it," Gabizon muttered, as she returned to her computer.

***

Jasmine was sitting opposite Violetta in her little receiving room. "I need another story," she said. "I need to talk to Sebastian."

"Oh, no," Violetta said, "not him."

"If we talk about him, he'll just turn up, won't he," Jasmine said.

"No," Violetta said. "It doesn't quite work like that." But then there was a knock at the door. Violetta rolled her eyes and went to answer it. Soon Sebastian had joined them, and she had persuaded him to tell a ghost story.

"Are you sitting comfortably?" he asked. Jasmine nodded. Smiling to herself that Sebastian had remembered the phrase. Violetta poured herself more sweet wine. "Then I'll begin," he said, "It was a long time ago, back in the old country when Vampires were as common as grasshoppers in summer hay." The story Sebastian told was about two vampires, a man and a woman. As Jasmine listened she started to picture the two vampires as something like Bonny and Clyde. She felt a shiver go down her spine. The vampires spread terror through the small communities up and down the land in those ancient times.

Everyone was frightened of them, except one man. The man was a great physician, with healing powers so strong his patients were healthy enough to live forever. The two vampires learned of the physician's healing powers and, one night, they paid him a visit.

At first they tried to torture him into bestowing the gift of immortality upon them. The man was enthusiastic in causing pain, but the woman was not, and the healer noticed this. He used this insight to drive a wedge between the two vampires. He convinced the woman that anyone could become good, even a vampire. The man just laughed at this and redoubled his efforts to loosen the physician's tongue. All he cared about was gaining the gift of immortality. The physician was very physically strong, and he resisted the torture, and all the while he did not give up his attempts to convince the woman that she could be redeemed.

At last, when the physician was at the edge of his endurance, his words started to have an effect. The woman began to change, began to see what was happening right in front of her, and she saw that it was wrong. The man, on the other hand, ignored the physician's words and just became more and more bestial. The woman turned on the man, stopped him torturing the physician and chased him away. The physician forgave her sins, and then he taught her the secret of eternal life. The woman was thankful, but she was also sad. She asked the physician what the point of eternal life was, if she would have to spend it in the dark, feared and hated by everyone. The physician pitied her when he heard about her curse, that she was only able to endure the night. He decided to help her. It took many years, but he was able to use his magical skills to make a beautiful and precious ring that allowed her to go out in daylight.

The woman waited for morning, and after so many years of darkness it was so beautiful that all she could do was stare at the heavens. She sat under a tree and gazed up.

She watched the sun climb high in the sky, and she watched it set. It was just as beautiful when it went down as it was in the morning, and while she was lost in the spectacle, watching the last glimmerings of the sun dip below the horizon, a shadow fell over her. It was a man but she didn't recognize him until he spoke.

"Do you remember me?" he asked. It was her former partner, the vampire. "I watched," he told her. "I watched when the physician taught you the secret of how to live forever. I too will now live forever, but what use is that if I must skulk in the shadows."

"It is your curse," the woman told him. "An eternity of darkness."

"Not if I have that pretty ring that your friend, the physician made for you," the man said.

The two vampires, fought all through the night. The man had eaten many villagers and he was strong, so he slowly won the fight. He was about to kill the woman when the sun rose again. The man was forced to flee, forever banished to the shadows. The two vampires fought that night and they have been fighting ever since.

"What a fascinating story," Jasmine said. "Thank you Sebastian."

"I'm glad you like it," he said.

"Are you kidding?" Jasmine said. "It's great. It has so many dualities, male and female, wild and civilized, dark and light, fighting over a ring that will unify them."

"It's all just an old fairy story," Violetta said. "Though I must admit, I don't think I've heard that one before."

"I know Jasmine likes ghost stories-" Sebastian started to say.

"They're for my boss," Jasmine interrupted. "This is my work."

"-so I've been doing some research," Sebastian continued, ignoring Jasmine's interjection. "The ring in this story is particularly interesting, don't you think?"

The question was intended for Violetta but she didn't answer. She gazed at Sebastian and took a sip of sweet wine, but she didn't answer him. "Well, you've had your story, Jasmine," she said. "Shall we tell him to fuck off now." She giggled a little.

"And eternal life," Jasmine said. "What a great story. Maybe, just for tonight, Sebastian can stay a little longer, if he promises not to be too annoying."

Sebastian stayed a while, and Violetta brooded while he chatted to Jasmine. She found herself, once again, lost in thought. She thought about her father, about how she had hated him back then. She hated him more now, of course. Back then, she even dined with her father. She remembered one winter evening going downstairs to the little jetty projecting from the front of their palatial residence out into the water of the canal. A servant called her over a gondolier and she was sitting at the table with her father in less than half an hour.

"Napoleon is a tyrant who has robbed this city of its independence," Her father had said, over dinner, "He is clearing the old buildings and looting the artistic and architectural treasures." She remembered his words so clearly, as if it were just a few nights ago. The strange tricks, played by a simple human mind, ill designed for eternity.

"Much of the looted art will go to museums, where the common people can see it," Violetta said, "Venice is archaic and atrophied. If it wasn't Napoleon doing this, it would be someone else." She was just playing with her food. He had ordered them both veal cutlets but neither of them were particularly interested in what was on their plate.

"Perhaps," her father said, "but there is one item that must not be given to Napoleon."

"What are you talking about father?" Violetta had asked. She hadn't known then what it was her father was looking for.

She remembered how frightened he had been that it would leave Venice though, before he could get his hands on it, but he hadn't told her exactly what it was he had been looking for. She had assumed it was something huge, imposing, a painting maybe, or a sculpture, but perhaps her father had been looking for a ring.

CHAPTER 12

An old secretary reached for the Roladex on the desk in front of her, an ancient rotating file device used to store business contact information. Even in technology-averse Italy, it was an anachronistic piece of office technology. The Rolodex had a sparse population of specially shaped index cards, with contact information for one person on each card. The cards were notched to be able to be snapped in and out of the rotating spindle. The secretary extracted one of the cards and held it close to her bifocal glasses. She punched the number on the card into her phone, a green plastic design with an angular handset. It had looked futuristic in the 1970s when it was bought, but was a museum piece now. The other end rang and rang. She waited six rings, always six rings, and then hung up. She waited twenty minutes, it was always twenty minutes, and rang again.

"Hello," she bellowed into the receiver. "It's Mrs. Melori." She paused nodding her head as the person on the other end of the phone spoke.

"Yes," she said at last, when the other person paused for breath. "I know you prefer things in writing, but this matter is urgent. It's about your file. The police are looking at your file-" The woman was interrupted by a burst of shouting on the other end of the line. She had to hold the receiver a little away from her ear.

***

"Vi," Jasmine said. "There's something I'd like to talk to you about."

"Go right ahead," she said, "but I have still not agreed to be referred to by that ridiculous contraction. I do not want my nickname to be Vi."

"If it helps, you can call me Jazz," Jasmine suggested. "It's what the other kids call me at university. Not my boss, of course, but the other kids."

"What was it you wanted to say to me, Jazz?" Violetta asked.

"Erm," Jasmine rubbed the back of her neck, "it's embarrassing. Very embarrassing in fact."

"You are starting to intrigue me," Violetta said.

"It's about Sebastian," Jasmine said. "I know your feelings about him are complex, but mine are too. In fact I think I'm starting to be attracted to him."

"I see," Violetta said, with a brief nod.

"I'm sorry, Vi," Jasmine said.

"No. It's not your fault," Violetta said, with a dismissive wave of the hand. "In fact it was only a matter of time. He is a very magnetic individual and not physically unattractive. It's almost inevitable that you would develop feelings for him, but I can't stress this enough. You must not give in to your feelings.

You must not allow any kind of romantic entanglement to develop between you and him."

"I don't have a good track record in resisting my romantic impulses," Jasmine said with a smile.

Violetta did not return the smile. "You must resist him," she said. "He is good at heart, I still believe that, despite all the evidence to the contrary, but he is debased. He has given himself over to debaucheries. He would drag you down, if you were to enter his orbit."

Jasmine nodded, then looked away. There was a knock at the door. "Speak of the devil and he shall appear," Jasmine said. Violetta left Jasmine alone in the drawing room while she went to answer the door. "And, I think it might be a little too late Vi," she whispered, her voice too low for her host to hear. "I think I've already been dragged into his orbit."

Violetta returned, leading Sebastian into the room. "Ah, the enchanting Jasmine," he said.

"Well why don't you take a seat," Violetta said. "I can't remember the last time you graced this house with your presence so frequently."

"If you think I should return the invitation," Sebastian said, "you are quite welcome to call on me at any time that is convenient to you."

"That's not what I meant," Violetta said.

"Where exactly do you live, Seb?" Jasmine asked.

Sebastian raised an eyebrow. "She's been contracting names," Violetta explained. "Apparently it's more friendly that way."

"Well," Sebastian said, "as you might expect, I live right here in Venice. In fact I think I probably have a calling card about my person somewhere."

"Well dig it out Seb," Jasmine said.

"Yes, do," Violetta said, "Seb." Sebastian reached into an inside pocket and pulled out a heavy little oblong of hand-made paper. On it was printed his name, address, an email address, and a cell phone number.

"Ordinarily," Jasmine said, "carrying around a business card would qualify you as a grade 'A' nerd, and the gold edges would increase your nerd grade to 'A+', but I'm going to make an exception. Let's just call it your idiosyncratic style."

"All right," Sebastian agreed. "Let's."

"You must not visit this creature unaccompanied," Violetta said, gesturing at Sebastian.

"Of course not, Vi," Jasmine nodded. "You're coming with me."

"I am?" Violetta said.

"She is?" Sebastian said.

"You are," Jasmine said to Violetta. "She is," she said to Sebastian.

"I hope your larder is well stocked," Violetta said.

"And I hope you have a few bottles of fragolino," Jasmine said. "It's the only thing we drink."

"Actually," Sebastian said, "I don't have a thing in the house."

"Well you had better get yourself to the local supermarket, hadn't you?" Jasmine said. Then Jasmine gave Sebastian her number so he could call and let them know when he was ready to play host.

"It might take a few days to get the place shipshape," he said.

"I imagine it might," Violetta said, a note of distaste in her voice. Sebastian left soon after, claiming he was going to start tidying up right that minute, leaving Jasmine and Violetta alone.

"You are always coming to call on me, but I have not seen your place since your first night in Venice," Violetta said.

"You're welcome to pop round any time, Vi," Jasmine said, "but you have to give me a ring first."

"A ring?" Violetta said.

"I need some warning so I can clear away all the stuff I have lying around," Jasmine explained. "My place is a tip."

"You would like me to telephone?" Violetta said.

"That's right," Jasmine said. "It's time we swapped numbers, anyway. I mean, I have Sebastian's cell phone number but I don't have yours. How crazy is that?"

"It's because I don't have a mobile phone," Violetta explained.

"Landline?" Jasmine prompted.

"I fear it has been disconnected due to an oversight with the billing," Violetta said.

"Happens to the best of us," Jasmine said, "but why don't you have a cell phone?"

"I have never felt the need," Violetta said. "I'm not against the idea. I suppose I've just been terribly lazy. It's very remiss of me."

"So you want a phone," Jasmine said, "but you haven't gotten around to it?" Violetta nodded in reply. "Then let's go get one now," Jasmine said, brightly.

Violetta's eyes widened. "A cell phone?" she said.

"Yes," Jasmine said, emphatically.

"For me?"

"Yes."

"Now?"

"There's no time like the present," Jasmine said, with an encouraging smile. It took only a few minutes to run to the cell phone shop, but they had to run to catch it before it closed. "What kind do you want?" Jasmine asked. She could see the single shop assistant rolling his eyes at getting customers so close to closing time.

"I haven't the foggiest notion," Violetta said.

"What's your budget?" Jasmine asked.

"Really," Violetta said, slowly and clearly. "That isn't an issue."

***

They took Violetta's new smartphone back to her house and sat at the kitchen table together, switching it on and putting in the SIM card. The instructions said to charge it and that's how they had ended up in the kitchen. It was the only room in the house with electricity sockets. Violetta's cat was watching them intently. "What's this little fella's name?" Jasmine asked.

"I call him Zmeu," Violetta said.

Jasmine scratched him behind the ears and was surprised by how cold his fur was. "He's freezing," she said. "He must have just come in from outside."

"Be careful of him," Violetta warned. "He bites." Jasmine dropped the cat and typed her number into Violetta's phone. "Could you also add Sebastian's number to the device?" Violetta asked.

Jasmine paused for a moment but couldn't think of any good reason to refuse the request. "Sure," she said.

"It's strange..." Violetta said, but her words trailed off and she didn't elaborate.

"What is?" Jasmine asked, glancing up from the phone.

"That I have known him for so long," Violetta said, "and yet it is you who he tells his address and phone number to, almost as soon as he meets you."

"Have I upset you?" Jasmine asked. "Are you still interested in Seb?"

"No," Violetta said, too quickly. "Maybe. I don't know. Maybe at one time I was. But not now. I don't think so."

"I won't see him," Jasmine said, "if you don't want me to, I promise, Vi."

"That would be best, of course. But I think the fates might have other plans, and it is pointless to try and spite them," Violetta said. "They control the thread of life. Even the gods fear them and are subject to their power."

"I don't think Seb and me are fated to be together," Jasmine said, but a goofy smile was spreading across her face at the thought.

"No. Exactly my point," Violetta said, leaning forward. "When the fates intervene it isn't to bring people together. It is to force them apart. To mock them and to destroy them."

"What the fates force apart, Facebook can bring together," Jasmine said.

"Facebook?" Violetta said, "I think I have heard you mention this before, but I didn't ask you to explain."

"Seriously?" Jasmine was genuinely aghast. ""Everyone knows Facebook."

"Apparently not everyone," Violetta said.

"Okay. Let me show you," Jasmine said, swiping at the screen of the device in her hands. "It's most likely already on your phone." Jasmine found the Facebook application, punched in some details, and took a picture of Violetta with the phone's camera.

The cat watched intently as the two girls, laughing and joking, set up Facebook on Violetta's phone, and then connected them both together on Facebook as friends. Jasmine stayed for a few more hours, and then Violetta was alone again. She stood in the front door, watching Jasmine go, right to the end of the short garden path. Then she turned to go back into the house. Her father was standing right behind her.

"I think it's about time you put an end to all this," he said. Violetta didn't say anything. She just stared at him, defiance in her eyes. "If you don't," he said, "I will." Again, Violetta did not react. Her eyes had narrowed, the tiny flames inside burning a little brighter, but she didn't say a word. She didn't move, she didn't even close the front door. She just stood there, facing her father, her back to the world. "Make it soon," he said. Then he turned and disappeared into the darkness inside the house.

Violetta didn't move for a long time. She just stood there, in the open doorway, then went to the kitchen. She gathered up her new phone and held it in her hand. It had just finished charging and she could very faintly feel the warmth of the battery against her skin. The phone vibrated, snapping her out of a reverie so deep it was almost a hypnotic state. She brought the phone slowly up to her face and looked at the screen. There was a little message on the screen from Jasmine. "Night, night," it said. There was a picture of Jasmine beside the words. Violetta smiled, but the smile quickly faded.

She went to her room, to her closet. Inside were some handbags. She picked out a vintage kid-leather bag, a refined item from the Belle Epoque. Despite being more than one hundred years old, it looked quite modern. She dropped the phone and charger inside and put back the expensive bag in the wardrobe. The menace in her father's voice had been unmistakable, it sent shivers of fear down her spine. She knew from long experience that he did not make empty threats.

She lost track of time, just standing in the center of the room, but then she noticed a small patch of red light on the wall. It was a very dim reflection of the sky, which, on such a clear and cloudless morning, could be seen brightening in preparation for dawn. She rushed to draw the heavy curtains, then turned to look at her bed. It was huge and ornate, with the four vertical columns supporting an intricately carved wooden canopy. She knew she wouldn't feel safe in the bed, between the sheets, only under it. She got down on all fours and crawled beneath. There, with her heavy drapes closed, protected by her massive bed above her, she gradually started to fall asleep on the bare boards of the floor. "Monsters under the bed," she mumbled, in a long dead dialect of an obscure language.

CHAPTER 13

Violetta brooded alone the next night at her window, looking out into the darkness. Her thoughts drifted back to a time almost beyond remembering. The images still left to her of that far, far off and terrible time were dim, like everything had happened in semi-shadow. She remembered just fleeting moments, like the time she and Sebastian had been racing across country, traveling by night to avoid the enemy. Sebastian was at the driver's bench of their cart, holding the reigns while Violetta was in the back, among the few belongings they had had time to throw together. Violetta could feel the uneven road beneath her, could see Sebastian's silhouette on the driver's bench. His back was broad and strong, his voice loud and deep as he yelled encouragement to the horses.

"Why are you helping me?" Violetta asked, having to raise her voice so he could hear her over the thunder of hooves.

"It's not your fault you were born into the aristocracy," Sebastian said. "If you had remained in the castle you would have met the same fate as your father."

"The same fate," Violetta said cautiously, "What do you know about it?"

"I know all about it," Sebastian said, glancing at her over his shoulder. "I've just returned from the capital. The peasants' revolt is much worse there. They're all ungrateful scum, you know the type... farmers, students, friars, parish priests, the lowest of the low. We train them to fight the Turks, give them swords, and then they use our weapons and training against us.

The nobility has failed to lead. That's true. But that's their only legitimate grievance, and it's no excuse for rebellion. Hundreds of manor houses and castles have been burnt and thousands of the gentry killed, impaled. It's worse than the Mongols."

Violetta gasped at that. The country had suffered during the Mongol invasion, she remembered those times only too well. The whole region had been ravaged. It had felt like the end of times, like the end of the world. City after city was plundered, and the advance was only halted by heavy snow. The invasion had finally been turned back, and it hadn't been the end of the world after all. The country was rebuilt, of course, and once more divided among the clergy, the nobility, and the commoners. Rebellions came and went, they were part of life, but this was worse. Perhaps Sebastian was right to compare it to the Mongols. Perhaps this was the end of times, again.

"The gentry are being impaled?" Violetta said. "Barbaric."

Sebastian glanced back at her for an instant, but didn't dare take his eyes off the road for long. "Don't worry," he said. "There are soldiers on the way from the Republic of Venice, hired swords. Scum to fight scum. It'll all be over in a couple of weeks. But it's still far from safe. I think it's best we travel by night and hide out during the day time."

Violetta looked down at the giant box, the centerpiece of the jumble on the back of the wagon. "Yes," she replied. "I think that's best."

"And I think you should let me do the talking," Sebastian added. "That accent of yours will get us all beheaded otherwise. Maybe we should pretend you're mute."

"My accent?" Violetta said, touching her mouth as if to keep the offending words from tripping out and betraying them.

"Yes," Sebastian said. "You talk like a countess."

"But I am a countess," Violetta said, "among my other noble titles."

Sebastian laughed. "Just keep your mouth shut until all this bloodletting is over. It can't go on forever, and when normal times return your cut-glass accent will be an asset once again." They rode in silence for a while, until the horizon started to turn fiery red. "It's getting light, but we could go a little further," Sebastian said. Violetta just shook her head, her eyes imploring, her face a mask of fear. Sebastian nodded and took the next side turning. It didn't take him long to find a clearing in a small wood to hide in. Violetta climbed under the wagon, threw some dirt over herself and fell asleep, nuzzling into the soft earth with her shoulder. Sebastian watched her scamper under the wagon as the sky began to glow redder and redder. She didn't even glance in his direction, or say a word.

"You must be terrified," he said softly to himself, so she couldn't hear him. He made himself as comfortable as he could in the back of the wagon, amid the few things they had saved from their previous life at the castle, and he soon fell asleep too. He dreamed that he was being chased by the monsters of the myths he had grown up with. Vampires. Horrible deformed men with pointed tails and hooves. They were chasing him through the woods, pupils reflecting the light like wolf eyes, floppy leather wings hanging from their backs. They were gaining on him, getting closer and closer. Then he felt a hand on his back and woke with a start. It was evening, just after sundown and Violetta was standing over him, her hand on his shoulder, shaking him awake. "Don't be frightened. It's only me," she said.

"I must have been tired," he said. "I slept the whole day away."

"Good morning, I suppose," Violetta said.

"Hardly," Sebastian said.

"Well it's not as if I can say goodnight, now is it?" Violetta said.

Sebastian smiled. "No. I suppose not." They were sitting side by side in the crepuscular light, Violetta's hand still on his shoulder. "I think we should take a look at your father," he said, "while it is still light."

"Do we have to?" Violetta said.

"Yes," Sebastian said. "We have to make time to bury him before he starts to rot." He pulled back the sheet covering the stuff on the cart. There were canvas bags, hatboxes and a giant wardrobe. Sebastian opened the wardrobe, to reveal the corpse of Violetta's father. "He's rotting quicker than I thought," Sebastian said.

Her father had been killed with a piece of sharpened wood. A pitiful peasant's weapon, but enough to kill even a powerful nobleman. It offended Sebastian to see such a powerful man brought low by such a humble attack. He placed his left hand on the chest of the corpse and grabbed the end of the wooden shaft with the other, then pulled it out all in one swift and smooth movement. Violetta gasped in shock.

"I should have warned you I was going to do that," Sebastian said, and turned to give Violetta a reassuring smile. He tried to catch Violetta's eye, but she was staring at the remains of her father. Sebastian felt something move under his hand, the hand that was on the chest of the corpse. He snatched the hand away and looked back into the improvised coffin. His eyes widened at what he saw.

Sebastian felt horror reach into him and grab him by the heart. This was something that could not be. He had heard vampire stories, of course, but seeing one was an entirely different matter. He was already coiling to run, but he had an instant to gather an impression of the monstrosity. It was rattling out words in some strange dialect of a forgotten language. The thing was disorientated, its eyes darting around in confusion as its flesh solidified and crawled onto its bones. A hand, more like a claw, was fumbling at the edge of the box, limp and ineffectual.

And then Sebastian was running, his attention was riveted on the edge of the forest. He had to make it to the edge of the forest clearing, get in among the trees. Some instinct was telling him that the trees were the only chance he had for survival. He was half way to the edge of the clearing before he even remembered that he wasn't alone. Violetta was with him. He didn't stop running but he glanced over his shoulder. Where was Violetta? Surely she was running too. Was she close to him? Was the Vampire on his heels? He could only half turn his head to look back for a second here and a second there, for fear of stumbling as he sprinted across the uneven ground. The horses had caught a whiff of something unclean and were rearing and whinnying, but they couldn't run, Sebastian had tied them to a tree for the night. Would the vampire take them, and spare him?

Sebastian made it to the trees and only then dared to take a second to look back. Violetta, he saw with relief, was running towards him. "Yes," he yelled, "come on Violetta, run! Run!" She was skinny and weak and unused to physical exertion, her running was painfully slow. Sebastian was gripped by an even deeper wave of fear. Was he about to see this delicate creature overtaken and devoured before his very eyes? He could see that the foul monster was standing by the cart. It was making no move to chase Violetta. It was simply watching her go, but Sebastian was under no illusions. He knew that it was simply gathering its strength. He looked around for a weapon. He could feel Violetta's desperation to get away from the terrible, unclean thing and he suddenly felt compelled to help her, even if that meant fighting a monster from beyond the gates of hell. He saw a branch, about the right size for a weapon, sticking out of a tree at a good height for him to wrench it off. He ran over to it grabbed it with both hands and heaved. He felt it give, felt the fibers of the wood splitting and cracking, but it didn't come away.

He looked over at Violetta, still only half way across the clearing, stumbling and staggering, her legs hardly able to carry her. The monster by the cart had started to move.

Sebastian renewed his efforts with the branch, twisting and wrenching, and it came away, the end a sharp blade of fresh wood where it had split as it tore from the tree. He quickly stripped away leaves and twigs to make it easier to wield and turned to face the monster, stake in hand, but all he saw was Violetta doubled over, massaging her legs, but strangely not out of breath.

"Where did it go?" Sebastian asked.

"I don't know," Violetta said. "Probably back to the castle to avenge itself on the peasants that usurped it."

"You think?" Sebastian's eyes were darting around, looking for any sign of the monster.

"I'm not sure. But if it was here, wouldn't it attack us," Violetta said. "Now, shouldn't we get the cart and make haste away."

"Go back to the cart?" Terror could he heard in Sebastian's voice. He was still deep in shock at seeing his former mentor transforming into something so unholy. He knew all about vampires, of course, though he had never personally seen one, but he'd somehow thought the aristocracy must be immune to vampirism, that it afflicted peasant families who couldn't afford to do the burial rituals right. Sebastian had a feeling like something was amiss, something at the corner of his vision, something still there, in the dark.

In fact, though Sebastian couldn't see him, the vampire was right there, right beside him. "I always liked Sebastian," the foul creature said. "Stay with him. He will be a good ally in these times when slave rises up against master. I must go a different way."

"Go away," Violetta hissed, "before he shrugs off your magics and sees you standing there as plain as day."

"Good counsel, as ever, my sweet daughter," the vampire said to her. "I will go on ahead to Venice, and make things ready for your arrival. Look for me there, look for the sign of the bull."

"Who are you talking to?" Sebastian asked.

"Nobody," Violetta said. "I'm just breathing hard. I'm not used to running from vampires."

CHAPTER 14

Jasmine could feel her own pulse, and it was beating a little quicker at the thought of getting to see Sebastian's place. Sebastian hadn't turned up yet to escort them, but Jasmine knew he was coming. Just Violetta and her were in the room, sitting at the big wooden kitchen table. Violetta had offered her some macaroons almost as soon as she had opened the front door to her and they had gone straight to the pantry to get them. They hadn't made it back to the drawing room before opening the packet to devour them. "There's only one raspberry one left," Violetta said, snapping Jasmine out of her reverie.

Jasmine looked down at the delicious little meringue biscuits spilling across the kitchen table. They hadn't even bothered to get a plate before ripping the packet open. There was indeed only one raspberry one. "Don't worry," Jasmine said, "I'll fix that."

"What are you going to do?" Violetta asked.

But Jasmine was already walking over to a chest of drawers. "Where do you keep the knives?" she asked. Violetta didn't say anything, she simply pointed vaguely at some drawers. "Don't worry," Jasmine said. "I'll find them." There was a lot of noise as Jasmine opened drawer after drawer, each one full of clanking metal kitchen utensils and clinking glass and china. "Here we are," she said. From one of the middle drawers she produced a huge knife with a serrated blade and wooden handle. She came over to the table and placed the point of the knife against the wood so she could gently lower the blade through the raspberry macaroon. The macaroon was split neatly in two.

"Ooh, sharp," Jasmine said.

Violetta reached for the macaroon half nearest her and popped it into her mouth. "Delicious," she said. There was a knock at the door that could be heard quite clearly from the kitchen. "Let's both go to the door," Violetta said.

Sebastian was there looking, if possible, even more elegant than usual. "Very dapper Seb," Jasmine said. "This bodes well for the evening."

"He does seem to have made an effort," Violetta said. Sebastian did a little twirl to show off his look, then headed off, wordlessly motioning for the girls to follow him.

"So why do I feel like a lamb going to the slaughter?" Jasmine asked. Violetta didn't reply. She just followed Sebastian, leaving Jasmine to trail along in the rear. They didn't have far to go until Sebastian led them to a big wooden door in a crowded square. "I know this square," Jasmine said. "They set up a cinema here in the summer, and an ice rink at Christmas."

"That's right," Sebastian said. "My apartment is that one up there." He waved vaguely upwards at one of the upper floors, then inserted a surprisingly small key into the lock of the big wooden door. "I overlook the ice rink so I have terrible 80s pop music wafting up through my windows all through Christmas and New Year, but I also get a great view of the movies when they set up the open-air cinema."

It was a double door and Sebastian's key opened the door on the left. With both doors open it would have been possible to drive a car into the building. Inside, the entrance hall was equally huge, the walls marble and the floor highly polished. It was like the lobby of a museum. The far wall was entirely wood and glass, and the trees of a garden could be seen casting shadows on the glass. "This way ladies," Sebastian said and led the way up an enormous marble staircase illuminated by chandeliers.

"The place looks so run down from the outside," Jasmine said. "You don't expect it to be so grand inside."

"Run down," Violetta mumbled, "definitely run down."

Sebastian ignored her. "There is nothing surprising about this finery," he said. "Venice is like Bristol, Prague, Havana, or New Orleans, built with slave money, the profits from all kinds of other human misery. It's a lucrative trade you know, human misery. You can build a grand house on the back of the suffering of others." He paused, and smiled.

"Slavers?" Jasmine said, "The Venetians were slavers?"

"Oh, yes," he said, "The worst. The most prolific. They sold huge numbers into slavery. Merchants could get returns as high as 150 per cent, and that was after accounting for death, shipwrecks, and disease. Venetians sold people from Greece, North Africa, and also Eastern Europeans. Caravans of slaves were brought here, traveling through Alpine passes in Austria. Eunuchs were especially valuable, you know, so the Venetians soon started building castration houses across Venice to meet the demand."

"Ew, that's nasty," Jasmine said.

"He's an expert on human misery," Violetta said, cryptically.

"Here we are," Sebastian said, as they came to a landing after climbing innumerable stairs. Sebastian and Jasmine went into the apartment, but Violetta hesitated in the doorway. Sebastian noticed, then turned to watch, and enjoy her discomfort.

"Are you having second thoughts?" Jasmine asked.

Sebastian snorted a laugh, but then he seemed to relent. "Enter of your own free will," he mumbled, without putting any real emotion into it. Violetta almost stumbled into the apartment, as if an invisible barrier had been lifted. Violetta didn't say anything, just motioned Sebastian to keep moving.

It was a large apartment, and the tour took some time. The main living space was very open plan, with smaller rooms leading off. There was a bar with a huge assortment of exotic booze on illuminated shelving, a white plastic table, an Eames chair, and an animal-hide rug. And there were some modern items too, like a laptop and a phone on charge, hidden away in niches. The wood tones were white, and the shag carpeting a medium gray. There was even a conversation pit, making the room split level. There whole place was suffused by the warm glow from indirect, low lighting. "Music?" Sebastian said as he stopped by a retro bubble stereo and then the hiss and crackle of a needle on vinyl could be heard through expensive speakers, before Thank You

(Falettinme Be Mice Elf Agin) by Sly and the Family Stone started playing.

"This is a real man cave," Jasmine said.

"So this is where it all happens," Violetta said, and irritation, perhaps even something more, something approaching rage, could be heard in her voice. Violetta had been getting more and more agitated, the more she saw of Sebastian's bachelor pad.

"All what?" Sebastian asked.

"I can only imagine," Violetta said, "but you look fat and healthy. Well fed. Your lifestyle here certainly agrees with you."

Sebastian looked away. Jasmine felt Violetta's tone was a little unkind, even though her words were friendly. "You can hardly call him fat," she said in an attempt to take some of the tension out of the visit. It was immediately obvious that her attempt at a little joke hadn't landed, so she went over to the stereo and looked through the stack of vinyl beside it.

"What are you even doing here in Venice, Sebastian?" Violetta asked. "You aren't trapped here, not the way I am."

"I'm looking for something," Sebastian said, his words hardly more that a hiss, all the while keeping an eye on Jasmine in case she wandered close enough to overhear.

"In fact I think you are perhaps starting to suspect what it is I'm looking for."

"After that story you told Jasmine, yes I am," Violetta hissed, finally on the point of losing her temper with him. "You have to know that is just a stupid old legend."

"Then it won't matter if I keep investigation, now will it?" Sebastian said.

"It is dangerous to chase after legends, and you know that," Violetta whispered.

"It's a little rich, you... warning me... about danger. You are following your own dangerous paths," Sebastian said. "For example, I notice that you have developed a fondness for Jasmine. How upset you would be if anything were to happen to her. Such terrible things tend to happen to the people you have feelings for."

Jasmine felt the tension coming from where Violetta and Sebastian were hissing at each other. She went over to them, noticed how they both quickly fell silent, and looked from one to the other. "Let's go Jasmine," Violetta said, some of the rage fading from her voice, replaced by weariness.

"Right with you," Jasmine said, but from the way her eyes darted from Violetta to Sebastian and back, she was clearly torn. Sebastian made a 'call me' sign with his hand so Violetta couldn't see but Jasmine could. Jasmine nodded.

***

The next day, Jasmine was at the city's main library. It was right in the center of the ancient city. Just off the main square, its door in the very shadow of the bell tower. It was nestled between mask shops and the kind of cafes where a two ounce coke costs ten euros. The walls were so thick that heat couldn't penetrate. The air was as cool and fresh as a desert cave. The furniture was equally ancient and solid, which it needed to be, because some of the books they supported were enormous. They had to be moved around the library on a cart to avoid wrenching your back.

She was there researching ghost stories in the hopes of impressing her boss. The stories told by the local fishermen were a particularly rich vein. They distilled the fears and desires of the people of the time into a potent mix, and the stories had made it almost unaltered in form for generations.

A story she was particularly interested in was mentioned by one of the most famous of the region's collectors of folklore, an Englishman called Theodore Whitmore, in one of his collections. He had given the story the name 'Death's Head Moth' and referred to it often, but there was no sign of it in the literature.

After a whole day spent in the library, Jasmine gave up and stumbled out into the twilight. On an impulse she reached into her bag and pulled out her phone. She dialed Sebastian and listened to the phone ringing a while on the other end. She was about to give up when it was answered.

"Jasmine?" it was Sebastian's voice.

"Yes, you sound groggy, are you about to go to bed?" Jasmine asked.

"What?" She heard a snort of derisive laughter from the other end of the phone. "Hardly. The night is young, as they say."

"I need some help," Jasmine said. "There is a ghost story I'm interested in, but I can't find it in the library. It is mentioned in Whitmore, but only by name, the collection doesn't contain the story itself."

"Whitmore?" Sebastian said, all trace of grogginess leaving his voice.

"Yeah, that's right," Jasmine said, "and it's usually a good source, but it doesn't have this one."

"Where are you?" Sebastian asked. "I'll be right there."

"Oh, I'm still in St. Mark's Square," Jasmine said. "We can't meet here. These places are so expensive-"

"I'll be right there," Sebastian repeated, interrupting her. And, true to his word, he came striding across the square just a few minutes later.

"This way," he said brightly, shepherding her toward a cafe she knew to be sinfully expensive. He found a table for the two of them and they ordered a couple of delicious little cakes. Jasmine told Sebastian about the story she was interested in, and he nodded in recognition. "I know the story, he said. It is about the way that Venetian families are divided into two categories. There are the long-lived families, that is the families that have been here in Venice since the beginning, they have lived long here. The Venetians call them the Longhi, and the short-lived they call the Curti. There has never been much love lost between the two. The Venice that the Longhi built is reviled by the Curti. They see the ancient Venetians, the ones that built this place and now just collect rents, as parasites. They call them the frogs of the marshes."

"That sounds, quite cute," Jasmine said, as she took a bit of her delicious little cake.

"In English, perhaps," Sebastian said, "but not in the local dialect. These old families grew rich through taxing the trade of others, skimming off their cut of the wealth, as goods flowed through the Rialto markets. And, as I told you last time we met, the merchants didn't just trade in spice, they also traded in slaves. This slavery was practiced as a matter of course against Christian and non-Christian alike, but their most valuable slaves were the Morlachs. These were an ancient people from the dark mountains north of the Balkans. They were shipped in from Tanais, one of the earliest of cities. It was a far Venetian outpost, at the very edge of their scattered lands at that time."

"When was this exactly?" Jasmine asked.

"A long time ago," Sebastian said, "the mid 1300s, a time when the slave trade was in full swing. The section of the Venetian waterfront in front of the Doge's palace is still called Riva Degli Schiavoni, which means Slaves' Dock, because of the hundreds of thousands of slaves brought there and auctioned."

"I see," Jasmine nodded.

"Now I've set the terrible scene, the stream of enslaved people coming right through here," Sebastian said, "let me now tell the story. One day on Slave's dock a rebellion broke out. Now you have to understand that slave rebellions were very rare. The slaves were so terribly treated that they were too weak and terrified to put up much resistance. For the slaves to rebel, and risk harsh punishment, they had to be completely desperate. This rebellion started when a barge full of slaves was brought up to the quay, right below the windows of the palace. The first slave climbed from the boat, and all eyes were drawn to the man, a huge Morlach, but the other slaves would not leave the boat. They were too terrified of the man. After being locked up with him on the barge, they knew he was the devil. The slave drivers whipped and beat them mercilessly, but they would not get off the boat. The barge was a scene of Pandemonium, as the big Morlach watched from where he was calmly standing, alone on the quay. At last, the commotion attracted the Doge himself to come to the window to look down onto the chaos. As if sensing this, the huge slave looked up.

"Who lives here in this huge palace?" he called out.

"Amazingly, an answer came back. "I, Faliero. The Doge."

"Show me your face, Doge," the slave shouted.

"Faliero came to the window and spat down on the slave, just as he was pulled away by slave drivers, a huge smile on his face. "Now I have seen your face," the slave laughed, "I can always find you, and I can eat your heart and take your form."

"That very night the slave disappeared from the holding pens. Nobody knew where he had gone. The other slaves said he had turned into a death's head moth and flown through the bars of the cage. Faliero was frightened after the strange encounter, and decided to hide in the house of a fellow noble. He wore a mask and traveled by canal, so nobody would know where he was spending the night.

"The nobleman was woken by the sounds of struggle, and fearing for the life of his Doge, he ran to the Doge's quarters, his sword drawn. By the time he reached the Doge's rooms, he found that the struggle was over. The Doge was standing over his would-be assassin. He had skewered the man's heart with his sword and the man's face had been bashed in, but who could it be apart from the strange Morlach slave. The nobleman did not see the Doge leave for his palace, but he did see a death's head moth flying from the Doge's window. The nobleman would remember this later, at the trial.

"The trial?" Jasmine said. She hadn't meant to interrupt, but she was being drawn into the story. She couldn't help herself.

"Yes," Sebastian said, "you see Faliero was no ordinary Doge. He had been a naval commander and a diplomat before being elected to the throne, in 1354. He was a popular choice, and the electors had high hopes for him because of his political savy and experience. People expected him to make Venice great again, after a terrible naval defeat and the ravages of plague. People expected a just ruler and a peacemaker, but he was never the same after his encounter with the Morlach, what they got was somebody completely different.

"They got a highly ambitious man, dissatisfied with being only a Doge, whose power was curtailed by a council of electors. He looked at the kings of other states, and he was jealous. He immediately conspired to become an absolute ruler, like them. He somehow convinced the Admiral of the Arsenal, an important man who commanded the mighty Venetian fleet, to back him as he killed all the other members of the council, to seize power for himself.

"The plan was to go to the grand palaces of the city and eliminate the rest of the noblemen. He would then be designated 'Lord of Venice.' But a spy, and there were many in Venice, named Beltrame discovered the plan, and warned the council. He was awarded a thousand ducats for saving their skins, but he complained that the sum was insufficient. He was exiled to the Black Sea for his impertinence.

"Thanks to Beltrame, on the evening when the power play was to take place, the nobles were ready and the Doge was arrested, as well as the Admiral of the Arsenal and all the other conspirators. Summary trials were held the next day, and they were sentenced to death.

"There is no official account of the rest of the day's events, because the Doge's executioners pronounced a damnatio memoriae upon their victim, which is a special curse to wipe all record of what happened from history. Even Faliero's portrait in the great hall of the Doge's Palace is veiled, the only portrait among the many Doges pictured there to be hidden in this way, but some things are known. The executions of the other conspirators went smoothly, but not the execution of the Doge. The executioners were forced to chase him through the building, inflicting mortal wound after mortal wound on him, but he would not die. He would not fall down dead until he was eventually beheaded. His head was finally chopped off on the first landing of the main staircase of the palace, where the Doges usually took their oath. The head bounced down the stairs, but some say the body still had to be wrestled to the ground.

"Some say that the Doge was cursed, but some say that the creature beheaded at the top of the stairs was not the Doge. Some say the real Doge died the night he met the Morlach slave. And there is an ugly postscript to the story. Remember the spy who betrayed the Doge's plans?"

"Yes," Jasmine said, "he was paid with silver, but exiled because of his ingratitude."

"Weeks later, Beltrame, the spy who had frustrated the Morlach's bid for power, was found dead on the shores of the Black Sea, a death's head moth fluttering over the body."

***

A few days later, Jasmine shuddered again at mention of The Death's Head Moth, the next time she was reading Whitmore. It was a very precious edition, one she hadn't seen before, and it even included some photographs. As well as being one of the preeminent Victorian anthropologists, Whitmore it seemed had also been a pioneering photographer, and along with the written accounts he made of the legends told to him of the lagoon, he had also taken beautiful pictures of the sailors and fishwives who told him the stories.

The photos in the book she held in her hands were beautiful images created from the original daguerreotypes from the 1850s. They showed the lines of the people's faces, their costumes, and were very skilfully done. Mr Whitmore had obviously been an accomplished photographer. The photographs weren't spread through the text in the modern manner, but instead were collected in an appendix in the back with captions listing the date each photograph was taken, the name of the subject, and often a brief biography. One caught her eye for a moment.

5th May 1857, Aldo Maletti, Fisherman; was a witness to many events of the Venetian Republic Revolt, also told many traditional stories of the area.

She flicked through more photographs, each more fascinating than the one before. They were windows on a past time, with strange costumes and haircuts, the faces of people who lived hard lives and did backbreaking work. Then, right at the back was a picture of the illustrious Mr Whitmore himself, a self portrait? or did he have an assistant?

He was quite an attractive fellow, for a Victorian scholar with bushy sideburns. There was one more page, probably a small glossary. She turned it over and saw that it was, in fact one more photograph. The caption read.

12th August 1858, Violetta Romanziana, my photographic assistant.

It was a picture of a young woman. The woman was smiling in closeup, and there was no mistaking that it was her Violetta. It wasn't some relative, some great aunt. The resemblance was absolutely uncanny. But it couldn't be, of course, unless Violetta had a time machine hidden away in that weird basement of hers. Very strange, she thought to herself, and slowly closed the big heavy leather cover of the old book.

"I'll have to tell her about these photos," Jasmine muttered to herself, "When I see her." She left the library and went out into the hot sunshine of the square. She reached into her bag and plucked out her phone. She called Sebastian but there was no answer. "Must be out in the warm weather having fun," she muttered as she put her phone away.

CHAPTER 15

Violetta left the house and was wandering the streets, lost in her own thoughts. Sometimes the street lamps were dark because the city could not afford oil, but tonight they were giving off their dim glow. Often, when she was out walking, she couldn't help but notice how much Venice had lost of its old luster. It was no longer at the apogee of its trading might and the goods in the stores reflected that. Where once there were exotic spices and rich fabrics, now all she saw was fish, handcrafts and vegetables, the likes of which you could find in any village market. Maybe it was better that way though, she'd never much cared for the fine things anyway.

"You there," a voice suddenly said, snapping her out of her thoughts. "Girl." The voice, a young man's voice, was barbaric, the Italian mispronounced and ungrammatical in ways she had never heard before. Violetta turned to see who the strange sounding man might be talking to, only to find that she was alone on the street. The man could only be talking to her.

"Me?" Violetta pointed at herself.

"Yes," the man said, "I'd like to talk to you."

"Oh," she said, very much taken aback. "Why would you want to speak to me?"

"Scientific method," he said, as if that were explanation enough.

"Scientific method?" Violetta said.

"Yes. I am choosing conversation partners at random," he explained. "I count ten people, and this tenth person I invite to converse with me."

"I have never heard of anything like it," Violetta said.

"As I told you, it is a simple application of the modern scientific method," the man said. "If you are willing, we should converse. We have an hour before the hotel restaurant closes. The food is not perfect, but the wine is very palatable. I assure you I have no ulterior motives, but I will perfectly understand if you turn down my offer. I must admit that it may seem strange to you."

"What is your name?" Violetta asked. She hasn't spoken to a soul, apart from her father, if he even counted as a soul, for a long time. She was tempted to talk to this strange man, but she needed to take a little time before answering yes or no.

"Whitmore," the man said, "at your service." Violetta looked him up and down. He was tall, taller than most of the local people, but his features were weak, with a delicate jaw and large, watery eyes. His hair was mousy brown, thin and greasy, and he had grown the most extraordinary pair of sideburns, like wings projecting from his cheeks. He was dressed elegantly and was resting nonchalantly on a jet black cane with silver handle and foot.

"Whitmore," she repeated, feeling the strange selection of vowels role around in her mouth. "You are not Italian, I take it."

"No," he said. "I fancy my Italian is almost perfect, but it comes from practice, dedication and the application of the scientific method to the study of language." Violetta smiled. His Italian was absolutely terrible. He was only pronouncing half the letters and coughing out aitches and gees as though he had something stuck in his throat. His intonation was monotonous as if the words were being ground out by a mechanical device.

"So where are you from?" she asked.

"I am a subject of the British Empire," he said, "born and bred."

"I see," Violetta nodded. "I have never met a subject of the British Empire before, and so I will consent to sit with you in the restaurant of your hotel for the purposes of conversation."

"Thank you," Whitmore said, with a smile. He led her to a respectable hotel and they found a table. The kitchen was closed but they were brought a glass of wine each and some bread. Whitmore produced a writing pad from one of the large pockets in his knee-length frock coat. He wrote the date at the top and asked her to spell her name, forename and surname.

"You want me to spell my name? Is this to be a conversation," she asked, "or an interrogation?"

"A conversation," he said sheepishly. "Most definitely a conversation. Please only divulge whatever details you are comfortable with. I'm only taking notes as an aid memoir. I am writing a book about Venice, you see."

"Then simply write Violetta. That's all you need to know."

"Certainly," he said.

"What would you like to converse about?" Violetta asked.

"Anything," Whitmore said, "but my personal hobby horses are history, architecture and photography."

"Photography?"

"Yes," Whitmore said, his face lighting up. "It is the most amazing new process where light is captured on a chemical plate."

"I don't quite follow," Violetta said, and their first conversation developed into an explanation of how to make photographs. Despite herself, Violetta was intrigued. Whitmore told her that he would be happy to demonstrate his equipment and suggested a meeting the next day at noon.

"That's not really ideal for me," Violetta said. "I have business to attend to during the day and I won't be available until some time later."

"Then I have an even better idea," Whitmore said. "Meet me here for dinner tomorrow and I'll bring along some of my photographs to show you."

"Why not," Violetta said, "but tomorrow night, allow me to choose the retaurant."

***

The photographs were rather poor by later standards, with chalk-pale faces and harsh lighting, all deep blacks and bright areas, but they were like magic to Violetta. She had never seen anything like them. They had something that not even the most skillful portrait artist could capture, some essence of the subject. They seemed to say something about the person's soul, though she couldn't have said what that was.

Violetta and Whitmore became firm friends, and later in the season spent some time at the Lido together. Whitmore loved it. It was a boat ride from the city streets of Venice, but it was also a wild place. More and more tourists were coming to engage in the new fashion for Adriatic sea bathing. The waters were considered marvelous, like calm, warm oil. Not like the rough and cold waters of Northern Europe at all. There were only a few wooden shacks on the beaches in those years. It was an undeveloped and natural place. They talked together about all the new ideas coming from Europe, about history, and about philosophy, and Violetta learned about photography.

"I'm reading the Stones of Venice by Ruskin," Whitmore said, one night, as he rowed her down the Grand Canal.

"And what does Mr. Ruskin have to say about these stones?" Violetta asked, gesturing at the buildings along either bank of the canal with the wine glass she held in her hand.

"Nothing good," Whitmore said. "He talks about the noble Romanesque architects, who built story above story, as at Pisa. He complains of the Palladian architects of Venice who dare not do this."

"This is amusing," Violetta said. "This Ruskin is an idiot."

"Well," Whitmore said, spluttering in shock. "Actually he is one of the foremost thinkers on architecture of our time."

"Tell me more," Violetta said, and took a sip of her wine. "This Ruskin's idiocy is entertaining."

"In his view, these buildings are built in the image of the Greek temple because the architects were incapable of creating anything better," Whitmore said. "For him, the Greek temple is a simple structure, all of one height. He sees nothing more than a low gable roof being borne on ranges of equal pillars."

"Idiocy," Violetta said, with a smile, and sipped again at her wine. "Does he say more."

"He has much to say on the subject of craftsmanship," Whitmore said. "Though I wonder if I should even tell you. I am somewhat scandalized at the irreverent nature of your comments on the writings of Ruskin."

"Please, please," Violetta said. "Go on."

"He also says of Greek temples that they were built by slaves," Whitmore said. "The people creating them were not properly craftsmen but merely human tools. This creates an architecture with no stamp of the individual artists."

"Truly a long time ago," Violetta said. "Slaves. Imagine."

"For Ruskin, the modern laborer is no different," Whitmore said. "While not a slave, he is still reduced to an unthinking machine."

"It's true." Violetta said, nodding her head. "So many lives wasted in unthinking toil."

"Ruskin sees a direct relationship between architecture and a society's moral state," Whitmore said.

"Ah, delicious, more idiocy," Violetta said, refilling her glass from the bottle beside her. "Tell me, what does Ruskin say that the architecture of Venice says about the moral state of we inhabitants."

"He says that the society of Venice lacks truth and vitality," Whitmore said. "He remarks on the inevitable decline of Venetian architecture. You see, as a society's morality wanes, its architecture invariably suffers. This explains the sad state of Venice's architecture, ruined, moldering and decayed."

"I see," Violetta said. Then she gazed at Whitmore, at his arms straining against his coat sleeves as he rowed. "Do you think we lack morals, here in Venice?"

Whitmore's cheeks reddened a little, and he looked away. He couldn't find the words to answer her.

CHAPTER 16

Violetta opened the door as usual but, before Jasmine could take an unbidden step inside, she placed her hand on Jasmine's chest. Jasmine raised a questioning eyebrow and cocked her head. "Just a moment," Violetta whispered, darting a look over her shoulder. "I must forewarn you that I have Sebastian here, and we are conducting some important business."

"Oh," Jasmine said. "I'm sorry. I should have called ahead. I can come back another time."

"No," Violetta said, "this concerns you. You should know about it. I have made a pact with Sebastian that he will no longer have access to this house, and he has agreed, but only if I best him at cards."

"Just tell him he isn't welcome," Jasmine said.

"It is not so simple. He must relinquish his claim..." Violetta's words trailed off. "Oh please just come in. I'll try to explain later." Violetta led her into the drawing room, to a card table. The playing top was covered with green baize, it had simple cabriole legs, recesses for gambling chips, and it was veneered in burr walnut. Sebastian was sitting at the table, shuffling cards. They were playing some game that Jasmine didn't recognize, with cards that looked somehow wrong, primitive. The aces seemed to show the four seasons. The kings were shown seated on horses and, except for the aces, all the cards had Roman numerals. Violetta sat at the card table and Jasmine sat in a small armchair nearby.

"Let's play a hand," Sebastian said.

"And then perhaps you'll go," Violetta replied.

"Well, that all depends on who wins," Sebastian said, with a smile, "doesn't it?" Sebastian hadn't acknowledged her but Jasmine could feel that he was all too aware of her presence. Why else would he speak English with Violetta? Neither of them had English as a first language and both spoke it with strange old-fashioned accents. And the longer Jasmine spent around Violetta, the more of her strange English and old-fashioned manners rubbed off. Jasmine was aware that she was something of a social chameleon, and didn't bother trying to fight it. Sebastian dealt Violetta her cards.

Violetta kept telling Jasmine little details about the game, as she was playing, but they didn't help Jasmine understand it. In fact Violetta's little tidbits of information just made the game seem even more complex and unintelligible. "It's like the Hungarian game Zsiros," Violetta told her. "Though the principles are unusual, it is quite simple to learn, and there is surprising scope for tactics." Jasmine nodded, even though she had no idea what Violetta was talking about. "The suits are a little different to what you may be used to. This one is Makk, they look like acorns, this one is Zöld, which are the leaves, and there are hearts and bells. The aim is to capture the majority of aces and tens."

"Okay, got it," Jasmine said. Violetta placed a nine on the soft green top of the card table. Sebastian then put another nine on top. Violetta played a king, and Sebastian played an ace.

"Do you concede?" Sebastian asked.

"Not quite yet," Violetta said.

"I can initiate another round by matching the first card played," she said to Jasmine.

"Right," Jasmine said, entirely confused.

The hands moving on the card table, and the cards being picked up and placed down started to blur in front of Jasmine's eyes. At the end of each hand, the two players made a note of their score. "Only the aces are worth anything at the end of the game," Violetta explained. Then there followed many more hands of the strange game, with its strange cards, each punctuated by the two players making a note of their scores on little pads, which looked like they had been stolen from a hotel, but Jasmine couldn't read the name below the crest at the top of each sheet of paper.

"This is pointless," Violetta said, what seemed like a very long time later. Sebastian let his cards flutter to the table, a slight snarl of disappointment on his face.

"Another draw," he said. "I suppose we know each other too well for either of us to emerge victorious."

"I want you out," Violetta said.

"I have a solution," Sebastian said. "Forget this stupid game. Instead of a wager. I propose an exchange."

"I knew it," Violetta said, dashing her cards to the table.

"What's going on?" Jasmine asked, but neither of them seemed to even hear her.

"Come on," Sebastian said. "You are so close. You can be rid of me forever. Just hand it over, and I'll go." Then he pretended to notice Jasmine for the first time, "Ah, hello Jasmine."

"Hello," Jasmine said, aware that a goofy smile was spreading over her face, but completely unable to stop it. Violetta looked at Jasmine, at her besotted expression, and then at Sebastian who was also smiling now, seeming almost to be enjoying the awkward situation.

Violetta got up from her chair and left the room. It was the first time that Sebastian and Jasmine had shared a moment unobserved that evening. Jasmine's heart raced. She had no idea what to expect from him. He had wanted this moment of privacy, she was sure of that. "You should not forge too close an attachment to Violetta, you know," he said. "Learn from my mistake."

"I have no idea what you are talking about, mate," Jasmine said.

"Mate?" Sebastian raised an eyebrow. Then he shook his head and smiled. "Have you really not realized who I am?"

"Nope, still no idea what you're getting at," Jasmine said. "You're going to have to give me more."

"All right," Sebastian said. He pointed at one of the mirrors. "Look," he said.

"Okay," Jasmine said, her gaze following in the direction he was pointing, "so the mirror is covered in a little curtain. That's a bit peculiar, I grant you, but it's traditional, isn't it? Something to do with avoiding the sin of vanity... I guess."

"Lift the drape," Sebastian said. "Go on... look in the mirror."

Jasmine hesitated, then went to the mirror. The velvet cover was surprisingly coarse, stiff and heavy. It took some effort to lift, and her arm started to get tired immediately as she tried to keep it out of the way to allow her to see herself. The mirror was old and dim with innumerable blemishes in the silver, but there she was. The young woman looking back at her looked confused. She didn't see what was important about the mirror or her reflection. She let the drape fall back to cover the mirror and turned to walk back over to the card table, but she stopped suddenly, a gasp of shock escaping her. Sebastian was standing right behind her.

Violetta suddenly returned, appearing silently in the doorway, and Jasmine's attention was drawn to her before she had time to think too much about how Sebastian had managed to slip up right behind her. She had been looking in the mirror the whole time, she should have seen him coming. But it was an old and cloudy mirror with a lot of dead patches, and Jasmine put it down to that.

"Come along now. Don't dawdle," Violetta said to Sebastian, handing him a book and sending him on ahead of her toward the door. Jasmine was left alone in the room, and she glanced back at the mirror, once again wondering how Sebastian had got so close unobserved.

"So now Sebastian is banished from this house," Jasmine said, when Violetta returned.

"Yes," Violetta said, "an idea I had been toying with for a very long time. I should have done this years and years ago."

"Why didn't you?" Jasmine asked.

Violetta didn't answer. She ushered Jasmine to a seat, filled her glass with sweet red wine, and leaned back. "What was that book?" Jasmine asked, after quite a long silence.

"Something he wants very badly," Violetta said at last.

"What, exactly?" Jasmine asked.

"There is a strange old legend that he is interested in," Violetta said. "It's crazy really. He is searching for the location of something lost, except it is not lost. It never existed. Anyway, he has been pestering me for access to those writings for some time now. He thinks that silly old book could hold the key to the location of the thing he seeks."

"Why is the book so silly?" Jasmine asked.

"Because it is most likely completely bogus," Violetta said. "It is an illustrated codex, hand-written in an unknown writing system. It dates from the 1420s, or thereabouts. It was written here, in Northern Italy, during the Renaissance. The thing is-"

"Wait," Jasmine said, suddenly sitting up straight. "You're talking about the Voynich Manuscript. Don't tell me you are talking about the Voynich Manuscript."

"Not the whole thing, obviously," Violetta said. "A couple of hundred pages of it are now in Yale's Rare Book Library."

Jasmine just stared in shock. "That book has to be worth... I don't even know how much it must be worth." Violetta went silent at that, and the silence dragged on for a few seconds. Jasmine soon recovered from her shock, and though she wanted to ask more questions about the manuscript, she knew now wasn't the right time.

She could see the effect just talking about it was having on her host. Jasmine racked her brains, trying to come up with some way to lighten the gloomy mood that had descended on them.

"Ah, wait," she said. "You'll get a kick out of this. I was reading a very interesting book the other day."

"Oh, yes?" Violetta said.

"Yes," Jasmine said, and smiled. "It was written by a Victorian anthropologist called Whitmore." Violetta seemed to wilt. "Do you know the name?" Jasmine asked, "He seems to have had some connection to your family. I think one of your relatives was even his assistant."

"Yes I know the name." Violetta said. Her eyes were ablaze, her mouth set in a grim line. She had obviously been gripped by some sudden and strong emotion.

"Are you all right?" Jasmine asked. "There is even a photograph. I thought it would cheer you up."

"I'm fine," Violetta hissed. "It's just that I hadn't thought about him in a long time."

Jasmine could tell what she had said had been even worse than the mention of the Voynich Manuscript. Violetta fell silent again, and this time Jasmine didn't dare to try and lighten her mood. She decided to just sit silently and let her work through whatever was going on with her.

Violetta's confusion and shame transported her back into the past, to a conversation she had once had with her father. They were in the mountains. She wasn't entirely sure she remembered things from her youth correctly anymore, but she was absolutely sure of that, at least, they had been in the mountains. She also remembered his hated presence, right beside her, a patch of cold in an already freezing room. An area of dark among the gloom. Her father.

It was mid-winter, and they were at the castle, which meant it must have been a very long time ago. She remembered that they had been looking out the window, unglazed in those days, barbaric, designed to provide a good archers perch, no thought to comfort at all. But she couldn't remember the view from the window.

Had there been snow on the ground, or icy mud? Was it a view of the surrounding landscape to the west or the massive walls of the castle to the east? Those walls she remembered had been so tall they blocked out the view from all but the tallest towers. She simply wasn't sure anymore. She chose to remember it as a landscape thickly covered in snow. Then she remembered what it was that her father had said that had disturbed her so much. "This is how it spreads," he had said. "You have met a man, and you love him. That love will infect him, but he won't love you. He will love somebody else and that love will infect her."

"So he can't love me?" she had said. "His love will turn to hatred?"

"You hate me now, don't you?" her father had said.

"Yes," she had said, emphatically. "You are a foul old monster. I wish I could destroy you. You are the cause of all this."

"Your feelings for him will never fade, just as mine for you are eternal, but his will fade. He will fall in love with another. This is how it spreads."

"Can human emotions be so easily manipulated?" Violetta had asked, softly, almost to herself.

"Are we even human anymore?" He said, even softer. She looked out over the snow, was there snow? Anyway, it didn't matter much anymore. Her father had been absolutely right. She had fallen in love irrevocably. Forever. And he didn't love her back. So she just kept pushing him away.

"Violetta, Violetta," it was the voice of her friend calling her back to the present.

CHAPTER 17

Jasmine was eating pizza with Sebastian. The restaurant was selling more take out pizzas than anything else at the late hour Sebastian was able to meet her, but there were a few other night owls like them at tables.

"I'm not sure having a whole pizza is such a great idea for my figure," Jasmine said.

"Nonsense," Sebastian said. "It is good to be plump and healthy."

"Hey," Jasmine said, "watch what you're saying. Plump is pretty much an insult. Nobody wants to think they look plump and healthy."

"Then what do people want to look like?" Sebastian asked.

"Gaunt and elegant," she said, "like you Sebastian."

"Oh yes?" Sebastian smiled.

"Yes," Jasmine continued. "Hey, how did you manage that trick? The one where you came up right behind me and I didn't hear you or see you. I was looking right in the mirror, and I didn't notice-"

"Jasmine," Sebastian interrupted. "You have to have worked this out by now. I'm a vampire."

"What? Don't be stupid," she said. "Obviously you have a reflection. Everyone has a reflection. I just didn't notice-"

"I was right behind you," Sebastian said, as he put more pizza in his mouth.

"Yes, but..." Jasmine was staring at him, trying to work out why he was saying such weird stuff. Was he joking?

"Have you ever seen me during the hours of daylight?" Sebastian asked.

This made Jasmine hesitate. "I'm sure I must have," she said. "Don't try to confuse me. Let me think."

"Go ahead, think," Sebastian said. "By the way, did you know vampires can cast a kind of spell with their eyes. You can't trust what you see or hear."

"I know a lot about vampires," she said, not able to take him seriously, although he seemed in deadly earnest. "I know a lot of different stories about vampires, and I also know that one important fact, that is the same across every story is that they... don't... exist."

"They do," Sebastian said, dabbing at his chin with a paper napkin, "and I'm one of them."

"Okay, fine," Jasmine said. "Let's say I believe you, which is stupid... but for the sake of whatever little game you're playing, let's say I do. So if I am put under a spell by a vampire, if I can't trust what I see or hear, what can I trust?"

"Trust your heart," Sebastian said.

"Vampires don't exist," Jasmine said.

"They do," Sebastian said. "I can see you aren't quite ready to believe it yet, but vampires do exist. They are no longer as numerous as they once were, that is true. Only the clever ones are left. Only the sly ones and the ones with great power."

"So being a vampire makes you clever, huh, and powerful," Jasmine said, with a smile. "I could see how that might be attractive, how somebody might want to be a vampire."

"No, it is a curse," Sebastian said, "becoming a vampire is the worst thing that can happen."

CHAPTER 18

Sebastian and Violetta blew into Venice on the winds of the Dark Bora. Strong gusts and blasts of wind, loaded with sheets of rain, plagued the city during the winter. The air grew even colder and denser at night, and the Bora blew all the stronger. There was no bridge connecting the city to the mainland back then, so they had come over by boat. The boatman, hopeful of a tip from two wealthy young travelers, was helping Sebastian unload their few bags.

"I love the big city," Violetta said.

"Hmm," Sebastian was only half paying attention. The boat, only loosely tied to the jetty, was being tossed about in the freezing winds and he didn't want to lose anything to the waters of the lagoon.

"Oh yes," Violetta said. "No matter the lateness of the hour, there are always people about their business. I like that." Sebastian glanced around, at the people Violetta was talking about. There were fishermen mending nets and merchants busy with cargo. They didn't look like they were anywhere near finished work, even though night had long since fallen. They just kept on working by lantern light. "In the country everyone disappears indoors at nightfall, it's so lonely and sad," she continued.

Sebastian didn't answer. He was paying the boatman and, as he didn't speak Italian very well, had to concentrate to work out what the man wanted. "I think we should go this way," Violetta said brightly, as soon as he was done and had their bags on his back, in his hands, and one under an arm. Sebastian followed wordlessly.

He had never been to Venice before and knew it only as a city state in the south that exported slaves and mercenaries. They were freezing, or at least Sebastian was, Violetta didn't seem to mind the cold so much. She hardly noticed that Sebastian's teeth were chattering from the cold winds, and she paid no heed at all to the driving rain and sleet being blown in their faces.

They didn't have a very clear idea about where they were heading either. They were wandering through dark, narrow little alleyways, gusts buffeting them at every corner. They could hear the wind's high pitched groans and shutters banging. There was a crash and some debris flew as a roof tile blew off and smashed. There were more noises coming from above too, less identifiable, as the wind played with washing lines, chimneys, and anything else projecting from the buildings. There was no guessing what the wind would rip free and hurl down on their heads next.

"What does that even mean, the bull?" Sebastian asked.

"The sign of the bull," Violetta corrected him.

"All right," Sebastian shivered. "But what does it mean."

"I don't exactly know," she said, "and I don't even know if it is a good idea to find it. In fact, it may be the opposite of a good idea."

"It's late anyway," Sebastian said. "Why don't we find some rooms, then keep looking in the morning?"

"But we travel by night," Violetta sounded almost hurt, "to avoid the peasant rebellion."

"There are no peasants in Venice," Sebastian said, through teeth clenched against the cold, "just fishermen, slavers and princes. There's no need to hide anymore. We can go out in daylight."

"Oh," Violetta said.

"And if we leave it any longer we wont get a room," he added. "We have to turn up at a respectable hour."

Violetta reluctantly agreed and they searched for a house offering rooms, soon finding one hidden among the alleyways. Violetta bargained with the woman who ran the place and it didn't take long before she had a room for them. "Your Italian is very good," Sebastian said, as soon as they were alone together.

"You will be able to talk to our landlady too," Violetta said. "She says her German is quite good."

"I'm not a fan of that language," Sebastian said, "but if needs must. I certainly can't speak a lot of Italian, but why are we sharing? Was there only one room left?"

"Yes, that's right," Violetta smiled. "I told them we were man and wife."

"You did what?" Sebastian gasped, took a step back, and fell over one of their bags.

"It was the only way to get the room," Violetta told him, as she helped him back to his feet. "They would never have given it to a couple living outside wedlock."

"I see," he said. "I suppose that's right. So what are the sleeping arrangements to be?"

"You take the sofa," she said to him. "I don't think you'll have any difficulty getting to sleep. You look tired."

"I'm exhausted," Sebastian said. He curled up on the sofa without removing a single item of clothing, not even his boots. He fell asleep in seconds, and Violetta stood over him, and just watched. Then, on an impulse, she ran her hand down his side, lingeringly. "I've grown accustomed to you, Sebastian," she whispered, and kissed his forehead.

***

Bright sunlight was streaming into the room when Sebastian woke. Violetta was nowhere to be seen. There was no sign of Violetta in the bathroom either. He called her name but there was no reply. Then, on a whim, he went to the bed and pulled back the blankets, still pristine and unslept in.

He started to get worried, started really searching the room. He checked in cupboards, then checked under the bed, and that's where he discovered her, so deeply asleep she seemed to be dead. She was wearing her clothes just as he was, still covered in soil from the journey. He tried to rouse her, but she didn't respond.

"You must be exhausted," he mumbled, "poor creature." Then he went to get some breakfast.

***

Violetta didn't get up until the sun had started to set. Finally crawling out from under the bed just as the light was growing dim and crepuscular. "There you are," Sebastian said. He was sitting at a small table near the window, nibbling at some bread and olives. "You've been sleeping the sleep of the dead."

"I have," Violetta said. "But I'm up now. I have to go out, and start to search for the sign of the bull."

"No," Sebastian said, shaking his head at her and wagging his finger. "You have had quite a fright, and you lost your father in the most terrible circumstances. I don't know why you want to find this bull thing, but there shall be no more skulking about after nightfall, do you understand me?"

"We're not going out?" Violetta sounded confused.

"No we're going straight back to bed and we're going to get up bright and early in the morning," Sebastian said. "you must be hungry."

"Not really," Violetta said, and went out onto the small balcony of the lodging house, a bare and moldy little space, with only a view of a small canal.

It was encroached on by other buildings on all sides. Night had fallen and candlelight could be seen in a few windows, the few that weren't already shuttered. Sebastian followed her out.

"I don't think our host has many guests," he said. Violetta turned to him. He was intimately close. There was no other option on the tiny balcony. It was little more than a ledge.

"Oh," she said, "why?"

"Look in the plant pot," he motioned with his head. Violetta saw that a plant pot was jammed precariously between the bars of the balcony railings, down by her feet. Then she saw that the plant pot wasn't empty, as she had first assumed, but she couldn't see exactly what was inside. Then she saw an eye.

"Eek," she recoiled, "what is it?"

"It's a baby owl," Sebastian said. "There are two of them in there."

"Oh," Violetta said, leaning forward again. "How delightful."

"Yes, I suppose." Sebastian said. "And they'll keep the mouse population down too."

"How very practical," Violetta said, "but owls are primarily important for their beauty."

"And these two will be beautiful," Sebastian said, "when they grow up." Violetta turned to peer into the pot again. The owls seemed to be getting used to her. She had always had an affinity with nocturnal creatures. Unsurprisingly, she thought to herself. The children of the night her father called such creatures. She banished all thoughts of her father and looked deeper into the pot. She could see two sets of eyes now. The slightly larger of the owls cheeped experimentally, as if investigating if she might provide some food.

"They are darling just the way they are," Violetta said. "I don't see any pressing need for them to be all grown up, just so they can be beautiful."

"Nor I," Sebastian said, after a pause. There was something strange about his voice, low and husky, that made her turn to look at him. He was staring intently at her, and she felt something inside her reach out toward him. She felt herself move imperceptibly closer to him, just as he leaned to her. Then they both moved as one, closing the remaining distance between them. Their lips touched.

Violetta had never kissed anyone before and she doubted that Sebastian had either, despite his play acting at being worldly and knowledgeable. They just stayed that way for an eternity, in each other's arms, their lips touching, mouths closed. Neither seemed to know what to do next, and it would never have occurred to either of them to kiss open mouthed, French style, such behavior was out of the question for a well-brought-up young lady of quality. They just hugged each other close. Enjoying being near each other. It was Sebastian who drew away at last.

"You're freezing," he said. "Perhaps you shouldn't be out here on this balcony. The air is still cold with the Bora winds." Violetta's eyes were rolled back in her head slightly. She was in the throes of some intense emotion. Sebastian could see that, but it didn't look like love somehow, not the way he thought of it. It looked more animal, more intense.

"I can feel your heart beating," Violetta said. "Your heart is so strong. So alive."

"Violetta!" Sebastian shouted and she seemed to snap out of whatever it was that had overtaken her. She was herself again. She was looking at him a little confused and embarrassed. She touched her head, as if checking for a fever.

"I feel a little strange," she said.

"Perhaps we should go to bed," Sebastian suggested. "We've crossed half of Europe to get here and we're both still a little exhausted and flustered. Our feelings are running high and naturally we are more susceptible to being overcome by impulses and yearnings. A good sleep and a good feed will see us regain mastery of our impulses."

He turned and went back into the room. "Go and wash," he commanded, falling easily into his role as male and in command, no matter the greater nobility of her birth. "You look frightful." Violetta went into the small bathroom and did as she was told. Then she returned in some demure nightclothes that she had been able to find in the few things that they had managed to bring with them. She went down on one knee, obviously intending to pull the sheets aside and disappear under the bed. Sebastian lunged across the room and put his hand on hers to stop her, but then he gasped.

"Your hand is absolutely freezing," he said. That's it. You're not spending another night cowering under a cart or hiding under a bed." He pulled the blankets to one side and indicated that she should climb in. She did as she was told again, very hesitantly.

"I don't remember ever having slept in a bed like this," she said.

"I know," Sebastian sympathized, "the place is a real flea pit, but needs must..."

"That's not what I meant," Violetta said.

"I'll be just over here," Sebastian said, ignoring her, and he pointed over at a sofa. Violetta lay back on the pillow and looked up at the ceiling, which had a painting of cherubs and kingfishers among the clouds. She could hear Sebastian changing for bed but she didn't look. The wind wasn't as bad as the night before but she could still hear it, making the timbers of the rickety old building sway and playing with the shutters. Then, a little later, she heard another noise. She couldn't identify it at first, but then she realized what it was.

"He's snoring," she whispered to herself and giggled. She got up in bed to look. She could see him sprawled on the sofa, his chest rising and falling and she could hear the snoring even more clearly.

Fascinated, she got out of bed and went over to have a closer look, creeping nearer and nearer, and listening as the snoring got louder. She reached out with the index finger of her right hand. She hesitated to touch him though, her finger stopping a few centimeters from his cheek. Even at that distance she could feel the heat of him, like standing near a fire.

She touched him, then snatched her finger back as he shifted in his sleep and his snoring paused for a moment. She touched him again, very slowly and very gently. The heat of him was intoxicating. She could feel it spreading up her arm. The sofa was large and Sebastian had curled himself up to the backrest leaving some of the seat exposed. Violetta was very slight and it suddenly occurred to her that she could climb onto the sofa with him. She could lie beside him.

Once she had had the idea it became irresistible. She moved very slowly and gently so as not to wake him. It felt like it took forever, but eventually she was lying right beside him, staring at his broad back and feeling the heat radiate from him. She put a hand on his shoulder. Then she snaked one of her arms round him. He shifted a little at the touch of her cold skin but didn't wake. She moved closer still, put her lips against his hot neck and tingles ran up and down her back. Then something took over, like an instinct, like breathing. Her mouth opened, her breathing was ragged, and her teeth were touching his skin, she felt the yielding surface of the skin against her hard, sharp teeth.

She had seen what her father had done, in that room, in the farmhouse, among the orchards, what he had done to the young man, little more than a boy. She knew it was wrong. She knew it was disgusting and nasty, yet here she was, her mouth open, her teeth pressing into his flesh, with more force every second, imperceptibly increasing. And then his flesh gave way, and the force that had penetrated the skin was enough to carry her teeth deep into his flesh.

It wasn't a big wound, but it was deep. Blood sprayed everywhere. She felt some instinct to clamp her mouth over the wound and suck all the blood down, so none was sprayed across the room, none was wasted, but finally she regained control. She recoiled from him, using all her will to fight the urge to bite deeper and drink in thirsty gulps. She stumbled backwards from the divan, falling to the floor, and spat out the huge gulp of blood that was filling her mouth.

It was only then that the enormity of what she had done hit home. She had bitten another human being, as if she was nothing better than a dog. And not just anyone, it was Sebastian, a brave young man who had saved her life, and who, she suddenly realized, she loved. There would be no chance of hiding what she was from him now. He would hate her and spurn her, he would probably strike her and tell her how dirty and feral she was. She stood, and ran from the room, only pausing long enough to grab a coat. She didn't even bother to put on shoes. She padded down the stairs, silent as a ghost, down to the front door, opened it and ran out into the night.

CHAPTER 19

Sebastian tucked into the food the landlady had prepared. It was a plate of stuffed duck which glistened with fat and was swimming in a sauce so full of red wine it was almost inky black. He had no illusions any more that it would fill him up, or make him feel stronger. He was dying. He was sure of it. His pulse was so weak that he could hardly feel it. He held his wrist, listening for the powerful, thudding flow of blood that he was used to, but many times couldn't find anything at all. When he did manage to find a pulse, it was so feint that he was never sure if he was imagining it or not. His strength was ebbing away and he was becoming an insomniac. Whenever he tried to leave the house, the brightness of the sun burned his eyes and all strength left his limbs. The last time he had tried to go out, eager to search for Violetta, tortured by the thought of what might have happened to her, he had feinted dead away and had to be carried back in by the landlady's son. The burly young man had dumped him in bed then gone off to work. He didn't get back till after dark, by which time Sebastian had recovered somewhat, just in time to toss and turn through another sleepless night.

"Does the food appeal to you at all?" the landlady asked.

"It's like ashes," Sebastian mumbled. "I don't mean to be insulting. I'm sure the food is good and that you are a wonderful cook, but this damn illness means I can't taste anything. I can't keep anything down. It's damnable."

"I've had my fill of this," she said. "I'm for calling the doctor."

"I hate those damn quacks," Sebastian said.

"I know young master but your situation is serious," the landlady said. "You look like the very death. I fear if we don't, that we might lose you."

"Do what you want," Sebastian said, unable to argue any longer.

"I will call him," the landlady said, as Sebastian pushed the meal aside and looked away.

"I'm so cold the whole time," he said.

"I'm calling him right now," the landlady said. "There's no more time to waste." She yelled to her eldest son, who lived in the same building with his wife and family so was always in earshot to be summoned, and sent him to fetch the doctor. Sebastian watched him go, then rose from the table.

"I'll take myself off to bed," he said, "though there's no rest to be found there. It is the very torture."

***

Sebastian was lying in bed, waiting for the house to go quiet. It was still a couple of hours away yet, but he would soon be left alone with his thoughts, once again unable to sleep. His landlady was on the stairs and he could hear her talking to her son, but then he heard a new voice. They were talking fast in Venetian, so he didn't understand. His door was opened and a heavy-set man was shown in. He was old, with thin hair, droopy ears, bushy eyebrows, and a long nose. His neck wasn't visible at all. In its place were heavy jowls that rippled and swayed with every movement and word.

"I'm doctor Scaffiante," he said. "I'm told you can't sleep, you are losing weight, and that you only speak German."

"I am not well," Sebastian said, "and I know a little German, it is true."

"I think I'm probably the only doctor in this city with any German," the visitor said.

"Thank you for coming doctor," Sebastian said.

"Your quite welcome," the doctor said. "Now let's have a look at you." The doctor lifted Sebastian's arms and let them fall, looked deeply into his eyes, and put a small stick into his mouth so he could get a good look at his tongue.

He took Sebastian's wrist and felt for a pulse, then felt for it at his neck. Sebastian was impressed. The only doctor he had ever met had only had a certificate good enough for the pulling of teeth and the letting of blood. This man was obviously much more educated. "You're cold as the grave," the doctor said.

"I know," Sebastian said, "and I never get warm, no matter how many blankets I pile on the bed."

"And your pulse is weak, damnably weak," the doctor muttered to himself. "I'm not sure I've managed to find it at all yet." Scaffiante stood back. Put his hand to his chin and stared at Sebastian, pondering the examination. "I believe you have Schuettelfrost young man," the doctor said at last.

"Schuettelfrost?" Sebastian had never heard the word before, and he definitely couldn't translate it. His German was far from perfect, and just wasn't up to medical terms.

"Yes," the physician nodded, "a serious condition but not incurable. Remain in bed, eat plenty of soup. I will create a medicine for you."

"Thank you doctor," Sebastian said.

"Not at all, young man," the doctor said. "I'm only doing my job. Before I go, I'll quickly bleed you to allow some of the evil humors that afflict you to escape." Sebastian nodded. It seemed an eminently sensible treatment to tide him over while the doctor went away and mixed some medicine. The doctor went through his bag and found a dirty knife, a blood-spattered bowl and some stained rags. The doctor talked as he prepared his equipment. "This is one of the oldest medical techniques," he said, "practiced by the Mesopotamians, the Egyptians, and the Greeks. Hippocrates himself practiced it, and Archagathus, one of the first Greek physicians to practice in Rome. He very clearly emphasized the value of bloodletting."

"I'm familiar with the technique doctor," Sebastian said. "I've been bled before. Did me the world of good, so please proceed with your work."

"That's the spirit," the doctor said, and continued talking, seeking to distract his patient from what lay ahead. "It may interest you to know that this procedure is modeled on the way women naturally purge themselves of bad humors. Blood, if it is not used up, stagnates and this upsets the balance of the four humors, blood, phlegm, black bile, and yellow bile, relating to the four Greek classical elements of air, water, earth and fire. Blood, of course, is the dominant humor and the one in most need of control. I must now remove this excess blood, the plethora, to restore the balance."

"Fascinating," Sebastian said. "Whenever you're ready."

The doctor spat on the blade of the knife and wiped it on his trousers. He positioned the bowl at the side of the bed and leaned closer. "Your arm, young man, if you don't mind."

"Not at all doctor," Sebastian said.

"Now there will be some discomfort," the doctor warned him. "You are quite likely to feel the urge to cry out or wail in pain. Don't fight it. This urge you will feel is the urge to unleash a primal scream and it is very beneficial in releasing evil influences."

"I see," Sebastian said, sounding uncertain, as the doctor tied cords round his arm, in theory to engorge his veins, but there was precious little reaction from Sebastian's veins. Then the doctor took a firm grip of his wrist with one hand and a firm grip of the knife with the other. He positioned Sebastian's arm over the side of the bed so it was above the bowl and placed the blade against his flesh. Sebastian flinched.

"Try not to move too much," the doctor said. "We want a nice, clean cut now."

"Whatever you say doctor," Sebastian mumbled through clenched teeth. He turned his head away from the doctor and the blade, staring at the wall and waiting for the pain. It came almost immediately, an intrusion, a burning, a tugging, a cutting, all in one. Much deeper and more excruciating than he had been imagining.

He screamed out, involuntarily beating the surface of the bed with his other hand. He screamed again as the pain intensified and whimpered as he realized the pain wasn't going to go away any time soon.

"That's the spirit lad," the doctor encouraged. "Now let's see if we can get a good bowlful. Hmm.. What's this now. There's some clotting I see. Some thickening. It's quite unhealthy blood you have. Made turgid with a heavy load of evil vapors. I'll have to make the medicine strong." Sebastian whimpered again. "Don't worry. You're in the best company. I've seen this condition in some of the oldest families of Venice. The old bloods I call them. It's a chronic condition but I don't lose many patients to it... There's a nice full bowl. All right, let's untie you and I'll be on my way. Stay in bed now, conserve your strength."

"As you wish doctor," Sebastian said, a little more comfortable now that he had been diagnosed. He had always had a strong constitution, and he expected to get better soon and belatedly start to search for Violetta, but that wasn't what happened. He didn't improve, he just kept fading. The landlady was forced to ask him to leave, as he hadn't the strength to find a job to pay his bills. Sebastian was very grateful when the doctor took him in, even though it meant he was now an invalid, living in one of the doctor's back rooms. His life had changed so much, so quickly, he just couldn't understand it.

CHAPTER 20

Jasmine was on her terrace, reclining on a lounger but wearing a cardigan against the cold. The sun had gone down almost without her noticing. She only realized it had gotten dark when she started to have trouble reading the textbook she had on her lap. The cat she had seen that first night had appeared on the roof of the building opposite again. She waved at it, but didn't pay it much further attention. She was trying to concentrate on her studies but it was hopeless in the dim light. She put the textbook down on the low wall around the terrace and phoned Violetta.

"Hello Jazz," Violetta said, before Jasmine had had a chance to say anything.

"Hey," Jasmine said. "I'm having trouble getting my research to come together."

"The ghost stories?" Violetta said.

"Yes, the ghost stories," Jasmine said. "There's a connection here, I'm sure of it. There's a thread that will tie them all together, but I just can't find it."

"I see," Violetta said. "So are you ringing so I can persuade you to have a drink instead."

"No," Jasmine said, fake shocked. "You absolutely mustn't do that. Only a bad friend would distract a young student from doing the research work her creepy professor has asked her to do to a ridiculously short deadline."

"So do you want me to hang up?"

"I didn't say that," Jasmine yelped. "What are you up to? Anything interesting?" They chatted for a while but didn't arrange to meet up. Jasmine put her phone down and turned back to her assignment. Sometimes she loved the broad scope of anthropology, but sometimes she hated it too. The sheer range of topics and approaches covered was sometimes bewildering. What other subject would allow her to explore subjects as diverse as forensic science, religious symbolism, language structure, and the similarities between the human brain and those of other animals? It was all so overwhelming sometimes. She decided to ring Violetta back, try a little harder to persuade Violetta to persuade her to go out for a drink. She turned back to her phone, on the low wall of the terrace beside her, but the phone was gone.

***

Violetta's phone rang, though it didn't seem to her like even just a few minutes had passed since she and Jasmine had been chatting. She smiled, pretty sure that Jasmine wanted to go for a drink after all. She swiped to accept the call."Hello Jazz!" she said, smiling from ear to ear.

"No. This is not your little friend, but she is close by." It was her father's voice.

"What have you done with her, you monster?" Violetta screamed into her phone.

"Don't worry my sweet," her father said. "I really have mellowed with age. I'm not the ravening beast I once was. Your friend is very much alive. I'm looking at her right now. She can't seem to find her phone, though that isn't surprising, seeing as I have it. I'm calling you on it right now. She's turning her disreputable little apartment upside down looking for it. Now she's looking in her jewelry case, a sad plastic little thing."

"Leave her alone," Violetta pleaded weakly.

"That's funny," the voice on the other end said. "If I remember correctly, that's exactly what I told you to do."

The line went dead.

***

Jasmine was searching through her fridge, behind the sweet chilly sauce, under a half-eaten bar of white chocolate. She had left her phone in the fridge before, but wherever it was it wasn't in the fridge this time. She went back out onto the terrace, where she had been doing her university work. Her plan was to think back, start searching again from there and find the phone, but there it was.

"Huh?" she said, out loud, oblivious to the fact that she was talking to herself. "There you were all along, just lying on top of one of my books." She picked the book up, it was Purity and Danger, one of the most influential books in her field of study. The phone started ringing, and Jasmine dropped the book so she could scoop it up. She saw the call was from Violetta, and answered.

"Thank the Holy Mother," Violetta said, on the other end. Jasmine could hear the relief in her friend's voice.

"What's going on?" she asked.

"I have to talk to you," Violetta said. "This is important. Promise me you'll meet me. Cafe Noir. Ten minutes. I'm already on my way."

"I suppose just one Spritz can't hurt," Jasmine said.

"Just be there," Violetta said, her voice almost a snarl. "Ten minutes."

***

Sebastian's phone rang. The number wasn't in the phone's memory, which was unusual, but he accepted it, sweeping the screen cautiously to accept the call. "Pronto," he said. He had been expecting a voice in Italian, or maybe English, but the voice he heard was speaking in the language of the old country. Shivers ran down his spine and it took him a moment to realize who it was, to concentrate and divine the meaning in the words.

"Violetta?" he said.

"Of course," she said, her voice sounded agitated. "Who did you think it was? I need your help."

"Oh really?" He said. "I thought I had been banished."

"Shut up," Violetta said. "Things are desperate or I wouldn't ask. Believe me. Are you at home?"

"No," Sebastian told her, his voice was uncertain. He'd never heard her like this.

"Go there," Violetta ordered him, "and I will arrive presently. And I will be bringing Jasmine."

***

Cafe Noir was already starting to get busy when Jasmine arrived and Violetta was already sitting at their usual table. "Sit down," she said, and slid a glass of spritz over to Jasmine. "I ordered you a drink."

"Thanks," Jasmine said, taking off her coat and throwing it over a chair, on top of Violetta's already discarded cloak. "So what's so important?"

"It's difficult to explain," Violetta took a pensive sip of her own drink. "Have a drink, you're going to need it."

Jasmine did what she was told. Her friend was very obviously agitated, and Jasmine was glad she had come to meet her. A friend who needed her help just couldn't be ignored, no matter how important the deadline. "Okay," Jasmine said as she put her drink back down, "what's going on?"

"You have never met my father, not really anyway," Violetta said.

"You said he was ill," Jasmine said. "Isn't that right."

"Yes," Violetta nodded. "I said that. But his illness is an illness of the spirit. He is no longer the person he used to be. I don't know if there was ever a time when my father was a man of good character with a strong mind, but he certainly isn't now."

"I'm not sure I understand," Jasmine said. "Has something happened to your father?"

"No," Violetta said. "He is a jealous and evil man, and he has taken an interest in our friendship. He disapproves." Violetta took a swig of her drink, as though she had finally gotten something difficult off her chest.

"I see," Jasmine said, though she didn't actually see at all. "I suppose that's a bad thing."

"Yes," Violetta nodded. "Unfortunately, that is true. It is very bad. My father uses violence to solve his problems, and I'm afraid he intends to hurt you. Maybe even tonight."

"Your father intends to hurt me?" Jasmine said. "Tonight?"

"Yes," Violetta said, "and I intend to do everything I can to make sure that doesn't happen."

"What?" Jasmine had forgotten her drink entirely. "Do you really think I'm in danger? From your father?"

"Yes I do," Violetta said. "You don't understand, you can't. You don't comprehend the threat he poses, I can see that, but that's because I never explained. It's my fault. If I had, you would understand."

"This is a little worrying, I suppose," Jasmine said. "So why does he object to our friendship?"

"He is very old fashioned," Violetta said, "very old fashioned indeed. He considers me... it's hard to explain. He considers me... something akin to his property."

"That's awful," Jasmine said, as some inkling of what her friend might have to deal with on a day-to-day basis started to dawn on her. "Is he violent towards you?"

"No, not physically, but he can see that my friendship with you is giving me the strength to pull away from him," Violetta said. "And that is something he can not allow. I didn't intend to let our friendship become so deep. It's a mistake I've made before, but I just have so much fun with you. I feel alive for the fist time in a long time. I have been selfish, and I have put you in danger."

"What kind of danger... exactly?" Jasmine asked, still having a little trouble processing what her friend was telling her. "What exactly are you talking about?"

"I'm talking about my father being in your house," Violetta said, "and I'm talking about how he has told me he intends to kill you if we don't break off our friendship."

"In my house?" Jasmine whispered.

"Yes," Violetta was having trouble meeting her gaze.

"Wait," Jasmine said, "do you mean in the building, or actually in my apartment?"

"I'm not sure," Violetta said, her tone very serious, "but he called me on your phone about twenty minutes ago, and he said he was in your house."

"That's not possible," Jasmine said, digging for her phone. "I was in my apartment twenty minutes ago."

"Exactly," Violetta said. Jasmine dove into her bag for her phone and fumbled to switch it on. She found the calls log and started to go through it.

"What the...? There are two calls here. But I only made one," Jasmine said, the implications still dawning on her. "I left the phone on the terrace. He must have climbed up to the terrace."

"That makes sense," Violetta said, sounding a little relieved, "so he hasn't gained access to the apartment yet."

"It absolutely does not make sense. None of this makes any sense," Jasmine muttered. "And if he's willing to climb up to the terrace, there's not much keeping him from simply breaking in."

"He is clever. He will eventually find some way in," Violetta said. Jasmine was having trouble concentrating on what her friend was saying. She dropped her phone back into her bag, not wanting to see it or touch it anymore. She couldn't work out how he had gotten past her phone's lock screen, or how he had climbed up to the terrace. "I really don't think you should go home tonight," Violetta said.

"What?" Jasmine said. "But all my stuff is there."

"You can go get it in daylight, tomorrow," Violetta told her.

"Why would that be any safer?" Jasmine asked.

"It will give me a chance to talk to him," Violetta said, though Jasmine heard a moment's hesitation in her friend's voice. It felt like she was holding something back, not telling the whole truth.

"I think we should just call the police," Jasmine said.

"Ordinarily I would agree," Violetta said, "but my father is influential. He has friends. What can we prove? Why would anyone believe us?" Again Jasmine got the feeling that this wasn't the whole story. "Perhaps nothing will happen," Violetta said after a moment. "His threats were vague. Perhaps if I never see you again, he will just forget you."

"I don't want that," Jasmine said, softly. "You are my friend and that isn't going to change, no matter what."

"Really?" Violetta finally managed to make eye contact.

"Yes." Jasmine said, reaching for her friend's hand. She could feel the cold of Violetta's flesh, even through the gloves she was wearing. There was a silence, and Jasmine took advantage of it to have a drink. Violetta followed suit, pensively. "This is awful," Jasmine said.

"Yes," Violetta said. "My father is a monster. I hate him. He corrupts and spoils everything. He turns everything he touches to the most obscene filth, including me. And the filth spreads and spreads, with no end, ever."

"Hey, hey," Jasmine said. "You are not bad or dirty, no matter who your father is or what he has done. You are your own person and you are beautiful." Violetta looked up, her eyes wide. For some reason, Jasmine had expected them to be glistening with pent-up tears, but they weren't. They were dry. "I don't really have anywhere I can go," Jasmine said. "The only other people I know here are the boys, and their apartment isn't even big enough for them. They sleep in a cupboard."

"You can't stay at your place," Violetta repeated, "and my place is just as dangerous, even more so in fact."

"Where does that leave me?" Jasmine asked. "A hotel room?"

"No. That's not a good idea," Violetta said. "He could find you and there would be nothing to keep him out of your room. The rooms are public, open to all."

"They have locks," Jasmine said.

"Yes, but..." Violetta mumbled, distracted. Jasmine had the feeling she had already decided on something but it was less than ideal and she was trying to think of something better. She waited patiently for her friend to speak.

"Sebastian's place," Violetta said at last. "I don't think he will suspect that, and I don't think Sebastian has allowed him entrance. I'm not sure, but I can't think of anything else." Despite the strange and confusing circumstances, Jasmine's heart jumped at the thought of spending the night at Sebastian's place.

"Oh," she said. Excited and unsure at the same time.

"I know," Violetta said, "The idea repulses me too. I can't think of anything more disgusting. But I can't think of any other option."

"I see," Jasmine said. "So, will I be safe to go back to my place tomorrow?"

"I don't know when it will be safe, but I will do everything I can to put this right," Violetta promised her. "I will give you your safety and security back. I'll do it as soon as I can, I swear."

"I guess we better go see if Seb is at home then," Jasmine said, "and see what he thinks of this idea."

"Yes," Violetta agreed, "but we must be careful that we are not observed as we leave."

"Really?" Jasmine snorted. "Isn't that a little melodramatic?"

"I'm afraid it is probably wisest," Violetta said, and some time later they both got up to go. Violetta turned her cloak inside out so that its navy blue lining was outermost, instead of the bright crimson of its fabric, then folded up her hat and put it in her bag. She scraped back her hair into a ponytail and tied it with a little ribbon. She undid Jasmine's hair and shook it out into a big mane of curls.

"Do you think this will fool him?" Jasmine asked. "If he's watching."

"It'll help... maybe," Violetta said. "When we get outside, I'm going to turn left. I won't be running, that would attract attention, but I will be moving quickly and purposeful. Follow me, concentrate on not getting lost and not losing sight of me. All right?"

"All right," Jasmine said with a determination that she didn't quite feel. Violetta turned and left so abruptly that it left Jasmine standing watching her go for a couple of seconds before she remembered to follow. The door had almost closed back into the frame after Violetta when Jasmine reached it.

Jasmine turned left as soon as she was outside and saw that Violetta was already five yards ahead. She wasn't looking back and she was moving quickly. Jasmine followed her at a fast pace, without falling too far back and without trying to close the distance between them. She soon realized they were taking a slightly circuitous route to Sebastian's apartment.

CHAPTER 21

Sebastian hadn't been sleeping. He was sure of that, but if he hadn't been sleeping, how had she managed to get into his room? The answer was obvious, he'd finally lost his mind. One moment he was alone, the next she was standing at the foot of his bed. It was dark but her skin was glowing with a pale alabaster light. She was a vision of fashionable beauty, not like the peasants and fish wives he had been surrounded with, their skin tanned like old leather by the rays of the sun. Sebastian recognized her immediately, of course, it was Violetta, a figment of his tortured mind come to taunt him. "You are weak," she said.

"Yes," he agreed, though he wondered if there was any point conversing with a figment of his imagination. She had a physician's bag with her, a heavy leather thing that opened at the top. She set it gently down on the bare wooden floor of the simple room where he found himself. Seeing it thorough her eyes he felt embarrassed, and even more embarrassed because he was so helpless. She bent, opened the bag and reached inside. The bag seemed to be virtually empty and she didn't have to rummage around for long before she found what she wanted. She produced a heavy, lead glass decanter. She struggled with the stopper for a moment before she had it open. Stopper in one hand, decanter by the neck in the other, she came round the bed till she was standing on his right. She was so close he could see the intricate patterns woven into her expensive skirts. He lifted his head to look into her eyes. They contained a thousand shifting shades of some color it was hard to identify, but which reminded him of fire. He began to wonder if perhaps she was real, after all. Could it be that Violetta had returned, come back to save him from poverty and illness?

"Lie back and open your mouth," she said. Sebastian did as he was told, and she lifted the decanter, obviously intending to pour its contents for him to drink. In the dim light, through the heavy glass, he couldn't make out what was inside.

"What is that stuff?" he asked. She paused, and a little shadow of disapproval passed over her face. She put the index finger of her left hand, the hand holding the stopper, on his chin and gently forced his mouth open.

"It will make you well," she said. "So what does it matter what it is? Will you drink it?" Sebastian nodded very gently so as not to dislodge her finger from his chin. He liked the feeling of her touching his face. She upended the decanter gradually allowing the contents to flow only very slowly. The stream of liquid was very slender, often breaking up into individual drops then becoming a thin flow again. Sebastian saw, even in the darkened room, that the liquid was bright red. He recognized the taste instantly. It was the metallic tang of blood. Vinegar and pig's or bull's blood he imagined, a popular traditional cure. He'd been given it before when he was a child, but never from such an expensive bottle.

She poured, paused to allow him a breath, then poured some more. She didn't stop until the whole decanter was empty. Then she put the stopper back in and returned to the foot of the bed, where she had left her bag. She replaced the decanter in the bag, closed it up and lifted it off the floor, as if preparing to leave.

"There," she said. "That should start you down the road to recovery."

"Are you real?" Sebastian asked.

"That's a good question," she answered. "I don't know if I am real, but I know that my mistakes are real. And I have to take some responsibility. I have to try to put things right, if I can."

Sebastian was confused. Violetta was being kind to him, but something was missing, as if there was now some distance between them, as if they had become estranged. He guessed he was just too befuddled to work it all out, that he would be able to work it all out when he felt better. Violetta had always been wise beyond her years, and it didn't surprise him that she knew the best medicine for his illness. "My condition, what is it?" Sebastian mumbled.

"Your condition, yes. You don't know what it is, do you?" she said. "You don't know the affliction you have, and will always have. However I know it only too well. There is no cure, I'm afraid, only treatment."

"The name," Sebastian insisted. "What is the name of the ailment. What have I come down with?"

"The name is inelegant in the extreme," she said. "I find it distasteful to talk of such things." Violetta was a lady of quality to be sure, Sebastian thought, and he knew he should not press her to talk of something she was unwilling to explain, but he couldn't help himself.

"I must urge you to try, because not knowing is a torture. I have been ill for so long, and constantly I imagine the worst and think I may die any instant."

"Then allow me to at least put your mind at rest about that before I go," she said. "You will not die of this. You are never going to die. Go to sleep now and I will return tomorrow with some more of my magical elixir. Until then." With those words she turned and let herself out. Sebastian heard a single step out in the hall and then silence.

"Until then," he whispered. He was feeling stronger already and looking forward to her return.

***

Sebastian seemed to have been alone forever when a gentle knock came at the door. He knew immediately who it must be, though why a figment of his imagination was bothering to knock was beyond him. "Come," he said. The door opened to reveal Violetta, returned just as she said she would. And, again, she was carrying her doctor's bag. Sebastian could see the doctor standing behind his visitor. He was still talking to Violetta in Italian. Sebastian could sometimes pick out Latinate words from the Italian, words shared by his own language, and, even though he didn't understand, he could sometimes get a sense of what was being said. It seemed to him that the doctor was thanking Violetta for taking an interest in his invalid.

Sebastian couldn't understand what Violetta said in return, but her dismissive hand gesture was unmistakable in any language. The doctor withdrew, leaving the two of them alone. Violetta crossed the threshold and closed the door behind herself. "I trust you are feeling better," she said.

"Much recovered, thank you," Sebastian grinned at her, strong enough now to prop himself up in bed. "I'm very glad to see you again."

"It is good to see you, too," Violetta said, "very good." Violetta was, if anything, dressed even more finely than the night before. The fabrics of her clothes were heavier, her hair more intricately done, and Sebastian noticed, even appreciated it, but he couldn't help wondering where she had been, what had happened to her that night, where had she gone? Why had she run away? Where did her new, expensive clothes come from?"

"You look troubled," Violetta said, as she produced the decanter from her bag.

"I've been worried about you, for I don't know how long. I have lost track of how long I have been lying here... a long time. You accompanied me here. But you disappeared, just as this cursed illness struck in fact, and it prevented me from searching for you."

"There is a lot to explain," Violetta said, as she unstopped the decanter. "I lost control of myself, and I betrayed you," she continued, as she pushed his head back and forced open his mouth, "but there's time enough to explain all that. We have all the time in the world, in fact." She started pouring the blood, and Sebastian gulped it down gratefully.

"What do you mean betrayed?" Sebastian asked, while she was replacing the stopper in the now empty bottle.

"I simply mean," Violetta said, "that I betrayed you, I caused all this."

"No," Sebastian said, "you were frightened. You ran, that's all. The important thing is that you came back."

"You are noble," she said as she took a seat on the edge of his bed and laid her hand on his chest, "so innocent, so trusting, so willing to see the best in people. But you must remember, that I bit you."

"Bit me?" Sebastian repeated, confused.

"Yes," she drew back her lips and clacked her teeth together in demonstration, "a bite. You must remember that I plunged my chompers into your flesh? Sunk my pearly-whites into your virginal skin?" Sebastian reached for his neck, where he had found the wound the morning she had disappeared. Violetta noticed the movement and smiled. "Ah, you do remember," Violetta said, stroking the jagged red line, "and here it is. Oh my, I did bite deeply. It was quite an experience for me, changed me. How was it for you?"

"I don't know what you mean."

"Perhaps not," Violetta nodded, "but I suppose you are beginning to be able to imagine what might have happened."

"Violetta," Sebastian said. "You seem so different."

"Tell me," Violetta said, "was there ever anything you ever noticed that was odd about me. Before I ran away."

"No," he said, "of course not. You are a lady of the highest quality. That's all I know."

"Think," Violetta commanded.

"Well," he said, "there was one thing. When your father was unfortunately killed as we left your home. In that ugly business, the peasant revolt. There was that thing, unless I imagined it. I have been delirious, but I remember that a few days later, the old man came back from the dead. He had become a vampire.

We both had to run for our lives. I always wanted to ask you about that."

"I am his daughter. I am a vampire too, you pea brain," Violetta hissed at him, annoyed that he couldn't put it together himself.

"But th..." Sebastian started to protest, but his words trailed away as the terrible truth started to dawn on him.

***

Violetta soon moved Sebastian from the doctor's care to a suite at her ancient and grand palazzo. She looked in on him as soon as he was settled in. "I have brought a decanter of your medicine," she told him.

"Thank you," he said, "but I shall not be drinking that again. It is not animal blood. Of that I am suddenly sure."

"No," Violetta nodded, "you are right. It isn't. It is something a little more potent. But if you don't want to drink, why did you come here? Why come with me to my lair?"

"I don't know. I didn't enjoy imposing on the good doctor. Not as the unholy creature I am now."

"Unholy?" Violetta snorted, surprised by the word.

"Yes," he said, "unholy. What else would you call a vampire? I have become an evil spirit, a creature of the night. It's time to put a stop to this. I shall simply stop drinking blood and continue to fade away. I want to die," he said to Violetta.

"Oh don't be so melodramatic. Look around you," she swept round his opulent rooms with a gesture of her hand, "you have everything. These sheets are silk, this furniture was created by a master, this painting is a work of genius."

"I know," Sebastian said, "and please don't think I am ungrateful. I know that you think you are helping me, repaying a debt to me, and these certainly are fine things, but I fear that I have lost my soul."

"Peasant superstitions," Violetta said.

"No," he shook his head emphatically, shocked at how much she had changed. "Something has changed within me. I can feel it. I will not extend my time in this world. I will not live at the expense of others. I will simply stop drinking blood and fade away."

"You have a lot to learn, Sebastian," Violetta said, placing her hand affectionately on his shoulder,

"What do you mean?"

"I mean that things aren't quite as simple as you might imagine. You will not die just because you don't eat. You will not die just because you don't drink, you can even stop breathing if your will is strong enough. But you will not die. I am proof of that. I resisted. I resisted for so long, until I finally gave in to temptation, and tasted you. Because of my weakness, you will never die. You will be forever young."

"I don't believe you," Sebastian said. "Everything needs sustenance. Even demons such as we."

"As you please," Violetta nodded. She gathered up the decanter and took it with her as she left his suite. Sebastian was left standing there, in his study. She had also given him a bedroom, bathroom and a box room for the few things he had brought with him, more space than most in the city had, and more than he had ever had before. It was all very generous, but it wasn't the first time he had been on the receiving end of the gifts of nobility. In the end, they meant less than a poor person sharing an apple. The poor person would feel the loss of giving away half an apple but a duke could give you free use of an entire wing of a castle and hardly notice. There was no generosity in it. It only meant that they wanted something from you and had decided to keep you close by.

His new study was a large room with divans, a desk, and a pair of large bookcases. The bookcases were so tall that a small ladder was provided to reach the top shelves. Hoping to distract his thoughts from the circles they were constantly spinning in, Sebastian wandered over to inspect the selection. There was a vast range of religious works, travel writings, the writings of the troubadours and many others. Among the expensive books were some works about legend, folktales, and ancient romances and in pride of place among them was a book with a title in a strange language, but which seemed to include the word "vampires", written by some kind of doctor. At least, the author called himself a doctor, Doctor Nicolescu.

For my benefit I suppose, Sebastian thought. He resisted the urge to pick the nasty old book up for a moment, then reached for it and opened it. He couldn't read it but there were illustrations inside. They were woodcuts, and quite inexpert ones, but all the more evocative for that. Page after page of the book was dark, inky images of impaling, torture, fires, and all kinds of other horrors. He threw the book onto the desk in disgust and went into the bedroom where he threw himself down on the bed.

***

Violetta looked in on him again the next day, and Sebastian was pleased to see that she hadn't brought her doctor's bag. "It's the first time I've seen you lately when you weren't carrying that bloody decanter around," he observed.

"Bloody decanter," she repeated absently. "That's quite fitting. But forget the decanter for now. You will soon start to feel weak if you don't drink from it, but not immediately. We still have some time."

"What would you have me do with my time?"

"I would have you enjoy your new life, do something entertaining. I know you like to hunt, and it is a pastime I have recently taken up."

"You have changed so much," Sebastian said. "But you are right, I know a little of hunting. I assume there is an abundance of game hereabouts, wild bore, dear?"

"Marvelous," Violetta said. "We shall hunt with owls, for rabbits and hares, or geese and ducks." Sebastian didn't reply, unsure what to think about her idea to go hunting. He intended to fade away, not enjoy himself hunting game, but there was no reason he had to fade away in bed. And he did enjoy being with Violetta. Unfortunately, this young woman was entirely different to the Violetta he had thought he had known. She was a vampire, a vampire who had turned him, by her own admission, into her undead companion.

"Let's begin right away," Violetta said, not giving him time to think. "It's not like you have much else to do, apart from famish yourself to death that is."

"I suppose we'll have to be back before sunrise," Sebastian said, his voice cruel. "For obvious reasons."

"That won't be necessary. I have a little lodge out on one of the islands in the lagoon. There are plentiful grounds to hunt in, well stocked with game.

We can stay there on the island until we tire of the hunt."

***

They were in a boat being rowed to the island within the hour, and it was less than an hour to the island itself. Venice was so close it could be seen from the small dock where they landed. They didn't start hunting that first night though.

Violetta simply showed him to the building that she called the hunting lodge. It had two floors and was comfortable but there were also signs of neglect, easy to spot even in the twilight of approaching morning.

The walls hadn't been plastered in some time and there were a couple of tiles missing from the roof. The front door was held shut with a chain and a padlock, and it had had time to become rusty.

Sebastian didn't think Violetta would be able to open it, it looked like it had rusted into a solid mass, but it didn't give her any trouble. "There's a trick to it," she told him, with a wink. She went inside and he could hear her dumping the chains on what sounded like a wooden table, but for some reason he hesitated to follow. After a while she seemed to notice his absence and her face appeared in the dark little doorway of the hunting lodge.

"You're taking your time," she said, though, inexplicably to Sebastian, she was smiling.

"I have the strangest feeling of dread and foreboding," he told her.

"Allow me to dispel that feeling for you," Violetta said. "Please enter of your own free will."

Sebastian felt the cloud of doom and foreboding lift and was able to take a step into the building. "What the..?" he gasped.

"Magic," she explained simply. "The bedrooms don't have shutters and the beds upstairs don't have heavy curtains, so we will have to sleep downstairs, in the pantry. It's the only room in the house where I can endure to rest through the day," she told him, "but you are welcome to try out any room that catches your fancy."

"No, The pantry will be perfect, if you consent to share it with me?"

"I do so consent," she said with a smile.

***

The hunt started the next night. Violetta produced a couple of owls from somewhere, but Sebastian had no idea where. There was no place he could see that they would be housed. He decided they had to be wild. "First you will have to train your owl," Violetta told Sebastian, confirming his suspicion. "Feed it a few tidbits while it stands on your gloved hand. Let it get used to you." Sebastian did as he was told, but the owl simply hissed at him. It was going to take some time to tame the contrary little creature, Sebastian thought. "Owls cannot focus on anything that is close to them, so don't just dump the meat on the glove. Also, if food is given from the glove, the owl will constantly bite at the glove looking for food," Violetta said, coaching him.

He held the tidbit out quite a distance and let the owl focus on it. He slowly brought it toward the creature and when it was exactly in front of his beak, Violetta gave a soft audible whistle. The owl opened its beak and gently took the tidbit.

They continued the training, night after night. At first, when the tidbit was coming in, the owl would snap and lurch at Sebastian's right hand. When the creature hissed and snapped, Sebastian halted the tidbit's progress towards it and counted to ten. Then resumed the approach. Eventually the owl started to learn that the nicer he behaved the sooner the tidbit got there.

Another task was getting the owl used to being approached and picked up. He would puff up, hiss, and snap for several minutes. Once Sebastian had gotten hold of him, and the owl was in position with both feet on the glove, Sebastian clicked his teeth to mark the event and then offered a tidbit with his right hand, just as Violetta instructed.

All seemed to be going well so it was time to introduce the lure, and then soon they progressed to some real hunting. They hunted at night, the island their domain, then spent the days cowering within the lodge, hiding from the sun, and time passed. Days turned into weeks, and weeks turned into months.

***

"This place has been here for a long time," Violetta said, as they were hunting one night. "It has been here since the dark days when people first came here. Nobody wanted to go into the lagoon to live. It was desperation and constant raids by barbarians, bandits, and forest people that forced them to abandon the shore and surround themselves with water. They became people of the lagoon, on this island and many others."

"Fascinating," Sebastian said, but the tone of his voice left no doubt that he found it anything but.

"You can't appreciate it from down here," she said. "You have to climb a tall tree, to get a bird's eye view. Here. This one will do."

"You want me to climb this tree?" Sebastian said.

"Yes, Sebastian," she said, "I want you to climb this tree. Now go on. Up you go."

"To see over all these other trees," Sebastian said, "I would have to climb almost to the top."

Violetta didn't answer, instead just motioning him to the tree. He found a handhold with his left hand, then reached up to take hold of another, slightly higher, with his right. Then he found a gap in the bark to wedge one of his boots into. He turned to look at Violetta again. "Are you quite sure that you want me to do this?"

"Yes," she urged. Don't be such a big baby. Go on, up you go."

It was a very difficult climb, and Sebastian had to test every branch before he trusted it to carry his weight. The tree was old and some of the branches were brittle. More than once he felt caterpillars and other assorted bugs squish beneath his fingers as his hands sought secure holds in the dark. Birds waited till he was almost on them before bursting from their perches, startling him, and half way up he felt something slither past his ear, some woodland creature, but he wasn't quick enough to catch a glimpse of it.

He kept doggedly climbing though, and was rewarded by an increase in the brightness of the moonlight as he climbed above the lower trees. Then his hand touched something strange as he was reaching for his next hold, something smooth. He looked up, and he saw that he had his hand on a boot. A small woman's boot with a high heel. In confusion, he looked further upwards, and saw Violetta's face.

"Boo!" she said.

He recoiled so hard that he lost his footing. He had only one handhold, a slender branch – all the branches were slender at this height. With all his weight on it, the branch broke clean off and he was tumbling backwards. His mind should have been instantly working at lightning speed, his eyes scanning for a branch to grab, some place to hook his leg, some way to save himself, but his thoughts were sluggish. The jolt of adrenaline in the blood that one of the living would feel just didn't happen. He plummeted to the forest floor, meter after meter. He hit the tree trunk on the way down crushing a handful of ribs and his neck broke on impact with the ground, but he didn't die. He felt pain, enough pain to make him scream, but he didn't die. He tried to reach for his neck, and estimate the damage. It was then that he realized he had broken both his arms. He yelled and screamed and cursed loud and long, and then he stopped.

Violetta's boots had entered his field of vision. He couldn't turn his head to look, but he knew Violetta was standing over him. Through all the pain, he still managed to wonder how she had gotten down from the tree so quickly. Then he heard her voice. "That looks painful," she said. "You're all splayed out like a marionette with the strings cut. Why did you let go of the tree?"

"I didn't let go on purpose," he yelled.

"I suppose not. Well that's enough lollygagging. On your feet. I still need to show you the view."

"I beg your pardon?"

"Get up," Violetta hissed.

"I can't," he wailed. "I think my neck is broken."

"I'm sure it is. That was very careless of you."

"Then how can I get up?"

"You must become whole again."

"And how the blazes do I do that?" Sebastian demanded.

"Think of how it feels when your neck is not broken. Think of how it feels when your arms are whole, in one piece and uninjured." Her voice was hypnotic, comforting and soft. "Whatever other injuries you have," she said, "wish them away. Become the young man you are. Become healed and healthy." On and on the words came, like a river, and Sebastian felt the sinews of his neck knitting back together beneath his skin, his bones aligning and fusing. He even felt his head drag across the grass as it assumed a more natural position. "That's the way," Violetta said. "How clever you are, how good you are at this. Look how quickly you can reconstruct yourself." Sebastian rose to his knees and then stood. He faced her, looked deep into her eyes. She smiled. "But why stop there?" she asked. "Look at my hands." She raised her hands, allowing Sebastian to see them more clearly. They were delicate and pale in the moonlight. But as he watched her nails seemed to get longer. They thickened and strengthened and her skin moved to accommodate them. They looked like the talons of eagles. "Copy me," she said. "Strong claws will make climbing the tree a lot easier."

Sebastian raised his hands till they were alongside Violetta's hands, and watched as they went through the same transformation. "How can this be possible?" he asked.

"What was it we decided?" Violetta said with a smile. "Oh yes. We decided it must be magic. Now climb the tree. I think you'll find it a little easier this time, and the view really is worth the effort."

***

They were hunting a few nights later when they heard the noises. There was a rustling in the undergrowth, a crackling of twigs, and low voices. "What was that?" Sebastian asked.

"People," Violetta said.

"Well yes, obviously people," Sebastian was a little annoyed at her stating the obvious, "but who? I thought we were alone on the island."

Violetta let her owl hop from her gloved hand to a low branch. Then she took off the glove and hung it over the branch beside her owl. She nodded to Sebastian to do the same. "That's right. We should be, as you say... alone," she said. "It is well signposted that trespassers are not welcome. It is well known in the lagoon that this is not a place to tie up at, or to explore."

The noises got quite loud as the people came toward where they were standing but then started receding, the people were passing close and then continuing on their way. They were heading in the direction of the house. Violetta took off her boots, and Sebastian quickly did the same. She padded off silently through the forest, intimately familiar with the location of every tree. Sebastian padded off after her. He could feel the sharp twigs and plants of the forest floor bite into the soft soles of his feet. He had to bite his bottom lip not to cry out in pain at the pinpricks of discomfort.

Violetta had soon gained on the people. It was a band of five young men, teenagers or in their early twenties. Sebastian could hear them now, and understand what they were saying. He found their Italian to be as easy to understand as his mother tongue, even though it had been pretty much a mystery his whole stay in Venice, but, of course, that was before.

"This island is accursed," one of them said. "We shouldn't be here." The one that had spoken was the only one wearing a hat. Even in the dark, Sebastian could see that it was a shapeless old thing that had been exposed to the elements for long years. They were obviously workers, fishermen perhaps.

"Wives' tales," one of his friends hissed. From his vantage point, behind the group, Sebastian could see that Violetta was right alongside the men, though hidden from them by foliage. She stopped behind a tree and reached out, unseen, for the nearest man. Sebastian saw her arm extend, at least twice as long as it should be, perhaps longer. As the arm extended, it became thinner, even more skeletal than it already was. She tapped the nearest of them on the shoulder, the other shoulder to the side she was hiding on. The man turned to look, and saw one of his friends standing there.

"What?" he asked, voice a whispered challenge.

"What do you mean... what?" his friend replied.

"You just tapped me on the shoulder."

"No I didn't. You're losing it. Try not to let this place get to you."

"Shut up back there," the guy in front hissed at them. Violetta ran ahead, hid again and tapped another shoulder, causing another bout of hissing and angry whispers among the men. The man in front, the leader, Sebastian judged, stopped and held out his arms in a gesture to halt his compatriots. They gathered round him.

"This is serious," the leader said. "There is treasure in the house on this island. Enough to make us rich. Some stupid nobleman owns this whole island. He obviously has more money than he needs. I have often glimpsed the house through the trees. The door is held shut with heavy chains. There is treasure inside, I'm telling you. Now stop playing and concentrate. There may be a watchman or two, and there might even be dogs. Be silent and careful."

The man set off again, with the others following. Violetta this time chose the man bringing up the rear to tap on the shoulder. The man instantly spun, but there was nobody to his side.

The man realized that whoever tapped his shoulder must be on his other side, must have reached across, a stupid childish trick. The man spun to his other side to confront his tormentor, his face a mask of rage. But there was nobody there either. Sebastian had seen Violetta withdraw her long spindly arm just in time, but to the man there seemed to be no hiding place near him, and no sign of anyone nearby to tap his shoulder. He had stopped to puzzle out his situation and, because his friends had kept moving forward, he was now completely alone.

"Guys!" he hissed, but his friends were too far away to hear. Violetta dropped her hand to the ground, snaking it towards the man through the underbrush, the dead leaves and detritus. The man couldn't see what was approaching him in the dark but he could hear it. He took a step back, scanning the ground in front of him for the source of the rustling. Even to Sebastian, a little distance away, it could be heard distinctly, like a snake slithering forward. The man's head twitched, had he seen something, something pale. He stepped forward for a better look, and a skeletal hand flew in his face, grabbing at his eyes, scratching his cheeks. The man stumbled backwards, screaming, he turned and ran, presumably back in the direction of whatever boat he had arrived on.

Violetta's arm shrank back towards her, regaining its normal dimensions, her hand returning to her through the undergrowth. The other men soon came running too, attracted by the terrified yells, shouting for their friend, the one who was already heading back to the boat. First came the man with the hat, then another man, then another man. Then finally, reluctantly, a little way behind, came the leader. Violetta stepped boldly out in front of him and said one simple word.

"Stop." The man came stumbling to a standstill, his eyes trying to make her out in the dark.

She caught his darting eyes with her own. He opened his mouth, took a deep breath, about to yell something. "Don't call out," she interrupted him. "You are the one who came here to my island, among my woods, where I keep my little house. You don't speak, I don't allow it and I am the mistress here, on my land." Her words were unbroken like a stream, her eyes intense. She was beguiling him, Sebastian realized. "It is my orders that must be followed and not yours, or those of any other ruffian who might think to invade my domain." On and on her words went, and Sebastian saw that the man was being completely bent to her will. "And for such a trespass," she said, "one of you ruffians must die. It is the old law."

Sebastian resisted for a while, but he was so hungry. Eventually he went over dropped to his knees beside her and watched her feed at her kill. He was so tempted to join her. He could feel the hunger tugging at him, but he didn't drink. The thief's friends didn't come back to see what had happened to him.

CHAPTER 22

When they got back to Venice from the hunting lodge on the island, the first thing Sebastian noticed was the book, still lying where he had discarded it on the desk. "This book seems to be about vampires," he said.

"That's right," Violetta answered. She was lounging on a sofa, admiring a scrimshaw he had whittled for her on the island. It was the least valuable item in the room, just a small stick with some designs he had carved, an owl and some trees, but it fascinated her above all else.

"What language is it written in?" he asked her.

"A long dead one," she said. "Precious few people spoke it, even before it died out." She put down her trophy and stood up. She crossed to the desk and picked up the book. "Go to your bedchamber," she said. "Get into bed and I will follow you in five minutes." Sebastian did as he was told and Violetta came in soon after, to find him comfortable in his bedclothes, tucked in beneath the covers. "You look so darling," she said. "I've come to read to you. Consider it a bedtime story."

"All right," Sebastian said, as Violetta perched on the end of the bed and started to read. "Wait," Sebastian interrupted. "I don't understand a word. Why aren't you translating."

"You must learn this language," she said, "and if I translated, you wouldn't learn."

"That's crazy," Sebastian said. "How will I learn if I don't understand?"

"Listen to my voice," she said, "just listen." And she was right. He started to understand, just as he had with the Italian of the thieves on the island, quickly and completely. He started to see images in his mind, images summoned up by Violetta and her ancient book.

It was a very different time. A time before the appearance of huge sprawling cities like Venice, with its tens of thousands of inhabitants. It was a time when even the biggest settlements, where kings and queens built their castles, were little more than towns, and most villages had only a handful of houses. Famines and blights were common, bandits were everywhere and there were vampires, many, many vampires. Vampires were as common as apples on the trees, so the book said. The writer of the book was a self-proclaimed expert on the proper ways of trapping, subduing, and finally putting to rest vampires, and he had decided to write down his lore, so that the knowledge would never disappear from the world. Sebastian found it repellent, but fascinating. Violetta finished the first chapter and closed the heavy book with an emphatic thump. "That's the end of chapter one," she said. "If you are a good boy, I'll read chapter two for you tomorrow."

"How is it possible that I understand this strange old language?" Sebastian asked.

"You understand because I understand," she told him, "and you were listening to me."

"That's not really an explanation."

"No," Violetta agreed. "It isn't." She thought for a moment, then looked into his eyes. "Magic," she said. "Isn't that what we keep saying. It must be magic."

"Necromancy and evil spirits, to be precise," he countered.

"No. Just magic." She leaned over and kissed him on the forehead, then got up, placed the book on the bedside table and left. "Goodnight," she said over her shoulder as she went.

"Good, night," he replied. Though it is actually morning that approaches and I will be forced to sleep through the day, he thought. He drew the heavy curtains around his bed. Then opened them a crack and reached for the book.

He opened it to chapter one, the chapter that Violetta had just read to him, and tried to read the words. It was hopeless. The words were so crusted with umlauts and accents that he had no idea how they should be pronounced or what they meant. The word for vampire, oft repeated throughout the text, he could recognize, but it was otherwise meaningless. But when she read it, he thought, I understood.

Outside, dawn was breaking. It illuminated the edges of the heavy shades at the bedroom windows. The tiny sliver of dim light was painful, burning into his mind, making him dizzy. He pushed the book over the side of the bed, hearing it thump on the boards of the wooden floor. Then he snatched the drapes closed and fell into a deep, deep sleep.

***

"Where does the blood come from?" Sebastian asked. They were in the main banqueting hall of the palace, but they weren't sitting at table. They were lounging on a divan at the edge of the room. The huge table was bare and the few things they had to eat were spread on the floor on small tin dishes. There were dates and nuts and oranges, fancy things, with sweet tastes. No honest food, as the peasants called it. At Violetta's side, nestled between her skirts and the arm of the sofa, was the decanter.

"I can show you, if you like," she said. She spoke absently, seemingly more interested in the expensive snacks. She reached down and grabbed a handful of nuts and popped one into her mouth, keeping the rest in the palm of her hand.

"I assume you have some poor wretch imprisoned in a dungeon," Sebastian said, "and, when they are bled dry, I assume you go hunting for fresh victims."

"Nothing of the sort," she said, popping another nut into her mouth. "It's all very enlightened. I've arranged quite an elegant little solution."

"All right, then show me," he said. "I will fill the decanter myself, and then I'll drink."

"That's marvelous news," Violetta said. "It has been interesting watching you waste away, but you're getting unattractively thin. This is exactly the pick-me-up you need. Let's go at once. We'll need an empty decanter, of course." She dropped the nuts in her hand back into the dish and stood up. Then she pulled out the stopper of the decanter and drank the contents in a series of huge gulps. Sebastian watched greedily, but didn't lift a hand to claim a share.

"Let's go," he said, "before I change my mind." Violetta led the way to the kitchen, where she rinsed out the decanter. Then she put on a coat, motioning Sebastian to do the same. "I no longer feel the cold," he said. "Or, rather, I'm cold all the time."

"I know," she nodded, "but one must still observe the social niceties. If we don't hold to the conventions of society then what's left. Why, we'd be no better than the wild people of the woods, running naked and barking at the moon."

"There are no wild people in the woods," Sebastian snorted.

"Not any more," she said, "at least not as many, but there were, and they were terrible. Be a good boy and put on your coat." Violetta put the decanter into her physician's bag and Sebastian heard it clink against some other implements inside. He decided not to think about that just yet. "Here," Violetta said, and handed the bag to him, "carry this for me would you." He made her wait while he shrugged on a heavy coat, then he took the bag, following only half a step behind as she left through the front door. It was late, but the streets were far from deserted. "Don't worry," she said. "It's not far."

She took him right to the center of town, to the Doge's Palace itself. "In there," she told him, "there is a prison. Criminals in the same building as the ruler of the city. The prison is in the roof. The metal roofs make them hot in summer and ice-cold in winter. It's barbaric, really."

"They're criminals," Sebastian said, as he stared up at the elegant building, "they deserve no better." He could hardly believe there were murders, arsonists and all manner of other scum on the top floor of this beautiful palace.

"Behind the palace," Violetta told him, "there is a small courtyard, accessible from the street." Sebastian followed her to it, and found himself in a tiny space, at the bottom of a shaft created by the palace walls. The dim moonlight, entering from above, descended four stories before it could reach them. "We have to climb now," she said. "Remember how I taught you? On the island?"

Sebastian nodded grimly. He concentrated and his hands became the talons of an eagle, leathery and scaly with wicked claws. Violetta started climbing, and Sebastian only paused to thread his arm through the handles of the bag, so he could carry it on his back, before he joined her in the climb. They reached a balcony on an upper story that hadn't been obvious when they had been looking up from below. There was a door leading from the balcony into the building and Violetta reached for it. It opened with the sound of a lock turning, though her back was to him, blocking his view of exactly what she was doing, but it sounded like she was using a key.

She went into the darkness of the unlit building but, when he tried to follow, Sebastian found that he couldn't cross the threshold. It wasn't fear. He was nervous but his blood was strangely calm. It was more like a hand physically blocking his path, a presence. It disturbed Sebastian, as though he could feel the force slowly seeping into him. He took a step back and the feeling was gone. Violetta's head appeared in the doorway, her expression slightly confused, then she seemed to realize what was going on. "This again," she said. "You're new in town, aren't you?"

"I don't know how long I have been here since you turned me into a creature of the night. I'm beginning to suspect a lot more time has passed than I realize.

You are now like somebody else entirely, no longer the same, no longer with the same fine feelings, the same goodness."

"Yes, yes," she nodded. "We know all this, don't we, but you have never been within the walls of this building before?"

"No."

"Most locals have," she explained, "on some official business or other. Oh well." She emerged from the door, her whole form now illuminated by the moonlight and stood aside. She then motioned to the door and curtsied slightly. "Enter of your own free will," she said, with a smile.

"But I felt a presence," Sebastian said.

"You'll be fine now," she said. She came round behind him and kicked him unceremoniously in the rear. "Go on in." Sebastian was glad of the dark because it meant she couldn't see his cheeks redden. Ladies didn't usually go kicking people in the posterior, at least not in his limited experience. He was so nonplussed that he didn't think about the presence and just stepped through the door. This time he was not held back. He entered the room and was surrounded by darkness. He patted his chest, where he had felt the force holding him back before. His new life was so confusing.

It was very dark inside the palace but he could see some feint glimmerings, moonlight on metal bars perhaps, but apart from that he couldn't make out any detail of the interior of the room. Violetta breezed past him surefooted, he could feel the air displaced by her skirts and coat. It was quite an impractical outfit for burgling that she was wearing, he thought. Even so, he had to follow her closely or lose her in the dark, and it wasn't easy because she was moving as fast as if the rooms were bathed in light. He didn't hear any keys jangling but she didn't have any trouble getting through the various doors that barred the way. She seemed to notice the trouble he was having seeing in the pitch darkness, the way he bashed into things as he tried to keep up. "You have talons for climbing," she said, over her shoulder, "but your peepers are no good for seeing."

"I'm sorry?" Sebastian said. "What was that?" He had no idea what she was talking about, and was annoyed that she had taken him off on this adventure without explaining things a little better. They could have at least changed out of their fine clothes and put on something a little more practical.

"Your eyes," she said. "Oh for pity's sake, do I have to explain everything. Look at mine, and copy them."

"But I can't see anything. How am I supposed to see your..." His words trailed off, because at that moment he did see her eyes. They caught the moonlight from a window and reflected it back at him, making two horrible little luminous mirrors. "Like a wolf," he said, "or a cat."

"Now you're starting to get it," Violetta said, encouragingly, as Sebastian's vision started to clear. He couldn't see as well as if it was daylight, but he could see a wide corridor with a marble floor and one or two plinths with small busts. Now that his eyes had adjusted or, more accurately, completely transformed, he could see Violetta. She was smiling, he saw. She motioned over her shoulder with a thumb. "This is the one we want."

She turned to a nearby door and Sebastian saw something strange. He wasn't sure if it was some trick of the dim light, but he saw the darkness start to gather around her, like a haze. She reached for the door handle and the darkness went with her, but a finger of it separated from the mass, like a tiny, misty dust devil and entered the lock. The door opened with the sound of a key turning and the darkness dissipated. "In we go," said Violetta brightly, then noticed Sebastian's inquisitive stare. "Oh, that thing with the lock? That's an advanced trick. I'll show you another time."

"More cursed, evil magic," Sebastian said. "I will not learn it." The room Violetta had entered was some kind of office or study. There were cupboards full of documents, writing equipment and supplies of materials to make ink.

It was quite spartan in comparison to the richly decorated corridor. Violetta went over to one of the cupboards and pulled out a ledger. She took it to the desk, struggling a little under the weight of the massive book, and let it drop to the desk with a thump. She opened the cover and started leafing through the pages. "Here we are," she said. "Today's lucky customers."

"What is this book?" Sebastian asked.

"Nothing interesting," she said as she ran her finger down handwritten columns of text, "just a list of prisoners currently in detention here."

"Prisoners?"

"Hm," she looked up, caught his eye. "Prisoners. Yes. That's right. I may have been transformed into a creature of nightmare but I do try to keep some scruples about who I bleed."

"Bleed?"

"Yes," she said, "a perfectly harmless operation where I take a pint or two of blood. I imagine it even does them some good, balances the humors, and all that. A pint or two is more than sufficient for my needs, and I restrict my activities to condemned criminals and other scum. It seems a very sensible arrangement to me. Under the circumstances."

Sebastian opened the physician's bag and looked inside. He saw the decanter, with which he was very familiar, and he also saw a metal bowl, a sharp knife with the blade bound in cloth, a few lengths of cord, and some gauze. "I see," he said.

"Now," she said, "all that remains is to find a likely subject to persuade to donate some blood."

"One of the criminals?" Sebastian said. "What particular kind of scum are we looking for exactly?"

"Well it's difficult to tell from these lists, but I'm looking for a robust subject, a man or woman in their teens or twenties, and a docile nature," Violetta explained. "The process takes some time and the easier the subject is to control, the better."

"How very practical," Sebastian said.

"And tonight it seems that we are spoiled for choice," Violetta carried on, ignoring his comment. "I particularly like the sound of this young gondolier who has been imprisoned for killing a rival in a bar brawl."

"I thought you said you wanted a docile nature," Sebastian said.

"This man should he quite docile," she said. "I think I know the type. He is driven by his passions, not given to too much thinking or questioning. I think you'll find that he'll do nicely." She closed the book and replaced it, then led Sebastian out of the room. She locked it behind her, using the same trick or force that he had observed before. They traveled through the building and went up a floor to a more secure area. The area was lit and there was a guard posted half way along one of the corridors. A corridor wide enough to swing a sword comfortably, Sebastian noted. Violetta walked confidently up to the guard. "Aldo, old man," she said with a smile. "How are my patients today."

"All sleeping soundly," he replied.

"This is my assistant," she said and nodded in Sebastian's direction.

Aldo didn't seem much interested. He just freed a big bunch of keys from his leather belt and used them to unlock the door. He led the way inside, lighting candles as he went, and then opened another door onto a more open area. The area had five very sound doors with small barred windows. "You take a look," Aldo said, "and I'll go get the lads." Aldo went unhurriedly from the room, leaving the doors open behind him.

While he was gone, Violetta went up to each cell window and peeped in at each prisoner. She motioned Sebastian to do the same. "You never know, there might be a good candidate hiding undocumented in one of these cells," she explained. Aldo returned about fifteen minutes later with two large brutes wearing the same simple uniform as himself.

"I've inspected the prisoners," she told Aldo, "and they all seem in fine health, as usual. All but one. I would like to take a closer look at the gondolier. I'm afraid he may need some treatment."

Aldo nodded. "This the guy you mean?" he asked. He unlocked the door as soon as Violetta nodded. His two goons immediately went into the cell. There were sounds of a scuffle and the landing of heavy blows. Aldo watched what was happening inside from the doorway. When things had quietened down, he stood aside and nodded. Violetta and Sebastian went into the cell while Aldo waited outside. The cell was a very bare room with unfinished stone walls, and the young occupant was immobilized in the center, restrained by the two goons.

"I'm afraid you're not well young man," Violetta said. "Sebastian, position the bowl below his wrist and pass me the knife, would you?" The prisoner started to scream, but his voice was cut off when one of the guards clamped a meaty hand over his mouth. Violetta caught his eye and started to speak to him. "Relax," she said, "I'm one of the most skilled doctors in Venice, a lady and a scholar. You are lucky that I am doing my rounds tonight, because I can help you with a little health problem that you have been having..."

Her words went on and on, relaxing the man, beguiling him, allowing her to bleed him efficiently, with the practiced hand on an amateur surgeon.

***

"I think you'll find the gondolier's blood to be quite interesting," Violetta said, later.

"Oh?" Sebastian said, the word muffled as he wiped a drop of blood from the edge of his mouth. They were in the grand dining room of her palace, back on their sofa, the snacks still spread on the floor where they had left them, and Sebastian had, at last, gotten over his squeamishness.

"What could be interesting about the blood of that oaf. It is mere sustenance to me now... now that I am a demon from hell."

"The reason his blood is interesting," Violetta said, "is because he is in love."

"Love?" Sebastian snorted derisively.

"Yes," Violetta said. "He is passionately in love, at least according to the court documents. So besotted that he killed a rival in a knife fight, gutted him like a fish."

"A violent and passionate brute," Sebastian nodded, and took another sip. "I hope he rots in that dungeon."

"That passion," Violetta said, "is in the blood."

Sebastian pulled the decanter away from his lips, the blood that was in his mouth dribbling down his chin. "The very thought of that is abominable," he said, spraying blood with his words.

"Don't waste it," Violetta shouted. She snatched the bottle away from him, her expression stern, then she softened and burst into giggles at the sight of his disgusted face. "You have no idea how many bottles of despair and desperation I have drunk. A bottle of passion makes a nice change."

"Appalling," Sebastian said.

Violetta took a sip at the neck of the bottle, wiped her mouth with the back of her hand and smiled. "I can feel it working," she said. She smiled at him in a way she hadn't smiled in quite some time, and he backed away from her, pressing himself into the corner of the divan the furthest point away from her he could manage without actually running away.

"I think I'm going to go to my rooms," he said. He got up and walked the length of the banqueting hall to reach the door that would take him to his apartment. Violetta's eyes followed him the entire way, a hungry fire burning within them. She took another sip.

"I'll be along in a moment sweetheart," she whispered quietly, so quietly that he wouldn't hear her. She waited until the decanter was empty before following him.

She noticed that he had locked his door. How sweet, she thought, and she smiled. Sebastian was waiting for her when she came through his door. He was standing in the middle of the room, his demeanor so stern it stopped her in her tracks.

"What do you think you are doing?" he snarled.

"I think you know," she said, her confidence returning as quickly as it had gone. "Don't you feel it. The fresh blood coursing through your veins, full of... potential."

"That is disgusting," Sebastian said. "I think any feeling I may have still had for you has finally died. You have blood dribbling down your chin-"

"I know," she said, "Isn't it glorious? I can almost feel my heart beating. I know it isn't real, but... I feel alive."

"Get out," Sebastian said. "If you still feel anything for me at all, get out, and don't come back till you have some sort of control over this creature you have become. I don't recognize this Violetta. Go away and don't come back until you have returned to yourself."

CHAPTER 23

"Well, look what we have here," Sebastian said. "Two waifs. I suppose I should send them away."

"We're in trouble Sebastian," Violetta said. "You have to let us stay with you."

"So you have decided to defy father... again," he said, "and you want my help."

"He isn't my father, and he isn't yours," Violetta said. "He is simply the source of this evil."

"You are welcome to use the place as if it was your own home, and I will help you in any way I can," he said, "but there is a price."

"Name it," Violetta said.

"If it's not too much trouble," he said, "I would like you to read me a bedtime story, just like in the old days."

"I don't understand," Violetta said.

"The book I want you to read is written in that dead language that only you can understand," Sebastian said. "I need your help. So, you scratch my back, and I'll scratch yours, as the saying goes."

"This is about the ring, isn't it?" Violetta said.

"Do we have a deal or not?" Sebastian asked.

"Yes, yes, we have a deal, you monster," Violetta said.

"Then come on in," he said. "Come in. Make yourselves at home."

"There's something I need to know first. Have you ever allowed my father to enter this place?" Violetta asked.

"No, never," Sebastian said. "Thankfully, that old horror is much more interested in you than in me."

"Good," Violetta said, "then we can stay here. At least for a short time."

"Hello Sebastian," Jasmine said, interrupting for the first time, after waiting for them to conclude their negotiations.

"Hello Jasmine," Sebastian said, with a relaxed and charming smile. "Come in."

He went ahead of them. He took them to the living room, to the conversation pit, and took a seat. The two girls joined him.

"Sebastian," Violetta said, "I have decided to take a very important step. I have decided to cut off all contact with my father. I have decided that he will never have any say in my life ever again."

Jasmine looked from Sebastian to Violetta. "He was on my terrace," she said.

"Yes, of course," Sebastian said. "It was only to be expected. But, like I said, if there is anything I can do, just let me know. A deal is a deal. So what is your plan?"

"We don't actually have a plan," Violetta said. "Yet."

"Violetta is going to talk to him," Jasmine said.

"Talk to him?" Sebastian said. "I'm not sure that's a good idea. He is a very jealous man, with a very short temper. And his attitude to family is positively medieval. If you go to talk to him, he'll lock you up in a tower for a hundred years."

"That isn't helpful, Sebastian," Jasmine said, "besides. How else is Violetta to deal with an abusive father? If she doesn't confront him, he'll just keep terrorizing her. And I'll be there with her."

"No," Sebastian said, suddenly less amused by the whole situation. "I would advise you, Jasmine, to stay away from Violetta's father. Whatever the solution is, your meeting him is probably not part of it."

"We haven't decided anything," Violetta said to Sebastian. "We're just talking. And thank you for taking us in. I know that father will not be able to bother us here. You've bought us some breathing space, Sebastian, and father will be angry with you when he finds out. You have gone out of your way to help us, and I am grateful to you."

"Yes, Sebastian," Jasmine said. "Thank you."

Sebastian hesitated for a moment. He looked from Violetta to Jasmine. "Damsels in distress," he said.

"Hey," Jasmine said. "We can handle ourselves. We're not damsels." They talked for hours, while Jasmine looked up information on abusive fathers on the Internet with her phone. She read that children with abusive fathers had often learned to believe that they deserved to be punished and that they didn't deserve to be treated with respect. They had become used to being treated badly and they didn't know what it was like to be treated well. Abusive fathers made their victims dependent by having to know where they were and who they were with all the time, controlling contact with friends, and controlling what their children wore, did and said, giving orders, making all the decisions, refusing to take opinions and feelings seriously, being

225

unpredictable and violent, making their children worry about how they will react to things, and hurting their friends, or family to get their way.

She also read about the cycle of abuse, that it had three phases: the tension-building phase; the explosion or acute battering incident; and the calm, loving respite. During the tension-building phase, the abused person tries to calm down the abuser in order to prevent his anger from escalating, and often feels guilty when she doesn't succeed. Her heart went out to Violetta. Had she been going through this? Had their meeting given her the strength she needed to take a stand?

She also learned that drugs or alcohol were involved in a lot of abusive behavior by a lot of abusive fathers. "Does your father drink or take drugs?" Jasmine asked Violetta.

"He is an addict," Violetta said. "He has always indulged his urges and desires, and they have mastered him." Jasmine nodded. It seemed a classic case, and Violetta's father's threats to hurt her friend, to hurt Jasmine, fit the pattern perfectly. It might also be an explanation for how skinny Violetta was, but Jasmine didn't want to jump to conclusions, she just wanted to help her friend to make a break from this man.

He was a man Jasmine had never met, but who she felt she was beginning to get to know. Jasmine was so engrossed in her research that she wasn't paying much attention to what Violetta and Sebastian were saying to each other. Her phone finally died after numerous warnings about a low battery, but Jasmine had her charger in her bag.

"Is there somewhere I can plug this in?" Jasmine asked Sebastian.

"Sure," he said, waving at a nearby socket. "Wherever you like."

"Day comes," Violetta said. "I must sleep."

"I'm knackered as well," Jasmine said, "but I'm more and more convinced that we are doing the right thing. We have to get you away from him. If you stay in that house with him, you'll never be free of his interference."

"How right you are," Violetta said, face set in a grim expression of determination.

"Let me show you two where I'm going to put you," Sebastian said. He showed Violetta to a spare bedroom, and made up a sofa in the main area for Jasmine. He showed her where the bathroom was, and showed her his well-stocked kitchen. "If you get peckish, please help yourself to anything," he said. Jasmine fell asleep instantly on the sofa.

***

She didn't wake up till three in the afternoon. Violetta was still in bed, and she couldn't find Sebastian anywhere. She knocked on his bedroom door, and opened it up, but the bed didn't look slept in. She made herself some breakfast, and tried to work out what to do about university. She rang the college and asked to talk to her tutor.

"I can't come in today, Professor Gabizon," she said.

"This is starting to become a problem Violetta," the woman muttered.

"I'm really sorry," Jasmine said, "and I know this is a big disruption, but I won't be able to come in for at least a week."

"What?" Gabizon said, she sounded aghast.

"I said I'm sorry, but something really important has come up," Jasmine said. "A friend of mine really needs me."

"Look, I'm really busy right now Jasmine," Professor Gabizon said, obviously angry with her. "Take the rest of the day, and ring me again tomorrow, around noon. We'll talk about this then, but you better be very sure your friend really needs you, and that he is worth jeopardizing your education over."

"It's not a he," Jasmine said, "It's a she."

"Just call me tomorrow," Gabizon said. "We have been making very good progress. Very good progress. I don't know where you found the stories from your last report but they are sensational. The problem is, you don't site any sources. Are you sure you can't come in today. I would love to talk about some of this."

"Okay, okay," Jasmine said, "but only for an hour or two. My friends seem to have wandered off for the moment anyway."

"That's great, Jasmine," Gabizon said. "Come in now."

Jasmine wrote a note telling Violetta and Sebastian where she was going and stuck it to a small table near the door. Then she left, closing the door to the apartment silently behind her.

"Shit, I don't have a key," she muttered, as the door clicked emphatically closed.

***

Jasmine had to ring the doorbell three times before Sebastian came down to answer it. "You are not seriously telling me you were still in bed," Jasmine said to him.

"Why not?" Sebastian said, and glanced at the sky, which was still bright from the sun, only just below the horizon. "Who's this?"

"I, young man, am Professor Gabizon. You must be Sebastian, the source of all the stories Jasmine has been discovering."

"Yes, that's right," Sebastian said, then turned to Jasmine. "Did you have to bring this woman round today?"

"The professor can be quite insistent," Jasmine said.

"Well, invite me in," Gabizon said, "or are you going to leave me waiting out here all night?"

"Come on up," Sebastian said, with ill grace, and led them upstairs. "Would you like something to drink?" he asked, as soon as he had ushered Jasmine and Gabizon to his conversation pit.

"My God," Gabizon said, "I haven't seen an interior like this since my younger, wilder days. I'll take a vodka and tonic, if you have one."

"I've got everything," Sebastian said simply. "Jasmine?"

"Oh, good grief, do we have to?" Jasmine said. "Shit, go on then, I'll have the same." Sebastian went over to the small bar in the corner of the room, leaving Jasmine and Gabizon alone. It was the first time she had been in anything like a social situation with the fearsome Gabizon, and she felt extremely uncomfortable. "There should be another friend hiding around here some place," she said. "I'll go and get her. She'll want to say hello at the very least, I'm sure."

She left Gabizon and went to Violetta's room. The curtains were still drawn, but there was nobody in the bed. That's strange, she thought. She took a step into the room, to get a better look at the bed, and her attention was caught by something. A shape, down on the floor, something sticking out from under the bed, a shoe?

A wave of fear washed over Jasmine, worried that something might be wrong with her friend. She dropped to the floor, looked under he bed, and saw Violetta. There was something strange about her, and Jasmine couldn't work out what it was at first.

Then she saw it, her friend was lying among piles of earth. Jasmine immediately reached out, grabbed her shoulder, tried to wake her. She wanted to tell her to get off the cold floor and get into the bed but she recoiled. Violetta was cold to the touch and she didn't seem to be breathing. Jasmine screamed, terrified for her friend, wondering what could possibly have happened.

***

Sebastian returned to the conversation pit with the drinks, only to see that Jasmine was missing. "She went to get somebody called Violetta," Gabizon explained.

"Ah," Sebastian said, with a nod of the head, though he seemed disinterested in the information. "So, Jasmine was collecting the ghost stories I told her for you?"

"That's right," Gabizon said, accepting the proffered drink and taking a sip. A little tension immediately left her face.

"Good," Sebastian said, leaning forward to put Jasmine's drink on the low table in the conversation pit. "Has Jasmine told you yet about the story with the ring?"

"That was in her latest report," Gabizon said. "That was what particularly piqued my interest. In fact, that's why I'm here, to find out more."

"Wouldn't it be wonderful if that ring could be found?" Sebastian said.

"Wonderful?" Gabizon snorted, "that's a strange word. Wait. Do you think the ring is real?"

"I do," Sebastian said. "I'm convinced of it."

"But you can't think it has magical powers," Gabizon said, "magic powers that are only of any use to immortal creatures of the night?"

"I think there is a ring," Sebastian said. "As to powers... well..."

He was interrupted by a scream, a scream that came echoing from Violetta's room. Gabizon immediately jumped up and ran to help. Sebastian waited a moment, rolled his eyes, took a sip of vodka, then followed at a more relaxed pace.

***

Jasmine heard the sound of feet on the stairs as Sebastian and Gabizon came running, but Jasmine didn't move, she just sat there, in shock. Gabizon was first into the room and came straight over to her.

"What's wrong?" she asked. "What's going on?"

"Violetta," Jasmine said, "She's under the bed."

Gabizon looked over at the bed, at the shoe sticking out. "Is she all right?"

"I don't think so," Jasmine said. "I think she's dead." Gabizon slowly went over to the bed, and Jasmine glanced away, down at the floor. She just couldn't look. But nothing happened. Nothing happened for quite a while. She heard Gabizon moving, doing things, but she wasn't sure what. Her brow wrinkled and she looked up. Gabizon seemed to sense Jasmine's eyes on her and looked away from Violetta, over her shoulder at Jasmine, and matter-of-factly told her.

"Your friend is a vampire."

Jasmine's eyes went wide. "What?" There was a silence. The air hanging in the room like lead.

"You have to have suspected," Gabizon said. "I know I did. I suspected the moment I stepped into this place."

"No," Jasmine said. "No. How could I suspect such a thing? This is all crazy. Her father got to her somehow. We have to call an ambulance and we have to call the police."

Gabizon just shook her head while Jasmine sat in the corner of the room, hugging her legs. Gabizon walked across the room, then wordlessly sat beside her.

It was then that Sebastian peeked into the room. He took one look at what was happening and retreated again. Gabizon stood up and left without a word, followed by loud noises from the kitchen. Then Gabizon came back with a table leg splintered into a point at one end, and, in her other hand, she held a meat tenderizing mallet. Jasmine looked up, her eyes puffy from tears. "What is going on?" she asked.

"There's no sign of Sebastian," Gabizon said, "but at least we can deal with this one. I had to improvise, and we'll have to be quick." But Gabizon had waited too long. Violetta emerged from beneath the bed, scattering soil across the floor as she appeared. She was still groggy and disorientated, her face confused, surprised that there was anyone else in her room, but she was definitely no longer inert. Then, still on all fours, she looked up and saw Jasmine. Then she glanced to the side, taking in the older woman standing in the doorway, and the weaponry she was holding. "I see you have discovered my little secret," she said, her voice tired. Then Violetta rolled onto her back and ripped at her cardigan and blouse, exposing a small patch of deathly pale skin, just above her heart. A couple of buttons came away, skittering noisily across the floor in the silent and dark room. "I won't resist," Violetta said. "By the way, you will need more than a stake and a hammer. I'm told the head must be removed, to make sure of permanently laying to rest the..." she paused for a moment, searching for an appropriate phrase, "subject of the procedure." Gabizon took a firmer hold of her tools. They were sweaty in her hands. She took a step forward.

"Stop!" Jasmine screamed. Then again and again. "Stop! Stop! Stop! Are you crazy? Put that pointy stick down before you hurt somebody." Gabizon stared at her in confusion. Violetta levered herself up onto one elbow, into a position where she was still on her back with the small patch of skin exposed, but where she could see Jasmine. "Vi," Jasmine said, "you were dead. You weren't breathing. You were cold as ice. But now you're okay. What's going on?"

Violetta looked up at Gabizon, the tall, skinny, old lady knew. Then she looked back at Jasmine, who obviously didn't. "Isn't it obvious? I'm a vampire. A demon of the night. Undead. I have to be put to rest."

"That's crazy. This is nuts. There are no such things as..." Jasmine paused, almost unable to bring herself to say the word, Vampires. This is a bad dream, just a bad dream."

"A nightmare," Violetta nodded. "becoming a vampire is not something anyone would voluntarily choose. It's something that is done to you. It's quite likely the worst thing that one person can do to another." Her voice was quivering with emotion, but her eyes were dry of tears.

"I just don't understand," Jasmine said.

"What happens to me isn't important," Violetta said. "What is important is that if my father even suspects that you have discovered my secret, then you are in very grave danger."

"Your father is also a vampire?" Gabizon asked.

"I don't suppose there is any point denying it," Violetta said. "Who are you by the way?"

"Her name is Gabizon," Jasmine said, when she hesitated to answer.

"Don't tell her my name," Gabizon said.

"Too late," Jasmine said, "and anyway, why not?"

"They have magic powers," Gabizon said. "They can beguile the mind. It's easier for them to do that if they know your true name."

"She's right," Violetta said. She got up off the floor, prompting Gabizon to take a step back. Then she sat meekly on the edge of the bed.

"But there are ways to harden your mind against this interference," Gabizon hissed, hefting her tenderizing mallet. "If you try your tricks on me vampire, I will pierce your heart and chop off your head. There is even garlic for your mouth in the kitchen."

"Just out of curiosity," Violetta said. "Where did you find a vampire hunter on such short notice?"

"Stop it," Jasmine said.

"Stop what?" Violetta asked.

"Stop acting as if everything is normal," Jasmine growled. "Nothing is normal. This is some bad fever dream and I'm going to wake up. I'm going to wake up."

"Listen," Violetta said. "You really are in danger. Real danger. You have to start listening to me."

"Are you convinced now?" Gabizon asked Jasmine. "She is a vampire and she must be laid to rest. You should stop listening to her lies and leave the room. They are very old and dry so they don't bleed much, but the ceremony will still be very disturbing, if you have never seen it done before."

"What?" Jasmine cried. "Are you still talking about killing my friend?"

"She is not your friend," Gabizon took a step toward the small girl perched on the edge of the bed. "She is a monster."

Jasmine turned to look at Violetta. "Are you a monster?" she asked.

Violetta didn't answer.

"My best friend the vampire," Jasmine muttered.

"Friend?" Violetta said, confused, "You still consider me a friend?"

"You still consider her a friend?" Gabizon said, equally confused, almost exasperated.

Sebastian was standing at the back of the boat, rowing across the lagoon. He could see the new gas lamps of the main island of Venice, an impressive and modern sight, most of them in St. Mark's square, and he could also see the dark shapes of the islands in the lagoon. Violetta was sitting in the boat

"Venice has a long tradition of exiling her problems to preserve her serenity," Sebastian said to her, the first words he had said during the trip, making her jump, "Including lunatics, lepers and amputees."

"But this..." Violetta said, gesturing at the dark shape of the island. "This horrible building, on its scraggy island. What a windowless, deformed, and dreary pile."

"It was an old monastery," Sebastian explained. "It was hardly built for comfort, but now the monastic cells have been adapted for use by women. And these women need help. They are unfortunate creatures who have succumbed to madness. San

Clemente, it's called." Their boat edged gently up to the landing stage of the island.

"So instead of criminals, we are to nourish ourselves from Venice's lady lunatics," Violetta said, "I'm not sure that is an improvement." Sebastian got out of the boat, went up to a locked gate in the wall that encircled the island, lit a lantern, and waved it in the air above his head. It took quite some time, but eventually the main door of the dark building on the other side of the wall opened and a figure emerged. The figure was male, and he made his way across the gardens to the gate. Even in the dark, the gardens were obviously immaculate, the hedges all right angles, the pale gravel of the paths gleaming against the dark foliage.

"We're expected," Sebastian said. It was the doctor in charge of the asylum in person. They inclined their heads politely and introduced themselves as he opened the giant gate. Sebastian introduced himself, using his title of doctor. He once again explained that he was concerned for the welfare of the inmates and introduced Violetta as his assistant. "We will only have time for your patients at the end of the day, after dealing with our usual clients," he said to the doctor. "I can only apologize for the lateness of the hour."

"Of course," the doctor in charge of the asylum nodded. "We will see to them during the day, but it would be useful to get a second opinion from other learned men and women, even at such a late hour. Why don't we get on with this, and then we can all get off home. Let's start the tour." The doctor led the way into the building, and then onto the galleries of cells. "We have no men, only women here. We'll start with the girls, eh?" he leered. "Fallen women, the lot of them. Or stone crazy. Some of them are more dangerous than any man."

"I'm sure," Violetta said.

"We can certainly start with the younger ones," Sebastian said. "I see no problem with that." They looked at prisoner after prisoner, most sharing three or four to a cell. They were the most pitiable of creatures, dirty, dressed in rags, bruised and battered, too. "They are in bad shape," Sebastian said.

"Yes, poor creatures, but better here than at home with their families," the doctor explained. "I cannot dismiss any of them from the hospital because the poverty at home means they could not be fed. Even when they recover, they must stay. It is a sad commentary on how far Venice has fallen from our former imperial might."

"Indeed," Sebastian said, surprising Violetta with the vehemence of his words.

"The really crazy ones, a danger to themselves and others, we have to keep in isolation," the doctor said. "They're down here." If the patients in the cells of general population were in bad shape, the ones who had been put in isolation were even worse.

"Perhaps this was a mistake. The wretches in the Doge's dungeon are in a better state than this," Sebastian whispered to Violetta. Where the other patients were bruised and dirty, these women had open wounds. Their clothes were little more than rags and they smelled. They smelled really bad, but it was their eyes where the real difference lay. Their eyes were searching and knowing at the same time, both empty and profound.

"I don't want the blood of any of these foul spirits any where near me," Violetta whispered to Sebastian. "I will have to return to the Doge's cells."

Sebastian opened his mouth to reply, then he froze, he had made eye contact with one of the women. The tiny, filthy form in the cell stirred, she looked over at the group of strangers, gawking at her through the tiny window in the cell door. All she could see was their eyes.

"Let her out," Sebastian whispered.

"Do you know her?" the facility manager asked, fumbling with his keys.

"Good question," Violetta said. "Do you know her?"

"She should not be in this foul place," Sebastian hissed. "She is obviously a woman of quality, can you not see that?" The lock clicked and the cell door swung inwards.

"Who is this woman?" Violetta asked.

"I don't know," Sebastian said, "but she belongs with us, with me, that's obvious, right?"

Violetta didn't answer. All she managed to do was raise an eyebrow. Sebastian arranged to have the mad young woman transferred to his custody, and the bribes had been insultingly small, considering they were, in effect, buying a human being. She was installed in a comfortable suite of rooms. Her bedroom was large and there was room for a table and four chairs between the bed and the window. Soon, Sebastian was sitting at the table, watching her as she slept. Violetta, in turn, was watching him from the doorway to the suite.

"I have seen that look in your eye before," she said.

"What look?" Sebastian asked, reluctantly taking his eyes off the young woman and glancing at Violetta in the doorway.

"That look," Violetta repeated. "It is how the curse spreads. It's love, you idiot. I know the look from my father's eyes, and no doubt that look is in my own eyes when I gaze at you."

"You're being melodramatic," Sebastian said.

"I wouldn't listen, either," Violetta said. "My father tried to warn me, but I wouldn't listen."

***

Sebastian was leaning over the railings of the cruise liner, Violetta right beside him. She was wearing her latest acquisitions from her annual pilgrimage to Paris, a smart blouse and a flared skirt combination, worn with a jacket against the cold. The outfit was topped off with a big hat with feathers at the brim. Their voices were low. There were people everywhere, distracted by their own noisy and tearful goodbyes, giving Violetta and Sebastian a moment of privacy in the tumult.

"You have to disembark," Violetta said, "or you'll be going to the new world with me." Violetta's ship to the new world was leaving directly from Venice. That was one thing about Venice. You could board ship just a ten minute walk from your front door. The moorings were right in the heart of the city. It would be leaving on the evening tide, just after nightfall. Sebastian had gone aboard ship with her to see her off, but there wasn't much time and he was expecting at any moment for the crew to call for everyone who wasn't traveling to leave.

"I still have a few moments," he replied, his voice soft and friendly, "and don't think I haven't thought about it. It's amazing what you're doing. Leaving Europe and going to the Americas. I have thought long and hard about whether I shouldn't be doing the same thing."

"Not just me," she said. "Look around. Half the city must be leaving on this boat."

"Good," Sebastian laughed. "You know how I hate crowds." Things had never been the same between them, not since that visit to the lunatic asylum, but Sebastian had to give Violetta credit for trying. She was almost her old self, the gentle creature that he had fallen in love with centuries before, but not quite. Their relationship had endured a long time, but it had never returned to the place it had been at the very start, before she had bitten him.

They were standing side-by-side, gazing at a view of Giudecca, the smaller of Venice's two main islands. It had once been a beautiful garden island, when they had first come to Venice, all those years ago, carried into town on the Dark Bora, but now it had been almost entirely claimed by residential buildings and industry. It was just after dusk, and the Giudecca skyline was a dark wall of buildings joined to each other at the shoulders and sprinkled with lit windows. "Well," Violetta said. "All the legal niceties have been taken care of. I'm sorry I had to sell the old place, throwing you out in the street like a dog."

"I've landed on my feet," he said. "That's the thing with our elongated existences. You can hardly fail to become rich. You should have come round to see the new place before going, it's quite cozy."

"I'm sure," Violetta said. "But I didn't want to have to say goodbye to her."

"Don't be that way," Sebastian said.

"The same will happen to you," Violetta continued, unable to help herself. "You will bite her, and she'll hate you. That's how it spreads."

"Whose to say I haven't bitten her already," Sebastian said. "Whose to say she doesn't already hate me."

Violetta stared at him. "This is not a subject for levity," she said. She suddenly lunged at him and embraced him, taking him by surprise. He hesitated, then returned the embrace. It was so close to the way it had been, centuries before, but it wasn't the same. Something had changed.

"It's time for me to get going," he said. "I'm rather afraid you'll have to release me, old girl."

"Shan't," she said, and he smiled at the petulant tone in her voice. There was time for a few more seconds of embrace before the ship left, he supposed.

"I'm never coming back to Venice," she whispered into the lapel of his jacket. "I have broken with this place, and with him, forever."

***

Violetta had left him the book by Doctor Nicolescu, and he opened it at random and started reading the words that, once strange, were understandable to him now, with a little effort. The chapter was called conversations with vampires. Doctor Nicolescu had been practicing his trade of ridding families of vampire relatives, and had already put dozens to rest in his career, when he was called on by a very poor family.

My visitors that day, Sebastian read, were of the very meanest type of peasant stock. They were suntanned and strapping from their work in the fields and dressed in simple clothes of drab colors. They looked hardly civilized at all, little better than the wild people of the woods, but they were fellow subjects of the queen, so I bade them enter.

They gave me many gushing compliments on my work and said that they had heard much of my vampire slaying. I explained that it is not possible to slay that which is already dead, and that the best that was to be hoped for was that the spirit could be made quiet. The unfortunate vampire had to be confined to their grave and prevented from bothering the living.

They nodded their heads respectfully, though I'm not sure they really understood, being very simple folk. They told me that they had recently lost one of their daughters. I told them that this was a common enough occurrence and nothing to shed too many tears about, they had others after all. But they informed me that the daughter had come back from beyond the grave. They said they had been warned that this was unnatural, and something should be done.

I, of course, could only agree. I emphasized to them most strongly that their daughter returning from her grave could have no possible, natural explanation. My services could not be offered without payment, which they understood, and terms were agreed between us. I then embarked upon a journey to their province at the earliest opportunity.

I have explained in great depth the proper procedures for hunting and capturing vampires in previous chapters and I will not reiterate those details here. The usual procedures, in the end, were sufficient to guarantee capture of the creature. But, I have to say that there was something different about this encounter.

The vampire was very cunning, but eventually the usual methods used by the wretch to evade capture were sidestepped and I had it in my power. The vampire was pinned by both wrists and ankles, in the manner I strongly recommend, and was at my mercy. I positioned the final of the five stakes mid sternum and to the left side, where the mass of the heart is greatest, and was about to drive it home. Then the creature caught my eye. Knowing this to be dangerous I looked away and my assistant slapped my face to prevent possession by her spirit. But she had not attempted the usual hypnotism. She had simply said four words. I will record these words here. She said: "I can help you."

I admit, I was quite confused. Previous to this encounter, no vampire had ever done more than try their tricks or, failing that, beg for their deliverance. She was the first to try to engage with me in a conversation. Despite myself, I was intrigued. My assistant was anxious to complete the procedure, but I insisted that we hear what she had to say. She was a very intelligent young lady, and quite articulate, considering where she came from.

When Sebastian read the conversations the doctor had had with this vampire, he thought he recognized something. A certain way of framing thoughts, a certain way of looking at the world. He suddenly thought he knew who this young vampire girl was. He did know that she was the only vampire in the book to survive an encounter with the terrible Doctor Nicolescu, and therefore it could have been her. It would certainly explain her affection for the book. It could have been Violetta.

CHAPTER 25

Ratchis walked slowly across town, just a twenty-minute journey, not in any hurry to see if his daughter had returned. He opened the gate and walked half way up the garden path. The house that he knew so well loomed above him. He reached out with his mind to the door, mentally grasping the handle. A tendril of darkness, only visible to somebody who was looking for it, emerged from his fingertips. It snaked ahead of him, seeming to be grounded like lightning, jumping from spot to spot. At last it touched on the handle of the door and the door sprung open.

"Are you at home child?" he whispered. He climbed the steps to the now gaping front door and went inside. He scanned the hallway then searched room to room. He saved the drawing room for last, somehow convinced that she would be within, working on a needlepoint sampler. He entered, the door swinging open ahead of him at his bidding. She wasn't inside. Ratchis felt rage flow through his body like rivulets of ice. "How dare you, you ungrateful and insubordinate whelp," he whispered. "I suppose you are with your new friend."

He turned on his heel and left the room, walked downstairs and left the house, the door slamming after him. He walked back through the narrow alleyways of Venice and up to the front door of Jasmine's building. The front door was locked and he had no key, but again the dark force emanated from his fingertips, slipped inside the lock and forced it to give way to him.

He entered and saw that the door to the ground floor flat was ajar. A tall woman in her early fifties appeared. She didn't bother to color her hair and she was dressed all in black. Her skin was prematurely wrinkled by the sun and had a ghastly tan color, like mahogany furniture. Ratchis had never understood the recent mania for tanned skin. It made everyone look like peasants. The woman opened her mouth to speak but Ratchis raised a finger, a small gesture but it cut the words dead in her throat.

"Mind your own business," he said, and carried on up the stairs. He had said it in that special way that everyone, eventually, obeyed. He had to catch her eye to do it, but she was far too weak willed to resist his suggestion for even a second. He didn't bother to look over his shoulder to ensure she obeyed, and he heard the woman go back into her apartment and close the door behind her. The door to Jasmine's apartment gave him a little more trouble. It's lock was a high-security model where three brass bars slid into holes in the door jam. The mechanism hadn't been oiled in a while and it was difficult to move, but it gave way in the end and he went into the apartment. He could feel from the silence that nobody was home.

He glanced into the bathroom to make sure it was empty then went into the only other room. He sat on the sofa and waited. He waited, inhumanly patient, staring ahead in the dark. He happened to be looking out of the patio window onto the terrace but he would have been just as happy to stare at a blank wall. He waited all night. He stirred slightly as the horizon began to brighten. The sun was the only force that held any fear for him. It forced him to rise from the sofa. "Where is your horrible little friend hiding you?" he mumbled to himself, the words icy and hard.

CHAPTER 26

At Sebastian's house. Jasmine, Gabizon, Violetta, and Sebastian were all sitting in the conversation pit.

"So everyone is a... Vampire?" Jasmine said.

"They are definitely vampires," Gabizon said.

"I'm afraid so," Violetta said.

"Both of us," Sebastian said.

"Welcome back, by the way," Violetta hissed at him, "after leaving me to the tender mercies of a vampire hunter."

"I ran, true," Sebastian said, "but I also returned."

"And they will kill to keep their secret," Gabizon warned, Jasmine, "Make no mistake."

"No!" Violetta barked, startling them all. "There will be no killing. Nobody is going to touch a hair on Jasmine's head."

Sebastian turned to look at her, scrutinizing her expression and body language. "I can see you have made up your mind sweet sister," Sebastian said. "You want to fight for this one, and it is a noble emotion, but our father is most insistent about such things. There is no saving Jasmine now, and he will also kill her champion here," he waved dismissively at Gabizon, "if he ever discovers her existence."

"Please stop with all the father and sister nonsense Sebastian," Violetta said. "It's abundantly clear to everyone now that we aren't actually related."

"So," Gabizon interjected, her voice hard, determined, commanding. "There is a head vampire. The father of the gang. The head of the nest. This is interesting information."

"Gang?" Violetta said. "I would hardly use the word gang."

"Then what?" Sebastian said, amused. "Coven, roost, gaggle? What is the collective noun for vampires?"

"Stop it!" Jasmine screamed. "This is no time for banter. My world is coming apart. I'm in one of my own damn ghost stories." There was a silence. Everyone was looking at everyone else, trying to see what was happening behind their eyes, trying to work out how they felt and what they were thinking.

"To answer your point, Gabizon," Violetta said, at last. "Neither I nor Sebastian will lay a finger on you or Jasmine. Our secret is yours to keep or betray, as you see fit. Speaking for myself, I would welcome a mob of pitchfork wielding villagers to come out from wherever they come from and put an end to my torment. For all I care, you can scream my true nature from the rooftops. I have only remained silent all these years out of embarrassment."

"Steady on," Sebastian said. "I, for one, would prefer things didn't get out."

"You will not lay a finger on them," Violetta said to Sebastian. "Do you hear me?"

"To be honest, I haven't decided," Sebastian said, "and what does the professor intend to do with her pointy stick?"

"I intend to kill you and your foul sister," Gabizon said, her voice a cold, hard threat.

"No," Jasmine said. "Is nobody listening? Nobody is killing anyone. I am going to get my normal life back and all this," she waved around her, indicating things in general, "shit, is just going to go away."

"Father is not just going to go away," Sebastian said. "He will hunt you till the ends of the Earth and to the end of time."

"Or," Violetta said, "we will hunt him."

"What?" Sebastian gasped in shock at her words.

"You heard me," Violetta said. "It is something I should have had the courage to do a long, long time ago. It would be relatively simple. We know where he sleeps. We tell our champion vampire killer here, and, when daylight comes, she goes in and ends the old monster, once and for all."

"I can't believe you're saying this," Sebastian said. "You're talking about our father."

"He is just an evil old man who infected me," Violetta spat. "He's no relative of either of us. He polluted me, and, through me, you too."

"Through you," Sebastian whispered. "That's one way to put it."

***

Gabizon started by carving symbols into the door jams and the window frames. "The carvings are best," she explained to Jasmine, "better than making symbols with piles of ash, or drawing them in charcoal. They're harder to wipe away."

Watching Gabizon at work, Violetta was taken back, back to the castle in the mountains, back to the peasant's revolt. She remembered the woman, the one who had crushed her father's throat with the edge of her hand. She had never seen a woman dish out such casual and practiced violence before. It had disturbed her to see it, a revolution in the natural order of things she had considered it at the time. Her father's cries for help came out as rasping whispers. There was a crowd of people, including the young woman, inside the castle. Violetta could not understand where they had all come from. Did so many people live out there in the sunshine beyond the castle walls?

Her father had been holding his hand out to protect himself, she remembered, just as the first rays of morning were flooding in the windows, making him slow, making him stupid, making him vulnerable. The woman and her friends had stormed the castle, aided by traitors from within. The woman's skirts were wide and voluminous, traditional for peasant women. Her skin was burnt a deep brown color by the sun, not like her own alabaster skin. She was vigorous, her arms strong. She was a terrible sight, truly frightening.

Her father reached forward, his sharp fingernails reaching for the woman's cheek, but she was young and full of life, much stronger than the desiccated and debauched remains of Violetta's father. She batted his hand away with an open palm, a sharp stake of wood was in the woman's other hand. Her father recoiled, showing real fear for the first time. How had all these peasants summoned the courage to storm the castle? Why was the world being turned upside down? Violetta had wondered.

Violetta was watching their confrontation through the columns of the balustrade that edged the landing, looking down into the hall below. She'd been watching her father close the shutters against the coming sun, preparing to go down to the basement, where she would follow him, and where they would both hide from the burning sun. She had no idea who, or what, this stranger was. She had heard rumors of an uprising, but she had assumed it would be put down, like all the others before it. She hadn't believed anything could ever intrude within the castle. If they weren't safe here, where were they safe? It was because of the traitors within the walls. The soldiers on the battlements, the servants in their quarters, who all had friends and family down in the village, and out in the countryside.

As the woman advanced on him, her father turned his head to call for help. He drew a deep, but rattling breath. But no sound came from his crushed windpipe. The woman punched father full in the face, sending a tooth flying, while her friends pulled him to the ground and held him still. His form contracted as though he was literally shrinking with fear, folding in on himself to avoid further punishment.

"You're just prolonging the inevitable old darling," the woman had said to him. Her words irreverent, even though he was her lord. "Stop struggling so we can get this done. Nobody's coming to save your miserable old skin." As she said that she drove her wooden stake through her father's left wrist.

A compatriot handed her a mallet and she hammered her weapon home, pinning Violetta's father's wrist to the floorboards of the hall. She pulled another stave from the folds of her big traditional skirt and drove it through his right wrist, hammering it down to secure him to the floor by both wrists.

He was now pinned to the floor by his arms and kicking feebly with his legs. His atrophied limbs, even kicking with both legs and all his might, were no match for the peasant strength of this woman, who obviously spent her days doing heavy work in the fields. Her colorful clothes were a complete contrast to the somber dress of the prone and writhing old man. She stood up and caught her breath, a little winded by the exertion of hammering in the wooden staves.

"Sarra," came a voice from her left, "are you all right to finish him off."

"Fine," the woman hissed. "Pass me another shaft of wood for the heart."

Violetta gasped in horror and, at the same time, breathed a sigh of relief as her father was staked. She couldn't stay to see what happened next, driven away by the rising sun. She crawled down to her tomb.

As Violetta watched the professor at work, Sebastian was staring at her. He remembered the day he had first realized he was no longer human, though he wouldn't admit it to himself at the time, preferring to think of himself as ill. The Bora winds had finally dropped and people could be heard outside the window putting their lives back to rights after having the winds almost blow all their worldly possessions away.

Sebastian remembered how he had put his hand to his neck. He remembered how it had come away bloody. He had a wound like a dog bite at the nape of his neck. He sat up on the sofa. It was shortly before dawn. He looked over at the bed to see if Violetta was up, but there was no sign of her. He quickly looked everywhere he could think of in the rooms, including under the bed, but his traveling companion had disappeared.

Sebastian stepped out into the dim morning light and knew immediately that something was wrong.

His eyes shut fast. The light was just too intense for him to overcome his automatic reaction to close his eyes. His legs suddenly went weak. They gave a little at the knees, and he straightened them with an effort of will but then his knees gave again, sending him stumbling sideways. He couldn't see where he was going and he held out his hand to fend off any obstacles. He fell to the pavement with a smack, slumped on his hands and knees. He could sense people forming a small ring around him, but he couldn't understand what they were saying and he was pretty sure they couldn't understand him either. He crawled back into the lodgings and felt a little better. He staggered up the steps to his room and blacked out.

He woke lying on his back with his arms crossed over his chest. There was a scattering of dirt around him and he felt hungry and stiff. He had slept through the whole day. It was already after dusk and there was still no sign of Violetta. He cleaned himself up, slewing off dried blood from his neck and the loose dirt that he guessed must have come from when he fell in the street. He went downstairs.

The landlady was waiting. She looked concerned. She made him some soup and cut off some bread. It was a generous helping of food, but it didn't still Sebastian's hunger.

"I'm not well," Sebastian told his host.

She didn't know what he was talking about. She stared at him concerned but uncomprehending while she fed him more soup. It took him only a few minutes to finish it, but even after his second large helping, he still had the same ravening hunger.

"My wife?" he asked. The lady nodded and said some words, too fast to understand, about money.

She seemed content, which meant Violetta had probably paid in advance.

CHAPTER 27

Accurso rang at the gate, but there was no answer. The house looked empty, no lights, no movement, everything locked. The shutters were even closed, though that wasn't unusual, even in occupied buildings. The house wasn't just empty looking though, it was deserted looking, with obvious signs of disrepair. The paint on the shutters was peeling, there were streaks of mold and water damage running down the face of the building. It had once been painted a warm terracotta color but the paint was now dull and faded. The garden was the worst though. It had been left to its own devices for a long time. It wasn't ugly exactly, with romantic trees and flowering creepers scratching at the walls, but it was wild.

After sunset, the colors of the garden were wintry and muted, bright green looked like yellowish gray and any darker color looked black. The bushes with their dark foliage and branches were mere silhouettes, the red brick walls were murky blood stains. The only touch of brightness was the overcast sky, where gray clouds were still edged by the setting sun. The garden had become an alien landscape where keen canine eyes were required for survival.

***

"It's like a last meal, don't you think?" Sebastian said. He and Violetta were sitting on one side of Sebastian's kitchen table, while Jasmine and Gabizon sat on the other. Gabizon nodded.

"Drink the cheapest wine you can stomach," Gabizon said, "and eat onions, as protection, it taints the blood."

"Actually," Jasmine said, "I could do with a glass of wine. So it has to be cheap plonk?"

"The worse the wine, the more it protects you," Gabizon confirmed.

"Fine by me," she said.

"I have to go," Gabizon said.

"Not before time," Sebastian snarled.

"Why?" Jasmine asked, ignoring him.

"I believe the alpha vampire of the coven should be our target," Gabizon said, "just as Violetta suggests. To do that, I need equipment, and my assistant."

"No," Violetta said. "You can collect your equipment, but you will not breathe a word about us, or my father, to another living soul."

"Living soul," Gabizon snorted, "interesting choice of words. So how do you plan to stop me?"

"I will go with you," Violetta said.

"I was planning to wait for daybreak," Gabizon pointed out, "which is problematic for you, for obvious reasons."

"We go now," Violetta said.

"If you go, I go," Jasmine said softly.

Both Violetta and Jasmine stared at Sebastian, while Gabizon took another swig of inexpensive wine.

"Well, I can hardly stay here on my own," Sebastian said.

"I'm not going to lose another friend," Violetta said, as they ate, "not again. Though I wouldn't blame you Jasmine, if you decided to run for the hills."

"No Violetta," she said. "I am not going anywhere. If you want to break your father's hold over you, I'm going to do everything in my power to help you." They finished their food and drinks and left the house. Jasmine was very aware of how dark it was. Darkness had become another world now, where the usual rules didn't apply. There really were monsters in the dark, and one of them was her best friend.

She looked to her left, at Violetta, as they walked. Her face had a determined look on it. She looked to her right, where Sebastian was walking at her other shoulder. His face was grim too. They walked side-by-side across the square and over the wide bridge at Accademia, before going to single file as they entered the smaller alleyways on the other side of the bridge. Violetta was leading the way, heading more or less directly toward Gabizon's office at the university, their goal. Nobody had said a word since leaving Sebastian's place.

"This doesn't seem the best way to travel," Gabizon said. "I mean, why don't you just turn into a couple of bats and flap your way home." It wasn't clear if she was speaking to Violetta, Sebastian, both, or neither. Nobody bothered answering her.

"This is all so nuts," Jasmine said, ducking her head slightly as they went under a low arch. It was just a reflex, there was no danger of her actually banging her head.

Violetta suddenly came to a halt. "Hey, where's Sebastian?" she asked.

"Behind me," Jasmine said, whirling round, but there was nobody behind her. She thought back. "The last time I saw him was back at Accademia bridge," she said.

"The evil old goat has him," Violetta said.

"Should we go back," Jasmine's voice wavered, "to look for him?"

"There is little point," Violetta said. "He has been spirited away. No doubt he is being secreted somewhere unholy. We could be searching for months and not find him." The two young women, alone in the dark, exchanged glances, while Gabizon walked a few paces down the alleyway. Violetta was right. It would not be brave to go looking for Sebastian, blundering around in the dark. It would be foolish. It would expose them to the same danger of being snatched.

"Give me your hand," Violetta whispered to Jasmine. Jasmine looked confused, overwhelmed by events. She was taking a lot of time to process the things that were happening around her. Everything seemed unreal, experienced through a haze of disbelief, shock and confusion. "Your hand," Violetta repeated. "I don't intend to allow you to be snatched away the same way as Sebastian."

"We should return to Sebastian's house," Gabizon said.

Jasmine proffered her hand and Violetta grabbed it. She tugged Jasmine along like a child. Jasmine remembered when she was a child, how she had followed unthinking, not looking, focusing only on the hand of her mother. But this hand was very different. Her mothers hand had been warm and strong, Violetta's was cold and weak. The arms that were pulling her along had hardly any strength in them. Gabizon followed behind and they reached the square in front of Sebastian's building. "Almost there," Violetta muttered.

Jasmine felt terribly exposed as they crossed the open space. She looked up into the dark, night sky. She thought she saw a shape move against the background of pinprick stars. "What was that?" Jasmine hissed.

Violetta didn't stop or look up. She just kept pulling Jasmine forward, eating up the distance between them and sanctuary. "Just keep going," she hissed back, "and dig out that key that Sebastian gave you." Jasmine was still fumbling for the key when they got to the door. She had one hand buried in the bag, searching around blindly, the other was still clasped in Violetta's icy fingers. Violetta's eyes rolled. "Come on," she urged. "We have to get off the street."

"I'm looking. I'm looking," Jasmine hissed.

Violetta grunted in annoyance and reached out for the door handle with her free hand. Darkness coalesced at her heart and then snaked along her arm. The darkness jumped from her wrist to the lock, which promptly opened with a loud click. She pulled on the handle and swung the door wide enough to stuff Jasmine through, followed by Gabizon. Violetta slithered after her and shut the door with a bang.

"Found it," Jasmine said, a note of triumph in her voice. She pulled the key out and dangled it in front of Violetta by the fob. Violetta snatched it and used it to lock the door behind them.

"How did you open that?" Jasmine suddenly asked. "We were outside and the door was locked. Then you did something and the door opened and we were inside."

"We'll be safer upstairs," Violetta said. "I know that the old goat has not been granted admittance to Sebastian's apartments. The building may be a different matter."

"What are you talking about?" Jasmine asked.

"There's no time to explain," Violetta hissed.

"Anyone could have allowed him access," Gabizon said, "a neighbor, a custodian, a real estate agent, anyone."

Violetta led Jasmine upstairs, less insistently now, more gently. She opened the apartment door with the key and motioned Jasmine inside before locking it again. All three just stood there, in the hall. None of them made any move to take off their coat or shoes, or to go through to the living room. They simply stood there, just inside the door, Violetta still with her fingers on the key, the key still in the lock.

"And what about Sebastian?" Jasmine asked.

"I don't know," Violetta said.

"What do you mean," Gabizon asked, "when you say you don't know?"

"I do not think that he will do any permanent harm to Sebastian, is what I mean," Violetta said, "but I don't know."

"Permanent harm?" Jasmine said.

"It is difficult to contain someone such as Sebastian," Violetta said, as she pulled the key from the lock, "or one such as me. You have just seen with your own eyes that no door can stand against me. It is the same with Sebastian. He can open any lock. To confine Sebastian, he will have to be..." Violetta paused, choosing her words. She looked at Jasmine, trying to divine her state of mind. Jasmine was pale with shock, "...incapacitated," Violetta said at last.

"He helped us," Jasmine said. "We have to rescue him."

"Reluctantly, I agree," Violetta said.

Gabizon didn't say anything. She just went to the bar and poured herself a vodka with shaking hands.

***

Sebastian was ashamed at himself. He had frozen in Ratchis's arms. He had felt the skeletal hand go over his mouth and he hadn't been able to cry out a warning. He watched the girls go, unaware that he had been snatched from among them. By a supreme effort of will, he managed to wrench the hand from his mouth for an instant. "Let me go," he screamed.

"I'm afraid that's no longer part of the plan," Ratchis said. "You've always been a bad influence on my daughter and it has to stop sometime." The hand was then firmly clamped back in place and Sebastian couldn't say a word, but the terrified and staring whites of his eyes spoke volumes. Ratchis dragged Sebastian off. Whenever a passer-by stopped to help, Ratchis mentally commanded them to be on their way.

CHAPTER 28

"He's going to pick us off," Jasmine whimpered. "One by one, like in a horror movie."

"I don't watch horror movies," Violetta said. "They frighten me."

"Are you kidding? You're a vampire."

"I don't think of myself as a vampire," Violetta said, a look of pain flitting across her face. "That is not who I am."

"Sure, sure, whatever. Right now," Jasmine whispered, "our big problem is that your pops is picking us off, one by one."

"Like in a horror movie," Violetta nodded.

"Exactly, Jasmine said. "So what are we going to do?"

"He can't be killed," Violetta's voice was quiet, stating a simple fact, "for he is, in a way, dead already."

"It is possible," Gabizon said, coming to joining them, ice jingling in her drink. "You have to cut off the head."

"Even that is temporary," Violetta said. "If you reattach the h-"

"Can he be imprisoned?" Jasmine asked, interrupting Violetta's grizzly description.

"Imprisoned?" Violetta said.

"Yes," Jasmine said. "Is there some special way to hold him in one place forever? Concrete him over, or nail his coffin shut, or something."

"You pin him down, like an insect," Violetta said, "With a stake through the heart."

"I have to go," Gabizon said. "we still need that equipment, and it is clear that it is not safe to travel a night. I will leave as soon as dawn breaks. In the meantime, we should sleep."

***

Gabizon had just left, a little before dawn, but Gabizon said time was of the essence and it was not a great risk as any vampires would be already fleeing home to their coffins. Violetta and Jasmine had let her go and were sitting in Sebastian's kitchen. They had found macaroons and were sharing them.

"We have to rescue Sebastian," Jasmine said.

"That's what he wants," Violetta said. "He wants us to come out of this sanctuary and go to him."

"But we can't abandon Sebastian to his fate, and I can't hide here forever."

"There is one advantage that we have, and it's something that your father doesn't know about," Jasmine said. "We have a vampire hunter."

"Maybe he saw her when he snatched Sebastian," Violetta said.

"So what if he did? She can go there in daylight. That is very advantageous to us. You can also go out in daylight," Violetta said, "but I can't. So we have to decide if we are going to do this together, or if Gabizon is going to do this alone. She seems very confident and capable."

"I think, if she goes alone, against your father, we will never see her again. Don't ask me why. It's just a suspicion," Jasmine said. "Our best chance of success will be if all three of us go. You, me, and Gabizon. I don't really know what we are going to do, or if we'll succeed, but we can't just leave Sebastian. I'm pretty sure he has him locked up back at the house, the house he wants you to return to."

"A lock would not keep Sebastian confined," Violetta shook her head. "He has done something terrible to Sebastian."

They both fell silent, Jasmine with her head down, while Violetta kept nervously glancing at the window, acutely aware of the dawning day. "How did he spirit Sebastian away so easily," Jasmine asked, not sure that she wanted to hear the answer.

"I don't think Sebastian has fed in a very long time," Violetta said. "I think I was getting through to him. I convinced him it was wrong to feed on human blood."

"You mean," Jasmine said, her words hesitant, "he was a killer, but now he isn't"

"It is not killing... but... essentially yes," Violetta nodded. "In contrast, my father has never ceased to feed. He sees nothing wrong in it, and it makes him strong. Not strong like you Jasmine, or like Gabizon, not strong like one of the living, but stronger than Sebastian."

"I see," Jasmine said. "I guess. So, you're saying that your father was stronger, because he drinks blood, and Sebastian does not."

"I really misjudged Sebastian," Violetta said. "For father to have carried him off like that he must have been quite light, quite weak. He can't have fed in years, probably decades. And I thought he was bringing unfortunate people here," she waved her arms to indicate the bachelor pad, "every week to kill them and drink their blood. He let me think that. He reveled in my discomfort."

Jasmine shuddered, her head drooped. Even if it was long ago, Sebastian had killed people in this room? She suddenly had an appalling mental image of Sebastian spreading out a plastic sheet on the floor, like a boogeyman serial killer in a Hollywood movie. She shook her head to free herself from the idea. But he had certainly killed people, that was becoming abundantly clear.

But that didn't mean he should be left to rot. "I understand now why this place repulsed you so much when we visited it before," Jasmine mumbled. "That first time he showed us round. And why you blow so hot and cold on Seb." Violetta didn't reply. Jasmine hadn't even bothered to raise her head and look at her friend, as if the words weren't really intended for her. She was silent a while. Then raised her head.

"Decades?" Jasmine said, suddenly remembering the word Violeta had used a few moments before.

"What?" Violetta was confused.

"You said decades," Jasmine repeated. "Just how old is Sebastian? How old are you?"

"Very old," Violetta said. "I don't know for sure."

"A hundred years?" Jasmine guessed.

"Longer," Violetta said. "Much, much longer. I am a creature of dark-age superstition, after all."

"Have you ever..." Jasmine hesitated, then steeled herself to ask what was on her mind, "fed. Have you ever killed anyone."

"One person," Violetta said, after a long pause, and immediately pain and disappointment flooded Jasmine's face at the words. She had been so hoping that, somehow, her friend would be innocent, even though she was a vampire. "It was Sebastian," Violetta said, her face slack. "I fed on Sebastian when he was a healthy young man with a good soul and with his whole life ahead of him. He had just saved my life." Jasmine's ears were ringing with shock.

"I have to go find Gabizon," she said.

"Wait," Violetta said. "Promise me you won't do anything stupid. Come back here before dusk. Come back to me before the day is done. I'm your friend, Don't leave me." By now the shutters were edged in bright sunlight and Violetta was forced from her seat at the table by the brightness. She crouched to the ground and backed out of the kitchen. Jasmine followed as her friend crawled to her bedroom.

When Violetta reached the room her stomach started to heave. Jasmine was torn. She felt concern for her friend but was also repulsed by the undead monster she now knew her to be. She was suddenly frightened now, too, at being alone with a vampire. Violetta was still clutching her stomach and retching, and then she vomited out some soil. She glanced over her shoulder at Jasmine, and wiped her mouth, embarrassed. Her shoulders sagged and, as a narrow beam of sunlight penetrated a crack in the shutters and fell on the shag carpet of her bedroom floor, she was reduced to crawling under the bed to avoid it.

Like a cockroach, Jasmine thought, and virtually ran from the dark house, out into the sunlight of dawn.

***

Jasmine went to a cafe, already open even at such an ungodly hour, and ordered a cappuccino. While the barista, a gentle old man, made it, she went to the perspex display cabinet full of croissants. It was the same system in every cafe, order your drink and grab your own croissant. The front of the display case was made of hinged panels, specially to allow customers to take their own, and there were serviettes in a dispenser to the side so you didn't get sticky fingers. She plucked out one of the serviettes, opened the perspex door on her side of the display case and reached inside. She selected one with cream, all on autopilot, unthinking, driven by hunger. She greedily took a big bite, squirting out a little bit of cream that lodged at the corner of her mouth, as the barista put her cappuccino on the bar for her. Everything was so normal, as if the events of the previous few days hadn't happened. It was so unbelievable, it was easy to think it was all just a dream, but it wasn't, she knew that.

She dug out her phone, and was about to ring Gabizon, then she put her phone away again, gathered up her coffee and what was left of the croissant and went over to a corner table in the back room. The front of the cafe was standing only, but there were five tables in the back. She sat and just stared into space. She felt a deep connection to her new friend, but seeing her coughing up lumps of soil as she crawled like a bug under the bed had strained her good will. And all the crazy vampire stuff and the drama with her father.

Maybe it was time for a clean break from all this, but that would mean abandoning Sebastian to his fate and she was now in the cross hairs of a supernatural killer. She wouldn't blame herself if she did make a clean break, if she did just forget them all, but it just wasn't that simple. She was mixed up in it all now, and nobody would believe a word, even if she asked for help, least of all the police. She was mixed up with Violetta, Gabizon, and most of all Sebastian. She felt stabs of fear and pain in her heart at the thought that he was being hurt. She dug out her phone, rang Gabizon and wasn't surprised when she answered almost immediately.

"Are you okay?" Gabizon asked before she could say anything, and then, "I shouldn't have left you there. That was wrong. But I have the things I need now. Where are you?"

"I'm at a cafe," Jasmine told her. "It's just round the corner from the nest of vampires you left me sitting in."

"The name?"

"I don't know," Jasmine said.

"It doesn't matter," Gabizon growled in her husky voice. "I'll find you."

Jasmine hung up and let the phone clatter to the aluminum tabletop, suddenly too weak to hold it up. It was over an hour before Gabizon arrived, and Jasmine hadn't moved in the whole time.

"How are you?" Gabizon asked.

"I'm a mess," Jasmine said. "I have no idea what to even make of it all. It's completely nuts, right?"

"Nuts?" Gabizon repeated. "Yes. Nuts. The question is, why did he kidnap the boy vampire?"

"Sebastian," Jasmine said. "Violetta thinks it's to make her come rescue him, and then he can get his hands on her again."

Gabizon looking round to see if they were being overheard, but the cafe back room was empty. "He must be killed. And the other two as well. All three will have to be killed."

"I can't agree with killing, Gabizon," Jasmine said. "I'm frightened half to death and I think I may well be going mad, but I still don't know if killing is the answer, even for the father."

"I understand," Gabizon said. "Killing is a sin, but it is not we who killed them. They are already dead. What we do is more like, laying them to rest. They are simply being given the peace that has been denied them. They are restless spirits and must be properly entombed. For their sake as much as ours."

"Part of me has no qualms about... entombing... the father," Jasmine said, "but Violetta is my friend. Besides, are you even sure you know what you are doing? Have you really done this before?" Gabizon didn't answer. Instead she let her hard eyes speak for her. "Violetta wants to be included in anything we decide to do," Jasmine continued, unsure if Gabizon's silence was a yes or a no. "We will have to wait for nightfall before we can talk to her."

"I have never heard of anyone befriending a vampire," Gabizon made a face, unable to completely hide her disgust.

"Me neither," Jasmine said. It seemed like she was going to go on, to explain or to justify herself, and Gabizon kept quiet, waiting to see what she was going to say, but no further words came. She just stared at the people coming into the cafe, grabbing a croissant from the display case, gobbling it down, ordering some tiny cup of coffee or other, knocking it back, paying and leaving, sometimes the whole operation taking less than a minute. The barista seemed to know them all by name, greeting each one as they came into the cafe, but how he'd managed to learn all these names when nobody was really talking to each other was a mystery. The front of the cafe was becoming ever more busy as the morning wore on but nobody came round the bar to the back to take one of the other tables. It was just a quick pit stop on the way to work. There was no time to sit down at a table, just a croissant and a jolt of coffee and then off. "This place is so alien," Jasmine said. "Italy, it is so unlike the UK, I'm rapidly falling out of love with it." Gabizon just nodded. "And there are no vampires in the UK," she went on.

"Sure," Gabizon said, but from her tone of voice she was obviously just humoring her. There was another long silence, broken only intermittently, which extended till midday.

"We have to decide what to do," Gabizon said at last.

"It's obvious," Jasmine said. "I think I just didn't want to see it before. If we want to save Sebastian, we have to go to the house."

"Even though that is exactly what our enemy wants?" Gabizon said. "Even though that is exactly what he will be expecting?"

***

"Shit," Gabizon said, as she and Jasmine neared the house. There were police standing in the small alleyway, at the gate.

"Police?" Jasmine said. "Why are the police here?"

"The monster obviously has mortal servants, to protect it when it is slumbering," Gabizon said.

"I've never seen them around before," Jasmine said. "And I have been here many times."

"Like you said," Gabizon reminded her. "He's expecting us. We have to find another way in."

"Or we abort," Jasmine said. "We abort mission, go back to Sebastian's place and tell Violetta what we have seen."

"Here," Gabizon said, and gave Jasmine the heavy leather bag she had been carrying. "Hold onto this. We are looking for another way in."

"There isn't another way in," Jasmine said. "I've been inside. I know the place. There isn't another way in."

"There's always another way in," Gabizon said, with a grim smile. "This way, to the other side of the building."

"What other side of the building?" Jasmine asked.

"The side that rises directly from the canal," Gabizon said, as she hurried off, forcing Jasmine to follow, carrying the surprisingly heavy bag.

***

It took a lot longer than Jasmine had expected for Gabizon to get a boat, and to find a place to climb the wall. The old lady was spry, but it still took her a long time to climb. "I have to pay more attention to my exercise regimen," she grunted, half way up the wall. With the heavy bag, Jasmine was having just as much trouble.

"This is crazy," Jasmine said. "It's getting too late. We have to call this off and go back."

Gabizon glanced at the sky, almost losing her grip on the crumbling brickwork as she did so. "Nonsense," she said. "We have plenty of time."

High up on the building, at the back, was a huge terrace that Jasmine had never seen before. It had a beautiful view of the city, and of the long shadows cast by the setting sun. "Let's get on with this, it's getting late," Jasmine said.

"Perhaps you're right," Gabizon said. "Give me the bag. We have to get into the building and there is no time to pick the lock." Jasmine handed over the bag and Gabizon rummaged around in it. She brought out a hammer, a big heavy one, designed for driving in stakes, crossed the wide terrace and went to the small wooden door that gave access to the building. She raised her hammer and slammed it into the door. There were sparks from the lock, bright in the failing light, and splinters of wood were smashed from the door frame and sent tumbling through the air. But the door held.

"C'mon, c'mon," Jasmine said. "Is it me, or is dusk coming quicker than normal."

"You're imagining it," Gabizon said. "But this door is a tough one. Here, take the hammer. Try with your young muscles." Jasmine reluctantly took the hammer and, as Gabizon got out of the way, moved to stand in front of the door. She raised the hammer, surprisingly heavy in her hand, threatening to pull itself from her grasp by sheer weight. She took a firmer grip of it and swung it at the door with a grunt. There was an impact that she felt in her arm bones and in her teeth accompanied by the thud of wood.

"I didn't even dent it," Jasmine said, turning to stare at Gabizon, eyes a little wild with panic.

"Try again," Gabizon said. "Put your back into it. We have to get inside, find the fiend's lair, and we have to put it to rest, all before the sun goes down."

"Maybe," Jasmine said, as she swung the hammer again, "this was not the best time of day to come, you know, just before sunset."

"Just get that door open," Gabizon said, and Jasmine swung again and again, punishing impact after punishing impact, and at last the door started to give.

"Yes!" Jasmine yelled in triumph. She slammed the hammer into it a few more times and the door finally swung in. "You couldn't exactly call this a stealth mission, but we have the door open."

"Put the mallet back in the bag, Jasmine," Gabizon said. And Jasmine did as she was told.

"Do you feel a dark energy coming from the open door?" Jasmine asked.

"Perhaps," Gabizon nodded, "or perhaps you're just spooked. You'd better let me take the lead."

"You're going in?" Jasmine said.

"What else?" Gabizon said. "Back down the wall? We've come to far to turn back. Or, at least, I have. If you want, you can go."

"No," Jasmine said. "No... Sebastian is inside here somewhere. We have to help him."

"That's the spirit," Gabizon said. "In we go." She walked slowly toward the small aperture and stepped through into the dark and silent house. "We won't waste time with the upper floors," Gabizon whispered. "Wherever he is, it will be closer to the ground."

"The stairs are that way," Jasmine told her. "They go down to the ground floor." Gabizon nodded and went in the direction Jasmine had indicated. She went down the stairs on the balls of her feet, as silently as she could, but her movements made sounds nonetheless. The stairs creaked, a small table, unseen in the dark, went tumbling to the floor, a bat in the rafters screeched. And the stairs seemed endless, down and down, steeper and narrower than Jasmine remembered. At last they reached the huge window at the bottom of the stairs, and Jasmine gasped at the sight of it.

"Is that moonlight?" Jasmine asked. "How can that be moonlight? The sun was out when we came into the house."

"This complicates things a little," Gabizon said.

"Complicates things?" Jasmine screeched. "Complicates things? We're toast. It's game over. Night has fallen, and Ratchis will be rising from his coffin, and he'll be coming for us. Right now, he's coming for us, and we're exactly where he wants us. What if-"

"Enough," Gabizon said, cutting off Jasmine's panicked babbling. "Remember, we are stronger than him, even if he has just fed, and faster. He will not want to challenge us physically. The important thing is to keep him out of your mind. Don't look him in the eye. Don't listen to his words. We just find him, and kill him, okay?"

"Okay," Jasmine said, glancing out the window again, and watching the clouds scud past the moon.

"We need to get down into the basement," Gabizon said,

"Through the kitchen," Jasmine said. "This way."

***

The basement, when they found it, was ankle deep in water. "Typical of Venice," Gabizon said. "What a shit hole." She reached into her bag and brought out a flashlight. She swept it around the room, letting it settle here and there, then allowing it to move on.

"He's not here," Jasmine hissed.

"He's here." Gabizon said. "Somewhere. There must be a secret chamber, or a tunnel. The entrance to a vampire lair doesn't need to be any bigger than a coin. He's here, and we'll find him."

"Okay," Jasmine said, as Gabizon took a step into the water. Jasmine held back, frightened, and battling a wave of disgust at the sight of the water, and also the smell of it. She thought she saw movement in it, and she stared into the depths, but the movement was at the surface. "I saw something," she hissed. "I think there are rats in the water."

"Rats?" Gabizon spun round to look in Jasmine's direction. "Did you say rats?"

"Yes," Jasmine said. "Is that so bad."

"The vampire can take the form of a swarm of rats," Gabizon told her, "or cockroaches, or bats, or any foul, verminous thing. How many rats did you see?"

"Just one," Jasmine said.

"Tell me if you see more," Gabizon called over. "If you see more rats, don't let them climb those steps. Kick them, stamp on them, do not let any crawling, creeping, or flying thing leave this cellar. What's that?"

"What's what?" Jasmine called. She stared into the dark, at the bobbing light of Gabizon's flashlight. She saw a figure, Gabizon, and beside her another figure.

"I have beguiled her," the second figure said. "She is a weak-minded fool."

"Ratchis!" Jasmine said, and turned to run.

"Stop," Ratchis called out, and Jasmine found she had no option but to obey. It was like his voice forced itself into her mind and took control of her body.

"Come back here," Ratchis said, and Jasmine turned and started descending the staircase. Ahead of her she saw Ratchis, and standing beside him, Gabizon, still holding her flashlight. "You can drop the bag," Ratchis said. "You won't be needing any of the things in there." Jasmine's hand slackened on the leather handle of the bag and it fell to the steps with a heavy smack. "That's right," Ratchis said, "keep coming." Jasmine came to where the steps disappeared into the water and she hesitated. She saw a frown appear on Ratchis's face. Her natural fear and revulsion at the sight of the water had held her back. It was more powerful than Ratchis' commands. "Come!" Ratchis snarled, and Jasmine's foot lowered, the tip of her toe touching the water. "I'm tired of waiting," he said, as her toe hesitated a few seconds more. He lunged across the water, coming right at Jasmine without even seeming to move his feet.

"I have to get out of here," Jasmine whispered.

"Wait right there," Ratchis' words were now like the hissing of a snake. He was just a few steps away from her, and there would be no help coming from Gabizon. She just stood like a statue, submerged up to her ankles in the water. It was up to Jasmine to protect herself.

She recoiled from Ratchis, reached into the leather bag, grabbed for what she hoped was a stake, but she could immediately tell from the weight that she had hold of the handle of the mallet. There was no time to search for a better weapon. She brought it out and swung it at Ratchis. The stairway was narrow and there was no time to swing properly, but she caught him across the side of the head.

Where the hammer hit, his brittle old bones immediately caved in, and he was thrown to the side. Jasmine tried to find the courage to hit him again, but couldn't. He was lying in the pool of light cast by the flashlight in Gabizon's hand. He looked dead. Just a skeletal old man, dressed in a heavy black suit of a type that hadn't been in style since the 1950s. He was face down in the water. If Jasmine didn't do anything he would drown, if he wasn't dead already from the blow to the side of his head.

Jasmine at last stepped into the water and felt the cold, cold as ice, immediately penetrate her shoes and socks, making her wince. She moved through the water until she was standing beside Ratchis' fallen body. She reached out her hand to turn him over, to see the damage she had done with her hammer. He was light, just bones, easy to turn. Jasmine looked down at his face, but there was no sign of the terrible wound she had inflicted. His eyes opened, and a moment later so did his mouth, exposing huge fangs in his upper jaw. Jasmine screamed, stepped back, lost her footing in the water and fell on her ass. Ratchis rose to stand above her, and he was speaking again. He was speaking a long monologue of words, about family, about his daughter, about strangers, about the young, about people like Jasmine, and Jasmine realized she was falling into a trance. He was hypnotizing her, his words worming through her mind. And her eyes became heavy, flickered for a second, her fingers went slack on the handle of the mallet and it slipped beneath the water of the basement floor. Her heavy eyes closed, just for an instant, and when he opened them again, Ratchis was at her throat.

She remembered how strong her words had been against Sebastian that one time. She wondered if she could repeat the trick. If not, she would be killed in a dark basement. "Fuck off!" she yelled, putting all her strength in her words, and felt her heart leap as Ratchis stumbled away. "Okay, I'm out of here," she yelled, as she got to her feet and started running. She ran up the steps, through the kitchen, and only came to a stop when she saw that the front door was open and a figure was standing in it.

It was Violetta. It was only a silhouette, but Jasmine knew it was her. "Violetta," she called out. "Your father is right behind me." And Ratchis appeared at the kitchen door.

"Come back," Ratchis shouted, and Jasmine span away from her friend and walked toward Ratchis. She managed to snatch up a vase as she passed a table, and she hurled it at him. It sailed over his shoulder and smashed against a wall. Violetta ran to her father and punched him in the chest. "Pitiful," he said. Your body is as weak as their minds. If you would only eat, you could become strong, maybe even strong enough to stand against me. Maybe."

Ratchis led the way down the stairs, at the head of a strange procession. Violetta was following at his back, punching and slapping ineffectually at him. Jasmine came last, walking like an automaton, her body no longer hers to command. Then Ratchis stopped. Something had unsettled him. "Stop this stupidity," he whispered at Violetta who was still pummeling ineffectually against his back, but she wouldn't stop her punches and slaps. "I said desist," Ratchis yelled, and he slapped Violetta so hard across the face that she gasped, and she fell down the stairs, tumbling into the dark. They heard a splash as she hit the water.

There was silence now, and Ratchis strained his ears, "Singing?" he said. He looked round to Jasmine. "Let's go down and see what is going on." He stealthily descended the steps, not making a noise, and Jasmine followed behind, like a drone.

The singing was coming from Gabizon, who was still standing in the water. "It's an old song," Gabizon said to Ratchis. "It's a song I know well. I think with the song in my mind, there will be no space for you. Do you like my song? Oh black raven, why you flying? Soaring high over my head. I'm not going yet to heaven. No, black raven I'm not dead." Gabizon walked purposefully toward Ratchis, who turned, fear in his eyes for the first time. "Sing the song with me, Jasmine," Gabizon said. "Oh black raven, why you flying? Soaring high over my head. I'm not going yet to heaven. No, black raven I'm not dead."

Ratchis was running as fast as his weak old legs could carry him now, running up the stairs toward Jasmine. "Out of the way, you ridiculous little girl," Ratchis barked at her. "I want you to poke out the eyes of that old lady down there. Do you hear me?"

"Oh black raven, why you flying?" Jasmine sang, her limbs relaxing, becoming less stiff. "Soaring high over my head. I'm not going yet to heaven. No, black raven I'm not dead." Ratchis bared his teeth, hoping to make Jasmine recoil in primal terror like she had just a moment before, but instead she raised her shoe, and because she was above him on the steps, she was able to stamp down on his face.

**

Violetta woke, felt her neck, which had been broken by her father's blow, knitting back together. Her lungs were full of the stinking water of the basement floor, and she coughed it out as she sat up and opened her eyes. She saw a scene of chaos in front of her. Jasmine was holding her father down, trying to stay away from his teeth, while Gabizon was searching around in the water at the foot of the steps. At last the old woman dragged the mallet from where it had been hiding, retrieved the leather bag that Jasmine had dropped on the steps, and joined Jasmine where she was holding Ratchis down.

Violetta couldn't say a word, all she could do was sit in the water, in the shadows, and watch. Neither Jasmine nor Gabizon were aware she was there, so busy were they about their work. But Ratchis knew, and he turned to face her. He mouthed a single plea, "Help me?" Violetta rose from the water and took a step toward the grim scene playing out in front of her, the only father she could remember being put down like an animal. "Help me?" Ratchis again mouthed. It was the second time she had seen this being done to him, and he had come back before.

Gabizon swung her mallet, driving a stake through the old man's right wrist. Then she did the same for the left. Jasmine relaxed a little and let go of Ratchis' arms. She took a step back, and watched as Gabizon worked. Violetta was at her shoulder, she suddenly realized. Jasmine reached out and her arm encircled her friend's slim shoulders. Violetta looked at Jasmine then back to her father. Gabizon was busy staking his legs. At last she put the last stake at the old man's heart. "this is hard work," she said. "If you have any last words for this monster, now is the time."

"You have me," Ratchis said, "but what will you do next? The old texts say beheading, but are they correct?" Gabizon is listening despite herself.

"Sing your song," Jasmine yells. "Keep him out of your mind."

"Oh black raven, why you flying?" Gabizon mumbled the words of her song, her hand shaking as it held the point of the stake at Ratchis' heart. "Soaring high over my head. I'm not going yet to heaven. No, black raven I'm not dead."

"It seems I have you at a disadvantage," Violetta said, as she moved to stand over the man, half submerged in the water, shafts of wood piercing his limbs. "Let's finish this."

***

It was Jasmine who found Sebastian, sitting in the study, with a stake driven through his chest. "He's in here," she yelled, and Gabizon and Violetta came running. "But he's dead," Jasmine said. Her head was lowered, a tear in her eye. Gabizon didn't say a word, but she took a couple of steps toward Sebastian, her leather bag full of vampire slaying equipment in her hand.

"He's not dead," Violetta said, to Jasmine. She went to where Sebastian was slumped in his chair. She took hold of the stake and pulled at it. She grunted and braced her feet, using all her strength. "I can't pull it out," she said. "Jasmine, come here, you will have to do it."

"No," Jasmine said. "Look, he's dead. What good will pulling that out do?"

"Trust me," Violetta said. She reached out, grasped Jasmine's right wrist and moved her hand into position to grab the length of shaft that was sticking from Sebastian's chest. Despite herself, Jasmine's fingers tightened round it. "Just pull," Violetta whispered in her ear. Jasmine did as she was told and the length of wood slipped easily from Sebastian's chest. Jasmine stepped back, and soon all three of them, Gabizon, Violetta, and Jasmine were standing in a line, looking down at Sebastian.

"So we aren't going to kill him?" Gabizon said.

"We aren't going to kill him," Jasmine told her.

"And we're not going to kill this one?" Gabizon gestured at Violetta.

"We are most definitely not going to kill this one," Jasmine said. Gabizon nodded, dropped her big leather bag on the floor and slumped into one of the chairs. Jasmine turned her attention back to Sebastian, and saw life in his eyes. He was looking at her.

"I knew you would come for me," he said.

"Welcome back to the land of the living," Jasmine said.

EPILOGUE

Jasmine was standing at the apex of Accademia Bridge at midnight. Violetta was standing beside her. One day the Serenissima will sink and bury all our memories, hopes, thoughts, and dreams. The lagoon will open like a huge chasm and devour all our petty achievements, Jasmine thought. And the rest will be silence, like a gentle breeze, and it will haunt us forever like forgotten ghosts.

"We're safe now," Violetta said.

"If this was running water, if it wasn't just a lagoon, would you be able to cross the bridge?" Jasmine asked.

"Please, forget that I am not one of the living like you." Violetta said.

"I can't," Jasmine said, "but that doesn't mean we can't be friends."

***

Far away, across an ocean, a crazy young girl was sitting in her car, a fast car, a muscle car, a sports car, but dusty and scratched. No matter how fast she drove, no matter how far she went, she could never outrun her past. She looked in her rear view mirror. A figure was approaching, walking unhurriedly across the dark parking lot, a figure she recognized. She turned in her seat and stuck her head out the car window. "Sebastian?" she yelled.

ACKNOWLEDGMENTS

One of the most important characters in this book is the city of Venice itself. We have had the great good fortune of living in Venice for many years, and have therefore been able to get to know it in winter, summer, fall, and spring. We see the tourists come and go, and we see the local Venetians celebrating their seasonal festivals and rites. We see the birds of the lagoon and the rats and alley cats, and we see the hungry waters, slowly encroaching on the ancient architecture, as it crumbles and molders.

We hope that you have gotten to know Venice a little through reading this book, and that it has touched your heart the way it has touched ours.

ABOUT THE AUTHORS

This is the first book written by Barbara Stanzl and Brett Fitzpatrick together. They have lived in Venice for many years, and have been involved in many creative projects, both together and individually, including photography, writing, painting, sculpture, and video production.

Cover design by Brett Fitzpatrick
www.brettfitzpatrick.com

www.kookyphotography.com
www.alleyesonvenice.com

ISBN: 9783751935234